THE TEATIME MYSTERY

An absolutely gripping cozy mystery
for all crime thriller fans

FAITH MARTIN

Travelling Cook Mysteries Book 6

Previously published as *Just Not Cricket*

Revised edition 2024
Joffe Books, London
www.joffebooks.com

First published by Robert Hale in Great Britain in 2016 as
Just Not Cricket by Joyce Cato

This paperback edition was first published in Great
Britain in 2024

Cover art by Nick Castle

ISBN: 978-1-83526-409-6

*For all of those who still like to honour the great
British tradition of teatime. Minus the murder, naturally!*

CHAPTER ONE

It was a perfect summer's morning in late June when travelling cook Jenny Starling pulled her small cherry-red van into the modest car park on the edge of Much Rousham's village sports ground and cricket field.

A large expanse of manicured green, it was surrounded at one end by mature horse chestnut trees at the top of a slight incline, which, along with a thick mist of cow parsley dancing amongst the tree trunks, hid most of the actual village itself from view. A long length of hedge composed mostly of native blackthorn, elder and hawthorns ran along two of the other sides, providing wind breaks. On one side of these, Jenny could just make out the silvery traces of a river running almost parallel to the field, which might have been the River Cherwell. Or then again, might not. Her sense of geography wasn't the best.

The hedges were thick with the fast browning flowers of May blossom, and a greenfinch sang lustily, if not very tunefully, from one such thicket. A narrow country lane, heading to another tiny and rather obscure neighbouring hamlet, comprised the fourth edge of the field, but Jenny doubted it saw much traffic, apart from the odd tractor or two. This roadway was lined by a tall chain-link fence, which circumnavigated the entire field. By the section of road, however, a plethora of pink-and-white striped weeds climbed and twined up the metal diamond struts vigorously, their trumpets rustling in a slight, warm breeze. Large patches of nettles and candy-pink willowherb, growing in five-foot tall swathes, further combined to hide most of the lane from view.

A quick glance at her wristwatch showed her that it was barely eight o'clock in the morning — which should give her plenty of time to set up. Already it felt distinctly hot, and she just knew that the rest of the day was going to be sweltering. Not ideal conditions for cooking in a cramped, confined space perhaps, but she was in too good a mood to even think of complaining.

Much Rousham's annual grudge match against their arch-rivals, the nearby village of Steeple Clinton, was due to begin promptly at one o'clock, and this year being their centenary, the cricket committee had voted to push the boat out somehow. This had manifested itself in the form of their hiring Jenny to provide gourmet nourishment for the gladiators, rather than relying on the always welcome, if somewhat erratic efforts of the cricketers' wives.

Now as she started to unload her van, her happy thoughts turned to which recipe she'd use for her strawberry scones, and which sponges she thought would best suit the occasion. Genoese were always popular, of course, but for sportsmen with a healthy appetite, perhaps a lemon curd cake or coffee and walnut might be better?

As she approached the small but picturesquely quaint wooden pavilion, which backed onto an area of the chain-link fence that was interspersed with hawthorn, she glanced around her in pleasure. The sun shone on the large green patch of neatly mown grass, and through the trees she could just make out the roofs of a small nest of thatched cottages. Everywhere wild daisies, pretty powder-blue speedwell and bright buttercups were blooming, and birds flitted about, gathering worms and caterpillars for their growing broods. A small pile of cricket paraphernalia, including wicket stumps, bails and balls, was laid out neatly alongside the green-and-white painted pavilion, obviously waiting to be set up, and it all combined to present a pleasant rural scene that could only be found in England.

And even Jenny, who'd never been much of a sports fan (and knew as much about cricket as she did about nuclear fusion), could just about understand and appreciate the allure of the occasion.

As she approached the wooden steps at the base of the pavilion, her arms laden with her favourite cooking utensils, she eyed the building thoughtfully. A set of three sturdy-looking steps led up to a narrow door, set squarely in the middle of the building. It didn't, Jenny had to acknowledge with a small sigh, look as if it was likely to possess a particularly generous kitchen. However, a large window on each side of the door suggested that there would at least be plenty of light inside, which gave her some cause for hope.

Just then the door opened and a man stepped out, smiling a warm welcome at her. He was tall and rake-thin, with close-cropped white hair and button-black eyes, a feathering of silver, short-cropped whiskers on his chin which led Jenny to estimate his age to be somewhere in the late sixties. Dressed in white trousers and a dark green shirt, his face had the creases and deep tan of a man who had lived his life mainly outdoors.

She saw his eyes widen as they took her in — a not uncommon occurrence, and one that she was used to. At six feet tall, with long, almost black hair and sky-blue eyes, her curvaceous figure could best be described as Junoesque. As such, Jenny was used to being viewed with considerable interest — especially by the male of the species — which sometimes bordered on the bemused. Not yet thirty, and looking considerably younger, she knew that she was not most people's idea of a professional cook.

'Hello, you must be the lady Mrs Enwright told me to expect. I'm James Cluley, the groundsman here,' he introduced himself gallantly. 'I've opened it all up for you and made sure that everything's in order. The electricity's on, and everything's had a good airing. I hope you'll find you've got everything that you need, but if not, just sing out and I'll see what I can do,' he promised. And so saying, he stepped to one side to allow her to pass.

As she stepped inside the narrow door, long benches and rather battered lockers lining the walls showed her that they were in the main changing room.

'The kitchen and storeroom are at the back, I'm afraid,' James said cheerfully. 'So you've not got much of a view of the cricket field.' He opened an internal door on a direct line with the main door, allowing them to step into a tiny dark hallway, with two doors facing them. The space was bisected by a rather dimly lit corridor, at the end of which were the toilets.

Of the two immediate doors facing her, the one on the left opened to reveal a cheerful if somewhat functional white-and-yellow painted room, housing the very modest kitchen facilities that Jenny had feared. On the plus side, it had a set of rather rickety-looking French doors on the side wall, which were currently shut, but which could be opened to let in a cooling breeze if needed. The first thing she did was to walk across and check them, but she found they were locked.

'Oh sorry, I meant to open them up for you. I'm the only one with the key,' the old man apologized, patting down his pockets absently. A small frown tugged at his white eyebrows, telling her that he was not finding what he was looking for. 'I keep all the keys. I can let you have that one if you like.'

'Oh, please, don't bother,' Jenny said, since the continued half-hearted patting of his pockets seemed to be coming to naught. 'Every fly and wasp in creation would probably come in if I opened them anyway,' she added philosophically.

He grinned in acknowledgement. 'Right you are. Well then, as you can see, we've got electric rather than gas,' James said, clearly proud of his little domain as he pointed out a strictly average oven with the usual standard grill and four rings on the hot plate. 'And of course, hot and cold running water.' He indicated a large Belfast sink. 'We're connected to both the national grid and the water mains.'

Jenny smiled gently. 'It's a lovely kitchen,' she said firmly, and tried to mean it. And then rather spoiled it by sighing at the single oven. 'Well, I've got no time to lose if I'm to get all my baking done in time,' she pronounced resolutely. And with that, she dumped her first load of equipment onto the small wooden kitchen table that stood squarely in the middle of the room and metaphorically rolled up her sleeves.

Taking the hint, the groundsman instantly became all business. 'Please, you must let me help you unload the van,' he offered generously.

Never one to look a gift horse in the mouth, Jenny promptly accepted the offer. And so for the next quarter of an hour or so, they worked in amicable tandem, scattering her accumulating cooking gear around the workspaces and offloading a large portion of her ingredients into the small fridge and a standing cupboard that James Cluley insisted on calling the 'pantry.'

Once they were finished, Jenny, always one to get her priorities right, instantly put the kettle on to make a pot of tea and busied herself with mugs, sugar and milk, which were to be found in one of the two painted cupboards that lined the walls.

'I understand that the tea is to be ready at four, or thereabouts, and will be followed by a buffet supper at seven thirty, once the match is over?' Jenny asked, just to be certain that Mrs Enwright had got the timetable right. If there was anything Jenny hated, it was to keep hungry people waiting.

James nodded. 'Yes. The match starts at a quarter past one, and we always stop for tea at four. But the timing of the supper buffet will rely far more on the state of play and the light, of course. Not that we need worry about that — the forecast is set to be fair all day.'

Jenny blinked, feeling somewhat baffled. To her, food was all that mattered, so fitting the consumption of it around something as unimportant as the vagaries created by a game of cricket sounded outrageous, but she was prepared to be magnanimous. Besides, she'd deliberately planned her savoury menu to be flexible. Her stuffed aubergines with tomato, onion, garlic, herbs, raisins, pine kernels and chopped parsley could be eaten hot or cold, and could be warmed through if needed. As could the spinach filo pie, quiches, and any number of other assorted pastries. The bowls overflowing with salad could be kept in the fridge until needed, and freshly baked bread smelt and tasted good no matter what, so Jenny would be fine. She'd had the foresight to prove a lot of her bread overnight, so those loaves and buns, at least, she could start baking right away.

She finished making the tea and poured out two mugs, handing one over to her new friend.

'That all sounds fine,' she said brightly, and took a grateful sip from her mug. 'So, I take it you'll be rooting for Much Rousham?' she asked with a smile.

James grinned back at her. 'I was born and bred here, so yes, of course I will,' he admitted. 'We've got a good team this year too, so expectations are high. Mind you, I've got in-laws playing for Steeple Clinton so I'd better not let my wife catch me out being too partisan.'

Jenny laughed. 'Uh oh. Like that, is it?'

''Fraid so. Anyway, I'd better let you get on,' James said, finishing his mug and setting it down on the draining board beside the sink. 'If you need anything, like I said, just let me know.'

'Thanks, I will.'

Jenny watched the old man leave before looking around her at the sacks of flour and sugar, and the butter warming on the windowsills to soften, contentedly contemplating a morning filled with baking. Already she was making a mental list of what needed doing first — which was, of course, to get on with the bread.

As the bread began to bake and she set about making the first of several batches of scones, Jenny began to hum softly to herself. The sun was shining, she had goodies to bake, and soon she'd have a lot of hungry mouths to feed. All was right with her world!

Jenny had just added a little rum to the mixture that would shortly become a gateau belle Hélène when she heard a cheerful 'Coooeee!' echo in from behind her, and turned to smile at the little woman who was standing in the doorway.

At barely five feet tall, with curly brown hair and twinkling brown eyes, she instantly reminded Jenny of a curious robin. She was even wearing a red-fronted dress (the rest of it being mainly navy blue) and she held in each hand a large plastic supermarket bag that clinked intriguingly as she raised them up slightly to show them off.

'Hello, you must be the fabulous cook that Margie's been going on about for the past week. I'm Caroline Majors, wife of the opening bowler, for my sins.' The fifty-something woman grinned and gave the bags another gentle shake. 'Me and the old boy have been put in charge of the booze this year.'

Jenny smiled and nodded. 'That's fine.' She didn't pretend to be an expert on wines or alcohol, and in her experience most clients preferred to see to that aspect of the catering themselves. 'I don't know if there's room in the fridge, though,' she added, with a worried glance at the small white appliance beside the sink, which was currently stuffed to the gunwales with her salads, sauces, milk and cream.

'Oh that's OK, I knew there wouldn't be — I've got iceboxes in the car. Won't be a sec, and I'll get them stashed.' So saying, the little woman darted back out, reminding Jenny even more of a robin. Within just a second or two (or so it seemed) she bobbed back in again with a pair of white coolers and set about her task of stashing the bottles away, chattering constantly as she did so.

'I think this year we're really going to give the Steeple Clinton lot a bashing. Well, we will if Tris is on good form and doesn't have too much of a hangover, the silly little sod,' she clarified with a chortle.

Jenny blinked.

'I'm not sure that he should be playing at all this year, since he's caused so much bad feeling, what with one thing and another, but he *is* the best batsman we've got, no matter what Max says, so you have to put up with it, don't you?'

Jenny thought it best simply to nod.

'Oh, and I do so hope that Michelle won't come to watch him play, but I suppose she'll have to. Mind you, it'll probably all end in tears before bedtime, as my old ma used to say. Or teatime, probably, in this case.' Caroline Majors paused, both to take a much-needed breath and to eye the bottle of supermarket rosé wine that she was holding suspiciously out in front of her. 'Bit of a cheap plonk, this. I can't think why the old boy got it.'

Jenny, furiously whipping up some meringue mix by hand, opened her mouth to ask who Michelle was, then closed it again as she was promptly told.

'Michelle and Max are supposed to be celebrating their ten-year wedding anniversary next month, but there's a nasty rumour going around that they'll likely be heading for the divorce courts instead. Not so sure I believe that myself,' Caroline put in judiciously, then added somewhat cynically, 'Michelle's the sort who knows which side her bread is buttered, if you know what I mean. So she won't take that lying down — if it's true. Still, let's hope it won't affect Max's fielding. He caught out Rolly Tompkinson last week when nobody else could!'

'Ah,' Jenny managed. She was beginning to get the hang of this. Obviously no social disaster was too bad, in Caroline's opinion, so long as it didn't affect the outcome of the cricket match.

It was starting to feel warm inside the pavilion now, and Jenny was glad that she was wearing a cool, flowing outfit that consisted of a multi-coloured maxi skirt that billowed around her ankles as she moved, and a short-sleeved cream top. Thin fabrics, with plenty of room for the air to circulate, were obvious choices for a day like today.

'I just hope the Steeple Clinton lot don't try and bring in a ringer, like they did last year,' Caroline was saying now with a snort, relegating some more cheap plonk to an inferior cooler. 'They tried to make out that a fellow with a summer cottage classified as a resident. Just because he played for his Cambridge college!' Caroline's curls bounced indignantly around her head as she tossed it back with a snort of glee. 'Not that *that* helped them any, as it turned out. Which served them right! We still had them all out for . . . what was it now?' She paused to cock a hand on one hip, her brow furrowed furiously in thought. 'Was it 106? Although this time the Lord of the Manor won't stand for any such nonsense for the centenary. And quite right, too.'

'Strict, is he?' Jenny asked, much amused by the woman's benign, non-stop gossip, and checked to make sure that her home-made 'instant' raspberry jam wasn't catching on the bottom of the saucepan.

Of course it wasn't. It wouldn't dare.

'Yes. Not that he's really the lord of the manor as such, or that trophy wife of his, heaven forbid, a real lady.' Caroline sniffed.

Jenny, who had already surmised as much by the way that her companion had deliberately exaggerated his title, bit back a smile.

'He just happened to buy the manor after the Dewhursts had all died out, that's all. Oh, and apparently he's been given one of those peerages for his services to industry, or charity, or whatever it is that the queen likes to dish out nowadays like Smarties. So technically he's a Sir, and he lives in the manor. But,' Caroline added with a sort of fond but chagrined grin, 'that doesn't stop Tris playing the role of the quintessential reprobate son for all that he's worth. And he does do it with such elan, you have to give him that.'

Jenny nodded. Tris again. The one who hopefully won't have too much of a hangover to play well. Little by little, more by osmosis than anything else, she was beginning to sort out the characters in Caroline Majors' own private soap opera.

'He's up from London for the weekend,' Caroline swept on. 'Not that you can call what he does working, of course. Playing with other people's money and losing it for them more often than not, or so I've heard,' she added darkly. 'Funny that, since he never seems to have trouble filling his own pockets.' A stockbroker then, Jenny mused. Or a banker. Given that description, he could be either. Or a bookmaker? Satisfied with the state of her jam and confident that it would set in time, she took it off the heat and set it to one side to cool. As she did so, a shadow passed over her, making her look up in sudden surprise, but it was only a young lad, passing by the back window outside.

Tall, with a mop of dark hair, he looked too slim for Jenny's liking, but he had a sulky, brooding profile that she suspected drove all the teenage girls potty for miles around.

As Jenny watched, he disappeared from sight around the back of the building, only to reappear at the front a moment or so later. Through the expanse of the locker room, she watched him through the front windows as he crossed over the field and started to help James Cluley fill the chalk machine.

'Nice-looking boy, isn't he?' Caroline, who, with a bottle of vermouth in each hand, had paused to follow Jenny's line of sight, smiled benignly. 'Only seventeen, and already breaking the village maidens' hearts. He's James's grandson, Mark Rawley. Took it hard, what Tris did to his granddad. Especially since he always used to hero-worship Tris,' Caroline said sadly and somewhat confusingly.

Jenny longed to ask exactly what it was that Tris had done to the lad, but didn't have a chance, as her chatterbox companion was already talking once more.

'Still, there you are, you have to live and learn in this life, don't you?' she said philosophically, if somewhat grimly. 'We all of us get our knocks.' And so saying, she stashed the last of the spirits in the final cooler and thoughtfully shoved it out of the way under the wooden table with the others, where Jenny wouldn't be constantly tripping over them.

'There. Now, my old boy will bring the beer and the lager when he arrives, but they can stand in big tubs of iced water outside, under the steps in the shade, so they won't be in your way, either,' Caroline said, making Jenny sigh with relief.

The small kitchen was already cramped enough without her having to make way for stacks of beer cans.

'Good grief, something smells good. What is that?' Caroline demanded as she straightened up, sniffing vigorously.

Jenny smiled. 'Probably the spiced apple and sultana fingers in the oven. They'll be done in another three minutes.'

Caroline's twinkling brown eyes swept up and down Jenny's majestic figure with definite approval. Her old ma had always said that you couldn't trust a skinny cook.

'You know, I reckon the boys are in for a real treat — no matter what moody Mavis has been saying.'

And with that rather devastating exit line, Caroline finally flitted off.

CHAPTER TWO

'Who was that masked woman?' Jenny muttered wryly to herself and with a little smile, as the whirlwind of chatter abruptly ceased and the pavilion fell blissfully silent. And who, for that matter, she thought with an even wider grin, was the cheeky Mavis, to cast aspersions on an unknown cook's prowess?

Jenny only hoped that this impertinent Mavis woman would be around and forced to eat her words (as well as Jenny's perfect cooking) later on this afternoon.

Leaving the first batch of breads to cool on a large baking tray, Jenny glanced at her watch. It was nearly noon, and perhaps a little early for lunch, but with two skinny men in eyesight, what did that really matter? Making up a tray that consisted of a little of everything that she'd baked so far, she made another two mugs of tea and stepped outside into the warm sunshine.

James Cluley's face lit up as she approached and he spied what she was carrying, but the young lad with him had his back to her, and thus hadn't yet seen her. They'd finished marking out the boundary lines, and were in the process of pushing a heavy roller over the ground nearest where the stumps lay ready, presumably to iron out any bumps on the pitch. Both men, not surprisingly, were beginning to sweat in the scorching heat, and Jenny made a mental note to herself to keep everyone well supplied with lemonade.

'I still say you should talk to Lorcan about it,' the old man's grandson was saying sharply. 'If even half of what he says is true, then he's the one who can—'

'Hello there,' James Cluley said loudly, very obviously and deliberately cutting off his grandson in mid-tirade before he could say more. The lad visibly jumped a little, and quickly looked around, his face an angry scowl. Not taking it personally, Jenny smiled at them both widely.

'Hello — I thought some elevenses might go down a treat, after all that hard work you've been doing.'

Mark Rawley's eyes dropped to the cake selection first, his eyes gleaming in a way that made Jenny smile. Budding Romeo or not, the handsome lad still had enough child left in him to be beguiled by proper jam tarts and strawberry scones.

'That looks lovely.' It was the older man who spoke first, however, reaching for his mug of tea. 'Thank you, Miss Starling.'

'Oh please, call me Jenny.'

'Mark, take the tray off the lady,' he admonished. 'Like your mum says, manners cost nothing.'

The boy flushed in embarrassment, mumbled something incomprehensible in typical teenage style, and relieved Jenny of the tray.

She smiled at them, but didn't tarry long. They were clearly in the middle of a private conversation, and a somewhat fraught one by the sounds of it, and she didn't want to be in the way. Nevertheless, as she walked away she heard the lad pick up exactly where he'd left off, and couldn't help overhearing what he said.

'Not that I entirely trust that lying, thieving little toerag either, but maybe there's something in it,' the boy grumbled.

'The money's gone, and the solicitors don't think we'll be getting it back, and that's all there is to it,' she heard his grandfather say flatly. 'You're just going to have to accept it, lad. Things don't always go your way in life, and it's no use thinking that they do, so you might as well get used to it now. Look, I know you're disappointed about uni, after we'd said we'd help you out and all, but you can still go. You'll just have to take out one of them student loans like everyone else, that's all. It may make things a bit harder . . .'

His voice faded in the distance as Jenny went back to the pavilion and contemplated the walnut bread that was in its second proving. Yes, it was risen enough and just ripe for the oven. She relieved the oven of its latest batch of savoury turnovers and popped in the bread.

Now for the meringues. Cooking in a single oven was a bit of a pain, but at least it kept her on her toes! In circumstances like these, timing was king.

* * *

As time wore on, the players began to arrive, and Jenny became aware of the growing noise coming from the changing rooms. She jumped as a discreet cough sounded behind her, and turned to see a tall, handsome man, with silvering hair and the beginnings of a slight paunch around his middle, standing in the doorway behind her.

He smiled and held out a hand. 'Hello. Max Wilson, the cricket captain,' he introduced himself, holding out his hand. Jenny shook it with a smile and introduced herself in turn. 'If you don't mind, I think it might be wise if we closed this door for ten minutes or so, just while we get changed,' he carried on. 'Just to spare your blushes!'

Jenny smiled widely. She couldn't remember the last time she'd blushed, but she was pretty sure that it hadn't been the sight of any naked man that had caused such a phenomenon. Actually, if she remembered right, the last time she'd felt herself blush had been when someone had tried to tell her the correct way to glaze baked carrots. And the ensuing tide of red that had followed this impertinence had been caused solely by her effort to hold on to her tongue!

'Of course,' she said obligingly.

'I'm glad you don't mind.' Max gave what he no doubt considered to be a very charming smile. 'Wouldn't do to get in the cook's bad books, would it?' And so saying, he moved back into the main room. And although he did, in fact, close the kitchen door behind him, thus cutting off her field of vision, the thin wooden barrier did nothing to shut out much sound. Which meant that she could clearly hear him talking to the woman who had arrived with him, presumably his wife.

'I don't suppose you know when Tris and Sir Robert will be coming?' Jenny heard him ask.

'And why should I know that? I'm not their social secretary.' The voice that shot back the answer was curt and clearly spoiling for a fight. It made Jenny wince — and she hadn't even been the recipient of it.

She sighed wearily. So it looked as if Caroline's gossip was right on the money when she said that the Wilsons' marriage was in a bit of trouble. Unless, of course, they were one of those couples who actually *liked* to fight. She could never see the point of that herself, but she had friends who swore that scrapping helped keep their marriage lively and cemented.

'I don't know why I have to come and cheer you on anyway. You know I loathe sport,' the female voice continued scathingly.

'Not all sport, or so I hear,' Max snapped right back.

There was a short, ominous silence after this evidence of retaliation, and Jenny frowned at the obvious rancour going on between them. She only hoped that the old wives' tale that marital spats had the ability to curdle milk was untrue, since she'd just set aside some home-made vanilla and elderflower custard to cool. She intended to make little individual trifles with it, with broken coconut macaroon bases and a white chocolate cream on top. She eyed the pale, cooling mixture thoughtfully.

It didn't look curdled. Which was good. If there was one thing she couldn't abide it was lumpy custard.

'Oh, don't be so childish,' Michelle Wilson's voice came clearly through the wooden walls once more. 'I'm going outside to set up a deckchair and do a spot of sunbathing. It's not as if there's anything else to do around here.' And she must have been wearing shoes with some sort of a heel, for the sound of her clumping off fairly rattled the wooden floorboards under their feet.

Jenny sighed over her custard. So this was the couple who were supposed to be celebrating their ten-year anniversary soon. She wouldn't want to be the caterer at that party, no matter what the fee! Anything she'd cook would be far more likely to end up being flung at a spouse's head than eaten with the proper respect that her food deserved!

* * *

Over the next half hour the spectators began to arrive, and the noise level just beyond her little kitchen rose to a general babble, making it impossible to pick out any individual conversations. Which was a circumstance that suited Jenny admirably.

So when there came another quick tap on the door and Max once again stood there, looking more handsome than ever in his white cricket togs, she wasn't particularly fussed to be told that everyone was now 'decent' and that she could come and go once again as she pleased.

Jenny did, however, need a specific spatula from her van, so she stepped out into the main room, and immediately found herself the focus of several pairs of interested eyes.

Caroline Majors quickly introduced her to her husband and several of the others. Most of the men had that surprised-to-find-themselves-interested look that most men wore when they first looked at her, and tried to remember why it was that only women who resembled stick insects were supposed to be attractive. Others were merely friendly, whilst one or two seemed to have other things on their mind.

And one of these was a forty-something, rather podgy, sandy-haired man called Lorcan Greeves. His grey eyes assessed her vaguely as they shook hands politely, and for a moment Jenny wondered why his name should sound so familiar, and then remembered Mark Rawley telling his granddad that they needed to talk to Lorcan about their financial woes.

Jenny smiled politely at the various men in cricket whites, and went off to her van to collect her spatula. When she came back, a very handsome couple indeed were standing at the foot of the wooden stairs, blocking her way.

The woman was a stunning redhead, only a few inches shorter than Jenny herself, with a slim athletic build and flashing green eyes. She was wearing a pair of elegantly fitted emerald-green trousers of such a super lightweight material that it was almost — but not quite — transparent, and that must have cost something well into three figures. With it she wore a tightly fitting powder-blue tube top that hugged her full breasts lovingly, and over that she had donned an unbuttoned pure silk blouse in various shades of green, blue and white, interlocked in geometric patterns. The whole colour scheme complimented her fiery hair and pale-as-milk skin perfectly.

She was also holding what looked like a glass of white wine in one hand, her blood-red nails contrasting sharply against the glass. This somewhat surprised Jenny — not because the woman looked teetotal, but because she had assumed that the booze was being kept back strictly for the buffet supper only. Still, she supposed peaceably, the sun had to be over the yardarm somewhere on the globe, and if the lady felt like she needed a stiff drink, who was she to judge?

'Don't be so damned spiteful, Tris,' the woman was saying heatedly, taking a rather large gulp of her wine and then reaching out to put her hand on her companion's arm in a more mollifying manner. 'Look, there's no need to upset your father just now. You know he's worried about work.'

So this was the famous Tris, Jenny thought, amused, and regarded the Lord of the Manor's disreputable son thoughtfully. In his late twenties, Jenny gauged, he was around her own height, with dark brown, slightly curly hair and dark blue eyes. He had the elegant but masculine strong-chinned, dark-browed, classically handsome features that were usually depicted on the front of the old Mills & Boon novels.

His body was lithe and fit, and probably boasted a six-pack. He looked young and sexy and immortal, and exuded a powerful allure that no doubt turned any female head within spotting distance.

And he almost certainly knew it.

Now he flashed a lazy, white-toothed smile at his companion, one which effortlessly combined sardonic humour and mild irritation.

'Oh come on, Mummy dearest,' he drawled, making Jenny do a classic double take, since the last thing she would have guessed was that this precocious pair could possibly be mother and son. 'You and the old man were washed up long before—'

'Oh, Tris, *there* you are at last.' Another woman, tall, slender and blonde, waved from one of the deckchairs that had been set up against the pavilion and facing the pitch. 'I've been looking out for you for ages.'

'Michelle,' Tris said, giving the blonde woman a long, lazy and wickedly knowing smile. The look he cast over Michelle's bare arms and the length of her long, tanned legs hardly needed an interpreter in body language to translate the sexual chemistry that was sizzling between them.

Jenny saw the redheaded woman's face suffuse with a dark, ugly colour. And since she couldn't (even with the aid of the best plastic surgeon in the world) be any more than thirty-five at the most, Jenny surmised that she simply had to be Tris's stepmother. And from the way she was shooting daggers at the woman in the deckchair, whom Jenny guessed must be none other than Michelle Wilson, her feelings for her stepson were not necessarily maternal.

Which was all very interesting of course, except that Jenny had spinach and Roquefort quiches in the oven that would need to come out in a few minutes. So she coughed very loudly and pointedly.

Tristan Jones glanced up at her, his eyes meeting eyes every bit as big and blue as his own, and what's more, on his own level. Instantly, his look altered appreciatively as he assessed her curvaceous figure. She could almost read his thoughts exactly as sexual speculation lit up his face.

Jenny flashed him her clearest 'on your bike, sonny' smile and indicated the steps. Then she waved her spatula in the air, nodded at it firmly, and jerked her chin towards the pavilion doorway behind him. With a grin and a mock bow, Tris stood aside, exaggeratedly breathing in to allow her room to pass him on the steps.

The cheeky little sod.

His stepmother barely glanced at her, but also took a small step to one side, allowing Jenny to be able to brush past both of them.

As she did so, the woman hissed quite clearly at Tris, 'If you think your father will believe you, you're insane! He knows just what you are, Tris, and exactly what you're capable of. So if you're hoping you'll be able to fool him then think again. He has no illusions about his precious only son, let me tell you.'

'Quite right, Mummy dearest,' Tris drawled. 'Alas, that's all too true. Unfortunately for you, he has no illusions about *you*, either, does he? Why else do you think he was so insistent that you had to sign a pre-nup, hmm?'

Jenny, hearing the other woman draw in a short, sharp breath, no doubt in preparation for delivering yet more vitriol, determinedly strode on through the fast-emptying changing rooms and into the safety of her kitchen, an angry scowl creasing her forehead.

If people were going to insist on arguing with one another, why couldn't they do it in private, she wondered grumpily. Jenny simply couldn't understand people's inclination to air their dirty linen in public. It was more common than ever nowadays, she speculated, not helped by the popularity of so-called reality TV shows. And of course people were plastering it all over social media too.

Irritated at other people's sheer bad manners, Jenny shrugged off her bad mood and emptied her oven of its latest goodies, then loaded it with the next batch, which was ready and waiting to go in. Then she glanced quickly at her watch. Good, nearly one o'clock. Soon they'd kick off, or start serving, or whatever it was they did in cricket, and hopefully then she'd get some peace and quiet around here.

So far she'd been subjected — vicariously — to a marriage on the rocks, an old man and his family's struggle with financial disaster, and now a mother-and-son spat that made Oedipus and his family look mildly dysfunctional.

Who'd have thought it of a run-of-the-mill village cricket match? If she'd had a more pessimistic nature, she might be wondering what was coming next.

Just then, she heard someone call sharply, 'Tris. I want a word with you,' and Jenny looked out through the open doors to see Mark Rawley stride up to Tris and scowl darkly.

'Round the back, now,' Mark snapped shortly, with a typical teenager's pugnacious belligerence.

Tris rolled his eyes and gave a shrug, which seemed to include both the women who were vying for his attention. Evidently dealing with a stroppy teenager was as good an excuse to bow out as any, for neither Michelle Wilson nor his stepmother made any comment when he muttered a graceless apology and left them.

For a few moments all was silent, and then Jenny, courtesy of the French windows, realized that the two men had come all the way around the back of the building and were now standing in the narrow egress between the rear of the pavilion and the chain-link fence. If she'd walked over to the French doors and peered to one side, no doubt she would have seen them.

But she hardly needed to do that in order to know that they were having a humdinger of a row. She sighed, and began to grate some nutmeg.

'I thought you were my friend!' she heard the boy yell forlornly, and couldn't help but grimace in sympathy. No doubt the young Mark had seen Tris — the rich, handsome son of the local squire, working in London, living in a fancy apartment and having his pick of women — as the ultimate role model. He'd probably been over the moon every time that lofty individual had deigned to so much as notice him.

Tris, to do him some justice, was trying to be conciliatory, but Jenny could tell that he was fast becoming impatient with the youngster's histrionics.

'Look, I told your granddad before he invested that there were certain risks. If you want to play it safe you can, but in today's markets especially, interest rates are low, and you just can't get any kind of decent return on your investment that way, unless you really want to go long-term. Which he didn't. I told him straight, if you want to make a big profit on your money, you have to take big risks. And I set up the deal in good faith. It wasn't my fault the market dipped when it did. Nobody could have predicted it. It wasn't anyone's fault. I've already gone over all this!'

'But you got your own money out in time, or so Lorcan says!' the young lad shouted angrily, as he continued to accuse Tris of first misleading his granddad, then of talking him into investing more money than he knew he could afford. Finally, he accused him outright of swindling James Cluley out of his savings by not warning him to get out in time.

In turn, Tris gave the lad a pithy lesson in the way of the world, and, perhaps worst of all to a lad of seventeen, advised him that he needed to 'grow up,' before breaking off the encounter by simply sauntering off.

A moment or so later Jenny saw the lad striding off as well, his face red and contorted with bitterness and rage. He was clearly trying not to cry, but not quite succeeding, and he had to dash at his face angrily with the palm of his hand. Jenny watched him lope all the way along the length of the hedge and then disappear under the horse chestnut trees at the top end of the field, where there had to be access back into the village.

No doubt he'd gone home to lick his wounds in private, away from prying, knowing, or worse still, sympathetic eyes.

Jenny sighed, and hoped that the lad had the good sense to stay away now. The last thing they needed at this particular 'grudge' match was yet more grudge.

* * *

The 'thwock' of leather on willow resounded outside as Jenny removed her last batch of strawberry scones from the oven. They were, of course, perfect, risen to just the right height and golden brown, the berries inside the mixture still bubbling a little with the sugar and heat.

She set them aside to cool, and then for the first time in ages sat down on one of the folding wood and canvas deckchairs in order to rest her feet. Perhaps not surprisingly, it squeaked rather alarmingly at this treatment, and Jenny reluctantly got back up and stood looking down at it thoughtfully. Perhaps she was just a bit too much woman for such a flimsy structure, she admitted to herself wryly. And it would be very embarrassing to have the damned thing collapse under her, dumping her ignominiously onto the floor.

Remembering that there was a storeroom next door where she might find a sturdier chair, she stepped out into the hall, and glanced through the outer door to the green. She'd heard from the conversation of the people sitting just outside on the deckchairs that Steeple Clinton had won the toss and were electing to bat. Whatever that meant.

She paused, and then watched as the unmistakably graceful figure of Tristan Jones ran up towards a man standing in front of some spindly pieces of wood, and threw a ball at him. The man with the bat made a swipe and seemed to miss. A man in a panama hat then put up his hand, one finger raised in a very imperious and portentous manner, and there was a ragged cheer.

'LBW,' someone muttered from just outside the open door. 'He will do it, every time. I've told him and I've told him . . .'

Jenny didn't wait to hear what the despondent player, now trudging back towards the pavilion, had been told, and nipped into the room next door instead. Here everything was dim and dusty, and Jenny looked automatically towards the windows, where the internal shutters were closed — hence the poor light. She made her way around the folded trestle tables and open shelves that were full of old cricket bats, balls, helmets, padded gloves, and a folded old-fashioned penknife, but a quick look told her that the shutters over the windows probably hadn't been opened in years.

And when she did, in fact, reach up to the one on the left-hand side, she could see that it was covered in a thick layer of dust and grime. What's more, a tentative tug on the handle told her that it was stiff and reluctant to move. Rather than force it, she turned away with a sigh.

As her glance ran over the shelves, she noticed a piece of wood that had split at one end, producing a sharp, pointed shard. It had probably once been an old cricket stump, but now it reminded her, in some macabre way, of a stake that might have been used in one of those old Hammer Horror vampire movies, where Christopher Lee roamed about, constantly on the lookout for a tasty virgin.

Shucking off such whimsical thoughts, she set about searching for, and finally finding, a rather more substantial folding chair. Holding it tucked under one arm, she hoofed it back to her kitchen, where she leant it against a wall and then thoroughly washed her now dusty hands.

It was time to start preparing the salads, then leaving them to get deliciously cool and crisp in the fridge. She checked that her range of homemade chutneys were up to scratch, and set about slicing tomatoes. She'd cut them into fancy shapes and scoop out the seeds and fill them with something tasty. Cream cheese and chives maybe.

Outside, hostile eyes watched broodingly as Tris Jones took another wicket, and applause rang out across the beautiful grounds.

CHAPTER THREE

Tristan took three more wickets in rapid succession, then handed over to another Much Rousham stalwart and trotted off to do some fielding. And if his chosen area just happened to take him to a point suspiciously close to where Michelle Wilson was lounging on her deckchair, nobody chose to comment.

From time to time, however, that lady's husband, who was fielding a little further away, glanced across at them. They weren't openly talking, as far as Max could see — indeed, they seemed to be oblivious to one another's presence. But since his wife was wearing sunglasses, it was impossible for him to see where she was looking, although her head seemed to be perpetually turned to watch the state of play.

But Max knew that her eyes were not on the cricket.

He forced himself to turn away casually and concentrated on the match just in time to see the ball come soaring his way, and made a perfect catch to run out Steeple Clinton's man for a duck.

He smiled in gratification at the smattering of applause that wafted appreciatively his way, and took the opportunity of the lull in play to saunter across to Tris and suggest amiably that they trade places.

His voice was just a little tight.

Tris, with a wide white smile, agreed affably enough and lazily moved away. In her deckchair, Michelle Wilson's eyes followed his pleasingly athletic figure all the way across the field, her eyes admiring his trim derrière in his tight white trousers.

She'd arranged to meet him later, after the buffet supper, when hopefully Max would be just drunk enough not to notice her absence for half an hour or so. But she was beginning to wonder, from the way Max kept hovering around, if he was beginning to suspect as much. So they'd have to be careful. She knew that neither one of them could afford to slip up. Not now.

Not that she was all that worried about her marriage breaking up, but she wanted to make sure it ended in a way that resulted in her getting a good settlement. And, perhaps more importantly, she wanted to be certain that she could be sure of Tris. Although she knew that many women were quite happy to be without a man, let alone an actual husband, she was not one of their number. For her, marriage meant security, position, and of course, a certain standard of living. And whilst Tris could certainly provide her with all three, she wasn't absolutely positive that she could snare him.

She'd learned, over the course of their affair, that Tris Jones could be somewhat slippery.

Max, carefully watching his wife languishing in her deckchair, slowly shook his head in disgust. Even here, right out in public, she didn't have enough sense to keep her infatuation for the younger man under control. Already he could feel several of the wives sniggering about it under their polite pretence at social chitchat, and it was more than he was willing to put up with. It was one thing to have your wife stray afield — in this day and age it had almost come to be expected. But it was another thing entirely to have her lose her head completely over a man nearly eight years her junior, and one who was so known for his Casanova complex that he was becoming something of a laughing stock himself.

25

Max suddenly realized that his hands were curling into fists tight with tension and forced them open. Then he turned away to smile pleasantly at the umpire.

His thoughts, however, were fast winging their way back to his cricket bag, sitting under one of the benches back in the pavilion. And just what was in the bag. It instantly made him feel better, and some of his rage abated. Because soon it would be time to put it to good use. And then he'd feel a whole lot better.

His wife wouldn't be so inclined to smile after that. And Tris sure as hell wouldn't, either.

* * *

In the changing room, Erica had set up a deckchair just inside the open front door to take the best advantage of the cooling shade, along with Caroline Majors and her friend Ettie Flyte, who had placed two chairs just behind her.

Erica had removed her multi-coloured blouse to reveal the short-sleeved tube top in shot silk underneath. What looked suspiciously like a diamond and platinum bracelet was wound around one twig-thin wrist, sparkling and flashing now and then as it caught the light.

Every woman in the room pretended not to notice it.

'I know why I'm not one for the sun,' Ettie, a sixty-five-year-old WI veteran said, glancing down ruefully at her extremely well-padded figure, encased in a large and rather loud floral print dress of dazzling hues. 'But I thought you youngsters liked to bask like lizards,' she said, smiling at Erica. She ran a hand through her short grey hair, and wondered if she might just casually slip off her shoes, which were beginning to pinch the corn on her little toe. But after one quick glance at the elegantly shod Lady of the Manor, who was wearing neat black ballet shoes, à la Audrey Hepburn, she conceded reluctantly that perhaps it wasn't appropriate.

Erica, assuming rightly that the remark had been addressed to her, forced herself to be pleasant. But it wasn't easy. What did she have in common with these tired, middle-class housewives, after all?

'We redheads tend to burn rather than brown,' she said, making no effort to stifle a bored yawn. 'Besides, I prefer to look "pale and interesting" as some poet or other put it, rather than follow the common herd and go the colour of a nut. It gives me an added cachet.' And so saying she eyed her milky white forearms with satisfaction.

Caroline managed to turn a derisive snort into a passable sneeze, and then suddenly applauded loudly as yet another Steeple Clinton man was caught out.

'Carry on like that and they won't even reach a century between them,' she murmured gleefully to her friend. 'It'll be an early tea, you mark my words. All the better for us.'

Ettie, not much of a cricket fan, nodded vaguely.

Erica, who was watching Max Wilson approach Tris and say something that made him swap fielding positions, hid a sly, feline smile. Now that was interesting. She hadn't been sure if Max knew which way the wind was blowing, but he obviously had some suspicions. And there might just be some mileage in that for her, if only she could think out how best to use it. Besides, anything that succeeded in putting Michelle's nose out of joint was always an added bonus, she thought viciously.

* * *

In her kitchen, and with one eye on the clock, Jenny was busy finishing the sandwiches and rolls, and she began to stack them attractively on large blue-and-white china plates, covering them with damp, clean tea towels to stop them drying out. She'd already unloaded the mint-green tablecloths, and now walked with them out into the main changing room.

There, Caroline Majors and Ettie were quick to help her set up and arrange the tables in the most efficacious way possible, to allow a milling crowd access to all sides of them. Jenny then began to load them with glorious food.

'I was just saying to Ettie, it's as well to set up early,' Caroline said, admiring the collection of quiches the large cook had just brought in on a mammoth tray. 'I reckon tea could be needed any time now, on account of the Steeple lot being almost all bowled out. Well, unless that Les Walton digs in and hits a few boundaries. He can be apt to do that,' she added darkly.

Jenny, carefully putting a gateau in pride of place in the middle of the display, sighed with relief at its safe transportation, and then stood back to survey the work so far. As every good cook knew, you ate first with the eyes, so an appetizing display of colours and textures all added to the gastronomic experience.

Perhaps a few more jam tarts? Their jewel-like colours *were* so impressive.

'Mind you, with Lorcan bowling, you never can tell what might happen. Les might be Steeple's best batsman, but Lorcan's known for being a bit of a wild card,' Caroline chattered on. 'Sometimes he can't bowl for toffee, and anybody's granny could get a century off one of his balls, and other times he can come up with a yorker like you wouldn't believe. Bit like that in his personal life too, or so I hear.'

Jenny, who had no idea what she was talking about, nodded wisely. 'Men can be like that,' she felt confident in saying, since, in her experience, she'd found that it could be said in more or less any eventuality, and hardly ever be challenged. Especially by women.

On cue, Caroline nodded eagerly. 'Oh, you're so right. Just look at that business over his engagement. First, his poor mother thought she'd never get rid of him again after his divorce — what with him moving back in with her and still living at home when he's in his forties. And you know what that nearly always means — he's back in the nest to stay. After all, it wasn't as if he couldn't have afforded a place of his own and everything if he'd wanted to, what with him being partners with Tris in that city firm and all. But then, just when she was resigned to being his unofficial housekeeper, he ups and springs that awful girl on her, and they're set to

28

tie the knot by the end of the month. No wonder his poor mother was at sixes and sevens, not knowing whether to be pleased or horrified. And then, to top it all, Tris goes and blows it all out of the water again.'

Caroline took a deep breath, shook her head sorrowfully over the shenanigans of others, and then looked down somewhat blankly at the mixed platter of teacakes, fruit fingers and Chelsea buns that she'd brought in from the kitchen all of five minutes ago.

'Oh well.' She popped the items in the last available space on the table, and then stood back to admire her handiwork and nodded in satisfaction. 'And if you ask me, he actually meant to do it, too,' she added, a shade defiantly.

'Meant what?' Jenny asked blankly, circumspectly rearranging the Chelsea buns into a more pleasing hexagonal shape.

'Meant to get caught out being so naughty,' Caroline said in surprise, but lowering her voice and looking around, as if expecting to see hoards of people, all with their ears pricked, trying to catch what she was saying. And in point of fact, although Ettie didn't seem to find the conversation particularly interesting, Jenny would have bet money that the same couldn't be said of Erica Jones. There was something in the slightly rigid set of the redhead's shoulders that told the cook that she, for once, was listening to Caroline's gossip avidly.

'Naughty?' Jenny echoed, still feeling a little baffled. They were talking about Tristan, and . . . was it Lorcan?

'You know, get caught *in bed*, with his best friend's fiancée,' Caroline hissed.

'Oh,' she said blankly. Then, realizing that much more was expected of her, added, 'Crikey,' somewhat helplessly.

'Yes. Of course, we all knew that she wasn't the right sort for Lorcan,' Caroline said grimly, and shook her brown head so emphatically that all her curls bounced pertly around on her head. 'Not at all his type, anyone could see that, so it was bound to be a disaster. His poor mother was at her wits' end about it, I can tell you. Which is why some of us think that Tris did it on purpose. You know, broke them up. To do Lorcan a favour, almost, as it were.'

Jenny smiled grimly. 'I'll just bet that Lorcan didn't feel particularly grateful about it,' she muttered sardonically.

'Oh well, you couldn't expect him to, could you?' Caroline agreed philosophically. 'But I dare say that Tris, being the sort he is, was very happy to do it! Still, Lorcan will soon see that he's better off without her. He'll get over it. He probably already has, although he won't admit it. Men can be so stubborn where their pride is concerned, can't they? Oh! Look at that! What did I tell you — he's just bowled out Les,' Caroline said with satisfaction, as the sound of a rather more robust round of applause came from outside.

'Oh, well done, Lorcan!' she yelled, making Ettie jump. Then added in a lower volume, 'That's it then — the whole lot out for . . . What's the score, Ettie?'

Jenny, who (like Ettie, as it turned out) wasn't particularly interested in the score, scooted back into the kitchen and began to gather up an army of cutlery. Sure enough, by the time she'd returned to the main room, the first of the men were coming in, and it was just gone half past three.

'Wow, what a spread,' she heard a male voice say admiringly, and felt a warm glow of satisfaction wash over her. She did so love it when people praised her food. It was the one thing that she never got tired of hearing.

'Can't wait to get tucked in to that lot,' another agreed, even more enthusiastically.

'We'd better get the tea urns on then, hadn't we?' Caroline Majors said crisply to Ettie, her friend. And Jenny, who wasn't in charge of beverages, nevertheless offered to help the ladies.

As she did so, she happened to glance through the French windows in the kitchen, where something had just registered in her peripheral vision, and she saw Mark Rawley walk past again. As he did so, he cast a look over his shoulder as he went by, as if checking to see that nobody had noticed him.

So he'd come back, Jenny thought, and she went to the fridge to pour several pints of milk into some blue-and-white jugs. From the changing room, the sound of voices began to rise, as people began to eat and socialize. She hoped that the young lad wasn't about to gatecrash the party, but after a few slightly anxious minutes had passed and there was no sign of trouble, she began to relax again.

She saw Erica leave her deckchair and greet a handsome older man, who was so like his son in looks that he could only be the errant Tristan's father, Sir Robert. Of Tristan himself there was still no sign, and Jenny wondered why he wasn't already the life and soul of the party. She'd heard enough people praising him and the number of wickets that he'd taken to realize that he was likely to be voted man of the match, and she judged him to be the kind who liked to revel in the limelight.

But it was hardly any of her business. She gave a mental shrug and checked the table. Most of the savouries were gone now, and people were starting on the sweet, but she went back for reinforcements of both and began plugging the gaps with more platefuls of food.

In her opinion, you could never have too much choice, although she had always found that it was the gentlemen in particular who could be relied upon to demolish the desserts. The women, on the whole, tended not to have so much of a sweet tooth.

She accepted the lavish praise that came her way graciously, but she couldn't help wondering if the doubting Mavis was amongst those congratulating her on the spread.

* * *

On the outskirts of the field, Marie Rawley moved silently along the hedge line, one eye on the people spilling into the pavilion for tea, the other on the lookout for her father. The last thing she wanted was for James Cluley to buttonhole her and ask her what she was doing there. Because one thing was for sure — he'd know that she was hardly likely to be there to watch the match.

And if her father suspected that something was going on, he'd want to interfere — either to forbid her from doing anything at all, or to muscle in and take over.

Luckily, her father was nowhere in sight, but she couldn't see Mark anywhere either, and that worried her. She just knew her son was up to no good, and after that last bit of trouble they'd had with the police, the last thing she needed was more drama.

Which was why she'd decided to take matters into her own hands and sort it all out.

She glanced at her watch and made her way slowly towards the pavilion, trying not to catch anyone's eye as she did so, and then slipped behind the building at the back. In the narrow space between it and the hedge-lined, chain-link fence separating it from the river beyond, she paused and bit her lip. Perhaps Mark was inside, stuffing his face? When all was said and done, he was still a teenage boy, and since he'd helped with getting the grounds ready, he would have felt he'd earned the right to help himself to a fabulous tea.

Perhaps his slipping out of the house had nothing more ominous behind it than an urge to pig out? She hoped that was the case. But now that she was here, she wasn't going to waste the opportunity to do what she came for. A mother determined to protect her child at all costs would be up for anything — and patience was no big price to pay.

As it happened though, she didn't have to wait very long at all.

Standing at the rear right-hand corner of the building, she saw her quarry begin to troop past on his way in to tea, and hissed out his name. He looked around, but it took him a moment to spot her lurking behind the building. When he did, he looked surprised.

Imperiously, she beckoned him over. He frowned slightly, not being a man who was used to being treated in such a manner, but after a weary sigh and a brief moment's thought, he supposed that he'd better go and see what the damned woman wanted.

She looked like she was ready to make a scene if she didn't get her own way, and right now that was the last thing the Lord of the Manor wanted. Sir Robert Jones sighed wearily.

* * *

Ten minutes later, Jenny had just put the penultimate batch of Bakewell tarts onto the table when she glanced outside, and through the far left changing-room window saw the curly head of Tris Jones. Beside him, in very close proximity indeed, was the blonde head of Michelle Wilson. So close were they, in fact, that it was clear to Jenny that the pair wouldn't have been able to place a matchstick between them.

She turned from the table, and as she did so, caught sight of the boy's stepmother and her husband, the Lord of the Manor, staring out of the same window. Erica instantly turned to say something to the man at her side, and in response, Jenny saw Tris's father scowl at him. Not that Tris noticed the fraternal disapproval being sent his way, of course. He was far too busy flirting with his pretty companion. And no doubt he'd probably have been oblivious to it, if he had noticed his father's ire.

Another person who'd also noticed the close proximity between his wife and her handsome companion was Max Wilson. But, Jenny noted with some surprise, he simply turned to the man he'd been chatting to, and, waving an apple and sultana finger to underscore whatever point he was making, carried on talking as if he'd seen nothing amiss.

Only the gleam in his eye, and the slightly twisted smile on his lips, told her that he wasn't feeling half so sanguine about the situation as he was trying to make out.

Jenny again shook her head and returned to her kitchen. She needed a cup of tea and a scone, but would make do with just the tea for now. There'd be time for her to eat after the match had resumed, and before she and any willing helpers had cleared away the tables.

'All right, ten minutes, everyone.' She heard one of the cricket captains call out the warning, and there was the usual disconcerted stampede for the toilets, which quickly formed into good-natured queues. Jenny smiled to herself and sipped her tea.

After nearly twenty minutes had passed, only a few of the older players still lingered in the changing rooms, reluctant to move so soon on such full stomachs. Besides, now that Much Rousham was batting, most of the team could simply sit or loiter about on the sidelines and watch and take it easy, until it was their turn to bat.

Erica was back once again in her deckchair just inside the door, whilst Caroline and Ettie began to stack the empty plates.

Tris Jones, Jenny saw with a smile, was hastily stuffing himself on the leftovers, and he winked at her over a strawberry scone, packed high with clotted cream and her raspberry jam.

'Very nice,' he said, but his eyes were on her, rather than on her food. His gaze was clear and openly salacious, and in a way, she found his uncomplicated sexual invitation entertaining rather than insulting.

She grinned widely at him. If she'd been the type to want an uncomplicated, one-off bout of recreational sex, she had to acknowledge that she probably couldn't do any better.

'On your way, sonny,' she muttered under her breath, but nevertheless just loud enough for him to hear her.

He grinned cheekily, taking the rejection in good part and moving off, still champing down on the last of his scone as he did so and snitching another one, which he took with him. She saw him blow a teasing kiss to his stepmother as he passed by her, and Jenny glanced at her watch. Time to start making good on the buffet supper.

She knew that all the men would enjoy barbecuing the meat — so she had made sure to provide them with the usual chicken legs, her homemade Cumberland sausages, Oxford herb sausages and her special chilli-flaked beef burgers. Men's affinity with the barbecue meant that she'd have a lot of the cooking taken off her hands, which, after a hard day's baking, was no bad thing.

Of course, she already had most of the bread baked, but she'd need to get started on some flatbreads to add to the tally. Vast salads could be assembled in no time of course, but she needed to start supplementing the trifles with some more desserts.

She checked the tea tables, not surprised to see that nearly all of the food had gone. Nevertheless she hastily tagged a Bakewell tart and bit into it. Made with proper *apricot* jam, of course. Not the raspberry jam which supermarkets would have you believe was the traditional filling.

'It was all smashing, Miss Starling,' Caroline Majors said, still stacking empty, crumb-laden plates. 'Everyone said so. Even Mavis, and she always thought that nobody's Victoria sponge could match her own.'

Ettie groaned with pleasure. 'Oh, that Victoria sponge. I had three pieces. I couldn't help myself.'

'I'm glad you enjoyed it! And please, won't you call me Jenny?' And she promised, once the buffet supper was over, to give both women a generous 'doggie bag' of goodies to take back home with them. (But she was careful not to offer the recipe for her sponge cake. Some things she intended to take to the grave, be she accused of selfishness or not.)

In her deckchair by the door, Erica sighed wearily at the plebeian level of the conversation around her, and rose elegantly from her supine position. 'Just have to pop to the loo a minute,' she said vaguely as she wafted past them. As she did so, she couldn't help but give Ettie's rounded figure a quick sneer as she went through, and behind her back, Caroline somewhat childishly stuck her fist up to her nose and wiggled her fingers at the elegant redhead's departing back.

Ettie giggled.

Jenny pretended not to notice, and began to fill a plate with one or two little nibbles for herself. After all, she was entitled — she'd been baking like a demon all day.

Out on the green, the match went on at its own leisurely pace. Max Wilson, as Much Rousham's captain, was first to bat.

It was quarter to five.

* * *

'Tris, I want a word with you.'

Tristan Jones, leaning against the left-hand side of the pavilion wall and nonchalantly eating his wonderful strawberry scone with lashings of clotted cream and jam, licked one of his sticky fingers and eyed his father with a lazy grin that hid his wariness.

'Well, here I am, Pater dearest, so feel free to bend my ear as much as you like,' he drawled, mocking his father's naturally upper-class accent ruthlessly, whilst waving his half-eaten scone in the air. 'Mind if I carry on munching on the old nosebag whilst you witter on? A fellow needs to feed before going out to commence battle.'

Robert Jones flushed angrily. 'Stop playing the clown for once. If you realized just how pretentious you sound when you try to be smart, you'd stop it quickly enough. Haven't you heard that sarcasm is the lowest form of wit?'

Tris sighed, and bit down hard on the scone, getting a dab of cream on the end of his nose for his trouble. It was a pity, he mused, that Michelle wasn't here. She could have licked it off for him.

Or Tracey, for that matter, the little dental hygienist that he'd spent the night with. Or had her name been Stacey? He sighed, and with the back of his hand, wiped his nose clean.

'So, what's up?' he asked, knowing that there was little point arguing with his old man when he'd got his dander up like this.

And one look at Sir Robert's flushed face told his only son that he was in the patriarchal bad books yet again. It wasn't, to be honest, a particularly rare occurrence, and he knew from past experience that it was best to just let him get it off his chest. It could be nothing more than the usual rant about him needing to settle down and produce a son and heir. But he rather thought, eyeing his father's particularly bellicose eye, that it was more than that.

'I'll have you know that I've just had some irate woman ranting in my ear about you getting her boy into trouble.'

Tris blinked, then laughed. 'I rather doubt it, Daddy dearest. Surely that's biologically impossible? Besides, I'm straight as a die, you know that. Boys definitely aren't my thing.'

'Don't be absurd,' Robert hissed. 'I'm talking about that Rawley boy.'

Tris sighed theatrically. 'Mark? No need to worry about him,' he dismissed casually. 'The boy's just had to learn some hard facts of life and he's still reeling about it. He'll pick himself up and dust himself off. You'll see.'

His father stared at him witheringly. 'That's not what his mother says. She's scared witless that he's going to get himself into some serious trouble with the law or something. Just what the hell's going on? She seemed to think I knew all about it, but I hadn't the faintest idea about half of what she said. But according to her, the boy's only seventeen. Please tell me you haven't been handling his money without parental consent?'

'Of course not!' Tris said, beginning to get angry. 'How daft do you think I am? If you must know, the boy's grandfather approached me. He wanted to put Mark through university — and quite right too. The boy's bright. Unfortunately, since they raised the tuition fees, he didn't have quite enough to do it, and he wanted my advice about how to invest his savings in order to get the best return in the short term. Even with a gap year, Mark would have to start a course in eighteen months or so.'

Robert Jones groaned. 'Don't tell me. You told him to invest in—' He suddenly paused, realizing he was about to break a cardinal rule of his business, and talk freely about stocks and shares in a public place. Instead, he waved a hand briskly. 'I take it whatever you advised didn't work out?'

Tris shrugged. 'Unfortunately not. What can I tell you — it should have done, but the old man was just plain unlucky. And before you start, I told him all about the risks, and I advised him not to invest the whole lot but spread his investments. I even went out of my way to explain to him about government bonds and blue-chip stock, even though the paltry few thousand he had to invest wouldn't even merit the interest of one of our interns. I only did it as a favour to Mark. The boy looks up to me. Looked up to me, I should say, since I'm out of favour with him at the moment.'

Robert shook his head. 'Well, get his mother off our backs, will you? If you ask me, she's unhinged. And that's not all. I've had Matthew on to me again,' Robert swept on, mentioning the senior partner in the law firm that they used to oversee their legal affairs. 'He's had yet another complaint about you.'

Tris sighed. 'Oh for Pete's sake, let me guess. This is about Fairweather Double Glazing?' He named a firm who had lost big when the market had taken an unexpected downturn at close of play yesterday. 'I told the Dorset people those shares will be up again within a fortnight. All they've got to do is hold on to them and keep their nerve. They only need babysitting along, and soon they'll be all smiles again. Surely Matthew is up for that? If not, pass the account on to Lorcan. He's good at babysitting nervous investors. That bland-as-milk way he has about him always settles upset tummies.'

Robert Jones shook his head, exasperated. 'No, it's not about them. But from what you're saying, I daresay I'll have them bending my ear first thing on Monday as well. This is Piers Mountjoy I'm talking about.'

'Oh that little twit,' Tris said carelessly. 'A real mummy's boy, that one. He's inherited so much money he doesn't know what to do with it, but he's desperate to be seen as a competent financial manager. He wants the rest of the family to believe that he's going to double the family fortune. I told him that what he really needed was to spread the risk with a fairly conservative mix, but he would insist on a highly speculative portfolio. He only saw the profits to be made, and totally ignored the risks. Don't let him worry you.'

'Not worry me? You've lost the man millions!' Robert then quickly shot a look around, in case anyone had overheard this extremely indiscreet outburst. Luckily no one had. Whilst stocks and shares was his lifeblood, most of the people there today were more interested in the cricket.

Tristan saw his father's worried look, and felt suddenly sorry for the old man. It must be awful to get old and lose your nerve. 'Relax, Pater, you'll worry yourself into a heart attack. Or worse. Piers is a pussycat. He'll just huff and puff but he won't cause us real any trouble. He wouldn't dare.'

'Tris, he's threatening to sue!' Robert said, frustrated almost beyond endurance.

'Oh, that! He's just bluffing,' Tris said confidently, polishing off the last of his scone and wiping his sticky fingers carelessly across his cricket whites to brush off the crumbs. 'He won't dare let it get to court — he'll be too scared that the rest of his family will get to hear about it, and start laughing up their sleeves at him for losing so much dough.'

'He shouldn't have lost it to begin with,' Robert Jones snapped. 'It's part of our job to protect our clients from doing something really foolish. You know better than most how many of them can be their own worst enemies sometimes. You should have steered him well clear. And if you couldn't, you should have handed him over to Lorcan. As you yourself pointed out, he's good at talking sense into people.'

Tris's lips twisted into a grimace. 'Lorcan can't handle the really big accounts,' he said. 'I can handle the likes of Piers — just leave it all to me. Don't you worry about it. I'll have a word with him on Monday. It'll all blow over.'

Robert looked as if he was about to blast off again, so Tris very cannily straightened up and abruptly inclined his head, indicating that he should look behind him. 'Best not to get into it here, OK, Pops? We're beginning to attract the attention of the locals and the last thing we want to do is start a rumour that the firm is having difficulties. Isn't that right?'

In point of fact, a few people were indeed beginning to look at them thoughtfully, no doubt sensing the tension between them, or reading their body language. And as his son had known that he would, Robert Jones instantly bit back the angry words that he'd been about to say, and turned away.

He did, however, content himself with a low growl and a final passing shot as he left. 'If you think you can continue to drag our good name through the mud and not pay for it, you're a fool, boy.'

Tris sighed, determined to have the last word. 'Oh, don't be such a drama queen! Nobody's dragging our good name through the mud. Everyone knows that trading in stocks and shares is just another form of gambling. Nobody in their right mind expects to win big all the time.'

'That may be,' his father said softly. Then, catching sight of James Cluley as he went by to confer with the umpire, he shook his head sadly. 'But when you lose people's entire life savings . . . Tris, you just can't keep on doing these sorts of things and expect to get away with it. You're playing with fire,' he warned his son helplessly.

But Tris merely shook his head. 'You worry too much.'

'And you don't worry enough,' his father shot back, and finally stomped off.

But as he walked away, Robert Jones knew that he was going to have to do something about his son. Something both definitive and decisive — otherwise his own position as head of the firm could be in jeopardy. He wouldn't put it past some of his so-called colleagues to try and vote him off the board. And with the firm's solicitors beginning to howl for his blood as well . . . It wasn't as if the firm was so big that it could afford to get a questionable reputation. As the commercial markets all knew, there was a big difference between having the nerve and being willing to take chances to make big profits, and being lackadaisical with other people's money.

The trouble was, he knew his son too well. Tris thought that he was invincible and untouchable. And he simply wouldn't be told — mostly because he'd had some truly spectacular successes to date. But these were beginning to be outweighed by his losses. And still he just wouldn't be told.

And if he, the head of the firm, didn't do something drastic soon, then they could be in real trouble.

CHAPTER FOUR

Lorcan Greeves glanced around, checking quickly to see if anyone had noticed his re-emergence back into the grounds. Satisfied that no one had, and that his meeting with his little friend had gone unnoticed, he made his way back to the pavilion, and found a shady spot on the grass in which to sit down.

Out on the green, he'd noticed that Max was still going strong, and from the scoreboard, that he'd made thirty-five runs already. Not bad. Not that he was interested in the outcome of the match particularly — he'd only joined the team in order to keep in with the 'right' people. He gave an inner snort. Whatever that meant!

He kept glancing surreptitiously to his right until he saw the figure of Mark Rawley slip along the outskirts of the field and head back into the village. He breathed a slight sigh of relief, and hoped that the lad would have enough sense to keep his mouth firmly shut.

But all in all, he was fairly confident that things should now work out as he'd envisaged. He'd never lacked for brains, after all. He was confident that the plan was a good one, and that so long as they both played their part, they would be safe enough.

And, in truth, Lorcan was convinced that the lad would see things through to the end. He was so full of youthful wrath and literally seething with a sense of injustice, that wild horses probably wouldn't be able to make him talk, even if things somehow went wrong.

Not that there was any reason why they should.

Lorcan's rather chubby face creased into a grim smile. Contrary to how the saying went, revenge was a dish that could be served either hot or cold. And whereas Mark might be boiling with rage, Lorcan had never felt calmer, or more cold-blooded, in all his life.

And overlying it all, he was aware now of an overwhelming sense of relief. All the frustration that had been weighing him down since his lover's betrayal, and that awful sense of futile helplessness whenever he thought of Tris, was finally gone.

He leaned his back against the warm wooden wall of the pavilion and waited for his turn to be called on to bat.

Life was suddenly good again.

* * *

But Lorcan might not have felt quite so sanguine about things had he bothered to turn his head towards the top of the field, where a lone female figure stood within the stand of horse chestnut trees, watching him with a writhing mixture of fury, resentment and dread.

Her talk with Robert Jones had hardly been satisfactory, and the Lord of the Manor's assurances that he would 'talk to Tris' had hardly filled her with confidence that anything would change, so she was already feeling tense and out of sorts.

So when Mark had tried to slip out of the house yet again without her noticing, he had been spectacularly unsuccessful, and she'd simply followed him back to the cricket field once more. But this time, he'd had no intention of seeing his grandfather, or helping himself to some fancy caterer's tea.

And her suspicions were doubly aroused when he'd taken the trouble to cross the farmer's field and then walk along the riverbank skirting the grounds, in an effort not to be noticed. He'd slipped in through the secret gap in the hedge and chain-link fence, not far from the stand of horse chestnut trees. All the locals knew about this shortcut of course, since fishermen had created it years ago to give them quicker access to the river from the village, without having to walk all the way around.

And why had he bothered to go to all that trouble not to be seen if he wasn't up to something?

But then she'd lost sight of him. So she'd simply taken up a position at the top of the playing field, hiding patiently in the cow-parsley smothered undergrowth beneath the majestic, flowering horse chestnut trees, and waited. And sure enough, after a while, she'd seen her son emerge from behind the mass of parked cars at the bottom of the field, where he'd obviously arranged to meet someone.

And it hadn't taken more than a few minutes before a man dressed in cricket whites had also emerged from the car park. And Marie had instantly recognized the squat, sandy-haired figure as that of Lorcan Greeves.

Which, she supposed a shade bitterly, made sense. Along with her family, Lorcan Greeves probably had as much reason to hate Tris as anyone.

Marie didn't have any trouble imagining just how much the resentment and hatred must have fermented in Lorcan's heart when he found out about Tris sleeping with his fiancée. And part of her didn't blame him.

But when Lorcan dragged her son into his schemes, it became a different matter entirely. Lorcan should have been man enough to go it alone — whatever it was that he was up to. So why hadn't he? He had plenty of resources, and the wisdom of nearly fifty years behind him, which should be more than enough for him to manage his own vendettas. So why would a middle-aged stockbroker, who was presumably big enough and mean enough to get his own back all by himself, need the help of a teenage boy?

Marie Rawley could only think of one reason. And that reason spelled trouble with a capital T.

Lorcan needed Mark to do something specific. Something that Mark excelled at. Something that Lorcan wasn't able to do for or by himself. And given what she knew about her son's proclivities, she didn't need to be a genius to know just what it was that he'd been asking Mark to do.

And Marie knew that it would mean prosecution for her son this time, if anyone found out about it. Mark had been lucky enough to get away with a warning the last time, but if he got caught again, especially doing something for Lorcan Greeves, then it would mean him gaining a criminal record. And what sort of future would there be for Mark then?

Forget about the mere disappointment of not being able to go to university after all — or being crippled with debt if he did go, after having to take out a student loan. If Mark spent time inside, then not having a degree would be the least of his troubles.

She'd seen the television programmes about young offender institutions, and read in the newspapers about what went on in that world — so she knew all too well what could happen. Young boys killed themselves in prison all the time. Or got hooked on drugs and got dragged down into a worsening spiral of addiction and crime. And she knew that Mark, for all his fierce anger and bravado, wasn't the kind of lad who'd be able to survive in a place like that. That sort of experience would crush his spirit like someone stepping on a Rice Krispie.

So she had to nip this alliance of theirs in the bud. And since she knew that Mark wouldn't listen to her, she needed to have a word or two with Mr Lorcan Greeves. He would listen to her all right — she'd damned well make him.

She felt her hands curl into fists. If he thought that he could use Mark for his own ends whilst keeping his own hands clean . . . well, he'd soon learn differently. He'd very quickly find out that whilst Mark might be a vulnerable, silly teenager, and thus easily manipulated, he had his mother fighting his corner. And she would not be such a pushover. Nor would she stand for her son being used in such a way.

So he'd better change his plans and leave her son out of it. Or Marie would make him.

* * *

Inside the pavilion, Erica returned to her deckchair, fastidiously brushing down her colourful green trousers of any lingering dust before resuming her seat. Jenny and the others now had the tables completely cleared, and were busy folding the legs back up, and stacking them, flat-pack, against the walls. On the pitch, Max Wilson watched the ball being bowled his way, and calculated his next move. He was instantly adjudged LBW by the white-coated umpire, and began the long walk of shame back towards the pavilion. Yet he didn't look particularly put out by his misfortune. Instead his eyes were fixed on the figure of his wife, lounging in her deckchair, amidst a line of the other cricketers' wives.

He began to smile slightly.

No doubt about it, the little chat that he'd had with her just before he'd gone out to start batting had left her badly rattled and severely shaken — just as he'd hoped it would.

She hadn't taken being served with the divorce papers very well, either.

No doubt she'd hoped, while his attention had been on batting, to relay the bad news to Tris. And he could just imagine how *he'd* have taken it.

If Michelle had thought that she could cry on her lover's shoulder, she must have been very quickly and rudely disabused of that notion. If all the sniping that had been going on between Tris and his father in recent weeks was anything to go by, they hadn't been getting on very well lately, and the last thing lover boy would want would be to get even further into his father's bad books. Sir Robert was still very much head of the home and head of the firm, and Tris a mere junior partner, way down on the totem pole.

So being cited in an acrimonious divorce might well prove to be the final straw that broke the camel's back. Who knows, Sir Robert might even wash his hands once and for all of the little shit.

So, all in all, Max was very much looking forward to the next half an hour or so.

As he passed some of the men on his team lounging on the grass just outside the pavilion, he nodded at them.

'Tris is up next. Where is he?' he asked casually.

For a few moments, everyone looked around, seeking out the distinctive curly-headed figure of their best batsman.

But Tris Jones was nowhere to be seen.

* * *

Mark Rawley all but ran down the garden path to his semi-detached house, his heart pounding with elation and, if he were to be honest with himself, a little dread as well. It was hard for him to concentrate on any one thing, since his mind was fizzing with thoughts and sensations. He felt like a giant, like someone who'd done something truly momentous. For the first time in his young life, he felt as if he was about to achieve something that he'd never forget. And that others would never forget, either.

Now all he had to do was be careful, just like Lorcan had warned him, and keep his mouth shut.

He pushed open the front door and headed across the tiny hall towards the bottom of the staircase.

His father called out to him in passing from the open kitchen door, asking if he was hungry, but the boy didn't appear to hear him. His face was pale and set, his eyes a little wild, and catching sight of himself in the hall mirror, Mark realized it wouldn't be a good idea to face his dad just yet. Instead, he put one hand firmly on the newel post and vaulted noisily up the stairs. He had things to do, and he couldn't wait to get started.

His father sighed, hoping that he wasn't going to spend the rest of the afternoon on that computer of his. Unlike his wife, Christopher Rawley had never expected his son to honour the promise forced out of him by his old school and the local coppers that he would keep away from a computer until he was eighteen. It stood to reason that was never going to fly.

He knew that Mark was considered to be very good, even a bit of a genius, in the world of IT. Kids nowadays seemed to pick up all that stuff easily, although he himself was still something of a Luddite when it came to modern technology. But from an early age, Mark had been a bit of a whizz at it, and in truth, Chris had always felt proud of him. But lads were lads, and he hadn't been all that surprised when Mark had got into that bit of trouble with the school. Annoyed by what he saw as 'teacher tyranny,' he'd hacked into the school's computer system and given all the 'swots, teacher's pets' and 'that toffee-nosed, brainiac crowd' a grade C. And all his mates, and those who notoriously struggled with academia, A pluses.

It had driven some of the parents into such fits of hysterics that it had secretly made Chris want to laugh out loud.

Of course, everyone else took a different, and much dimmer, view of Mark Rawley's 'creative' project. Although the headmaster had been very understanding, and in the end everyone had agreed that Mark had only done it in a sense of fun rather than out of malice, it had nevertheless been made perfectly clear to the Rawleys that what Mark had done was a criminal offence. If the school had so wished, it could have involved the police to a far greater extent than merely issuing him with a formal warning.

Naturally Chris had read the lad the Riot Act. And now, just to show that his son hadn't managed to pull the wool over his eyes, he craned his head back to peer up the stairs.

'And don't you be turning that machine on, Mark,' he yelled threateningly up at the landing, his voice hectoring. 'Remember the rules! I might be willing to turn a blind eye occasionally, but don't push your luck, son!'

There was a short, surprised silence, and Chris Rawley had to grin. No doubt the youngster had thought he'd been so clever. He remembered that, when he'd been Mark's age, he'd been totally convinced that both his parents had been blind, as well as stupid.

'OK, Dad, I won't,' Mark reluctantly answered.

But, in point of fact, Mark hadn't gone straight to the spare bedroom to turn on the family computer, as his father had surmised, but had headed for the bathroom instead.

In there, his hands now shook as they turned on the tap and he began to wash them. Only when he'd finished doing that did he force himself to meet his grim reflection in the mirror. And was again overtaken by a sudden wave of nausea that made him swallow hard.

'Oh, don't be so feeble,' he told his image in disgust. 'And grow a backbone, why don't you?'

Because Lorcan Greeves was right. There could be no regrets. And absolutely no weakening now.

* * *

Back at the cricket match, Robert Jones frowned at Max Wilson. 'What do you mean, he's not here?' Robert demanded. 'He's batting next. He knows the order of play, doesn't he?' he added testily. Although, even as he spoke, he had to admit that it wouldn't have been beyond Tris simply to have taken himself off to the local pub for a quick one. He'd simply say that he'd got tired of waiting and would saunter back in his own sweet time, wondering what all the fuss had been about. The boy had no sense of responsibility at all.

'He should do, I went over it with him just before the coin toss,' Max responded flatly. But his eyes roamed once again towards his wife, who was pretending not to notice him. Instead, she was talking desultorily to the woman on her left, who looked half-asleep.

'I'll check to see if he's in the loo,' one of the other players volunteered, and trotted off, but was soon back. 'No sign of him in there,' he reported. The umpire was beginning to look impatient, and one of the others players said that he'd be willing to bat next, if that would help.

Max nodded, then trotted over towards the pavilion as the match got underway again.

'Has anyone seen where Tris went?' he asked the first of the women in the line of deckchairs, and the Chinese whisper quickly ran up and down the field.

But nobody, it seemed, had seen Tris within the last ten minutes or so.

'Well, he can't have left,' Max said irritably. 'We'd have seen him if he'd walked off the pitch.'

'Then where is he?' his father demanded, his face beginning to suffuse with colour.

If there was one thing he hated, it was being made to look like a fool in public. And with everyone depending on Tris to catch up and then overtake Steeple Clinton's pitiful tally, the boy needed to have a damned good reason, other than impatience, for cutting out on them.

'I'll see if he's gone around the back, shall I?' James Cluley finally offered, nodding towards the pavilion. 'It's shady and cooler back there. If he ate too much at tea, he might have gone around to sleep it off before he was needed to bat.'

Max snorted at this — Tris was, after all, a fit young man, and was hardly likely to feel the heat, let alone the need to sleep off the odd cucumber sandwich or two. But it was the only place that they hadn't looked yet, so Max shrugged, and the boy's father sighed with impatience.

'Might as well,' Robert Jones agreed. And whilst he too doubted that his son would be found 'resting' back there, he did have to concede that Tris might very well be caught out entertaining a woman. That seemed to be about the boy's forte. He had no damned sense of discretion or discernment.

James Cluley dutifully slipped between the back of the pavilion and the hawthorn-lined chain-link fence, and did indeed promptly discover Tristan Jones lying down in the shade, about halfway along.

Except that he was lying completely, utterly still. And beside him was an old cricket bat, stained red on one side.

As James stood over him, looking down at the young man's body, the old groundsman could see that the back of his head had been dealt a very heavy and unforgiving blow indeed. It was clear he wasn't breathing.

Tristan Jones was as dead as you could get.

James Cluley, after one long last look, turned and walked very carefully away on legs that felt just a bit rubbery.

And although he could feel chills start to run through him, leaving him feeling a little light-headed with shock, if anyone had happened to see him in that moment, they'd have said that he looked, more than anything else, desperately puzzled.

* * *

James Cluley blinked rapidly as he stepped away from the shade and back into the bright sunlight beyond. His gait was still not quite steady as he approached the boy's father, and he had to fight a cowardly urge to simply turn around and walk away. Let somebody else do the dirty work instead. But he knew he couldn't do that. It simply wouldn't be right. He took a few deep breaths and tried to arrange the proper words, in order, in his mind. But how exactly did you go about telling a man that his only son was dead?

Robert Jones was now standing alone, since the others had wandered off to watch the resumed match, and the groundsman stiffened his spine as he approached him. Perhaps it would be better to ask his wife to be present? Or would that only make matters worse? Although Erica Jones had never struck him as the hysterical type, you never could tell how people would react to shocking news.

He was still rather fruitlessly trying to think of the best way to break the news when the Lord of the Manor spotted him shuffling about and looking lost, and somewhat impatiently spoke up first.

'He's not there then, I take it?'

The older man swallowed hard, and looked off somewhere slightly over Robert Jones's right shoulder.

51

'Oh no, sir, he's there,' James said vaguely.

His voice, even to his own ears, sounded as if it was coming from somewhere far away, and he blinked, then swallowed hard. But as he met the other man's vaguely irritated-looking gaze, he felt his gorge rise, and had to swallow hard once more.

There had been something so utterly *permanent*, so inhumanly intractable, about Tris Jones's silent and still body. James had never actually seen a dead person before today. And if he could feel the cold, creeping awareness of how *wrong* it all was, just how much worse would it be for the boy's father?

Robert's eyebrows rose. 'He's there, is he? Well, he'd bloody well better get a move on then. You told him he was up to bat, I suppose? It doesn't look like this chap we've got up now is going to amount to much,' he predicted gloomily. 'He'll be out for a duck if he's not careful.'

'No, sir. That is, I couldn't really tell him anything.' James Cluley shuffled his feet uneasily as the other man shot him a questioning look. 'And I'm very sorry, but he won't be coming to bat for us, either,' James heard himself say inanely, and then felt like kicking himself. What a bloody stupid thing to say, he thought helplessly. And tried again. 'We need to call an ambulance, Sir Robert.' He hesitated for just a moment, and then added, 'And the police, I reckon.'

* * *

Max Wilson was now sitting in the deckchair next to his wife and was talking quietly but seemingly quite viciously into her ear. Whatever he was saying to her was making her go slowly paler and paler, but conscious of the people all around them, she was saying little in response.

Her hands, though, as they curled around the plastic armrests of her chair, displayed stark white knuckles, and she was biting her lip, probably in an effort to prevent tears. One of the women sitting a few yards away was watching them curiously, and had obviously picked up on her friend's tense body language.

But for all that his attention seemed to be mainly directed at his wife, he also noticed the other two men talking not far away, and his eyes were particularly speculative as they settled on the old groundsman.

* * *

'What do you mean?' Robert asked James next, clearly baffled by the turn in the conversation, and for a second or two, couldn't seem to make sense of it. And then his face, which had been a trifle flushed, suddenly paled. 'You mean to say he's been taken ill?' he demanded loudly, attracting more than just Max's sharp ears this time. He began to move off quickly towards the pavilion. 'Why the hell didn't you just say so in the first place, man? We need a doctor. Max,' he suddenly called over to the cricket captain as he neared the wooden structure. 'Is Dr Warner here, do you know? Among the spectators, I mean?' he added, waving around vaguely.

'No, he's off on his holidays,' Max answered at once, scrambling up from the deckchair with a bit of an effort, and leaving his white-faced wife behind him without another thought. He walked quickly and curiously to catch up to the two older men. 'Why, what's up? Someone got sunstroke, have they? I'm not surprised. It's hot enough for it. One of the old folk, is it?' he asked, his voice almost cheerful, but his eyes going quickly from James Cluley to the powerful businessman, then back again.

'No, nothing like that. I don't really know what's going on,' Robert brushed this aside impatiently. 'James here says that it's Tris who has been taken poorly.'

The old groundsman desperately sought to catch Max Wilson's eye, perhaps hoping for, rather than sensing, an actual ally who could now safely take over.

'We need to call 999, sir. Do you have a mobile phone?' James asked urgently.

Max, of course, had, and began to take it out of his white trouser pocket. He unlocked it and dialled the famous three-digit number.

'I'll go and stay with Tris,' Robert said, and was astonished when the old man moved impertinently to block his way.

'Best not, Sir Robert,' James Cluley said respectfully but firmly. He may not be very good in a crisis, but at least he had enough about him to know that that was not a good idea. Not surprisingly, the Lord of the Manor began to argue.

He was not a man who was used to being thwarted, and certainly not by someone of James Cluley's status.

Max, who still had his eyes fixed on James's face, lifted the mobile to his mouth and began to talk quietly to the emergency services. His eyes were narrowed and thoughtful, and continued to dart about, as if unable to settle. Periodically, he spoke abruptly into the phone.

'No, I'm not sure of the nature of the incident, but it's obviously serious. Yes, I'll hold on. I can put a man out on the road, if you like, to help direct the ambulance to the back of the field, where the access is better. It's only a narrow lane, and hardly ever used. Yes, I'll do that.'

He nodded to one plump young man, who'd been sitting on the boundary and had clearly overheard the entire exchange. He'd risen to his feet, obviously keen to volunteer, and wore an enquiring look on his face. At a nod from his team captain, he walked rapidly across the field, heading towards the lane.

Sir Robert, in the meantime, was still staring at James Cluley, who was continuing to resolutely block his path. It was clear the groundsman wasn't about to budge, no matter how much Sir Robert was trying to badger him to do just that. Finally, realizing that it was hopeless, he stopped trying to force his way past.

'Look, I think I deserve at least an explanation, don't you?' the wealthy businessman finally said, but for once his voice lacked the authority it usually carried. His colour was now turning chalk-white as the gravity of the disaster began to seep in. 'If my son needs me, I should be there,' he added, more desperate than angry now. 'I may not know first aid, but just my presence may help assure him. Is he having a heart attack? Just what's the matter with him, man?'

James couldn't quite meet the other man's eye. 'I'm sorry, sir, but I believe your son is . . . I mean, I don't think that there's anything that you can do for him. That is — well, he's gone, Sir Robert. There's simply nothing that you can do,' he repeated helplessly. And again swallowed hard as the sheer enormity of it swept over him once again.

A man was dead. But somehow, James Cluley still couldn't quite make himself believe that it was true.

In the stark silence that followed this pronouncement, Robert Jones made once more to move quickly past the groundsman, but again the old man deliberately blocked his passage.

'Sir, I really don't think you ought to see,' James insisted grimly. 'There's something wrong about it. I mean, I don't think the police will want you to interfere with things. You know, like . . .' But here he broke off, simply not able to talk about things like disturbing evidence or contaminating a crime scene.

Max slowly lowered the phone he was holding to his ear and said quietly, 'Are you saying that it's not a heart attack or something?' His voice was hoarse now. 'You actually mean to say you think that there's been foul play, James?' he asked. Unfortunately, his voice carried quite clearly on the heavy, quiet, somnolent air, and soon the small crowd of people around them began to hum with a disconcerted murmur as the news began to filter through that some kind of tragedy seemed to be unfolding.

James Cluley, who was feeling more and more incapable of speech, simply nodded at the captain of the home team.

Inside, he felt truly sick with dread.

Sir Robert Jones looked vaguely around him, as if everything had become suddenly strange and alien to him, and then he stumbled to the nearest vacant deckchair and sank down heavily.

Instantly a few matrons hustled to his side to offer company and sympathy. Someone rushed off for a cup of tea.

* * *

Lorcan Greeves had been watching these events unfold from his position, lounging on the grass a little off to one side of the pavilion. Now he rose to his feet, with a little difficulty and a certain amount of huffing and puffing, and tried to stroll as casually as possible towards Max Wilson.

It wasn't easy to look unconcerned, however, when he desperately wanted to know what was being said. And even more importantly, what was being done.

He nodded a brief hello to one of the cricket players not currently in the match, which was still ongoing behind them, and finally fetched up beside Max.

'What's going on?' he asked quietly. And then, when the cricket captain looked at him with his usual mixture of impatience and disinterest, Lorcan shrugged a little shyly, and added affably, 'I thought I might be able to help with something.'

'Well, you can't,' Max said shortly. 'Not unless you're a doctor. Or maybe a faith healer who can raise the dead.'

Lorcan tensed. He could feel the half-hearted smile on his face freeze, and looked briefly away. But he was so used to other men treating him like someone of absolutely no consequence that the lack of respect barely touched him.

'Sorry? I don't quite follow you,' he said, spreading his hands to show his bafflement. 'Someone's been taken ill, I assume? But don't these dos usually have a St John's Ambulance man about or something?' he asked vaguely, looking around, as if he could conjure one up out of thin air.

He'd usually found that it paid to be irritating sometimes. People tended to say more when they were trying to get rid of you, and didn't realize how much they gave away when they didn't think of you as any kind of threat.

'I hardly think a local cricket derby rates something as grand as that,' Max said bitingly, looking worriedly at Robert Jones's slumped figure. He was trying to make sense of what was happening, and what it all meant, which was hard with Lorcan hanging around and droning on like a pesky fly. Like

James Cluley, he too was feeling sick with worry. If only Lorcan would sod off and let him think for a minute.

But the other man clearly had no intention of being so obliging.

'So who's been taken ill?' Lorcan persisted instead. 'A spot of sunstroke was it, I expect? I can see how that would happen. It's still so damned hot, and getting hotter, I reckon. Wouldn't be surprised if today doesn't turn out to be a record-breaker — the hottest on record, that sort of thing. You'd think once you were past four o'clock the heat would start to abate, wouldn't you? But I reckon we're all in for a really sticky night as well. It'll be impossible to sleep, you mark my words.'

'Oh for Pete's sake, stop rattling on! And it's a bit more serious than that,' Max hissed, exasperated. 'Tris is dead.' And then he amended hastily, 'At least, I think so. That's what James Cluley said, anyway,' he backtracked fast. It wouldn't look good to know more than he should.

Lorcan felt the colour washing out of his face, and his mouth went dry whilst his throat seemed to close up tight. For a second, he felt as if a constricting band had been looped around his chest, making his ribs start to ache, and then he drew in a long, shuddering breath.

'James Cluley?' he echoed stupidly. 'You say that Tris is dead?' And then, when his companion, perhaps alerted to something odd in his voice, suddenly took a closer look at him, he quickly half-turned away. 'How awful,' he managed to mutter. And, realizing just how inadequate that must sound, added, 'His poor father. Let's hope James has got it wrong. He's just an old man after all, he might have got things muddled.'

Max nodded automatically, but he rather doubted it. He doubted it very much, but he said, 'Yes, perhaps.'

Much to the cricket captain's intense relief, Lorcan then drifted off in that vague, silent, helpless way that was so typical of the man, but Max was just glad that he'd gone at last.

Right now he needed a clear head.

He had to think — how best to minimize the danger? What was likely to happen now? But, above all, only one thought was uppermost in his mind.

Just what the hell was he going to do about Michelle?

* * *

Lorcan wandered as far away from the crowd as he could get without looking conspicuous, and then glanced around. People were beginning to cotton on to the fact that something out of the ordinary had happened, and were congregating in little groups, chatting with a mixture of animation, pleasant alarm and, in some cases, genuine concern. Out on the field, the match was now being held in abeyance, with the umpire beginning to look rather comically cross. As he looked on, he saw him beckon the captain of the visiting team over, obviously demanding an explanation for what was interfering with the state of play.

Lorcan reached hastily into his trouser pocket and withdrew his own mobile phone. With a final glance to make sure that no one was within earshot, he selected a familiar number.

He didn't have to wait long for it to be answered.

'It's me,' he said flatly. And then, with a growing sense of panic, he hissed desperately, '*Just what the hell did you do?*'

* * *

Jenny was just eating the last of the mini-quiches — bacon and wild mushroom with a hint of thyme and sage — when the news of the catastrophe spread to the pavilion.

It was Erica's voice which alerted them all first, which had risen above the more general din.

'What do you mean, dead? How can he be dead?' she exclaimed.

Not unnaturally, this stopped all conversation within hearing distance, both inside the building and out, as everyone took a moment to process what they'd just heard.

Jenny also froze for a moment, and then, along with all the others, looked quickly across to Erica, and took in the fact that she had been addressing Max Wilson, who was standing just inside the doorway. She then saw him say something in response to the agitated redhead, but his voice was muted and pitched just too low for her to catch it.

Not that she really needed to as it turned out, for a moment later it was quickly repeated by the redhead.

'*Tris?*' Erica screeched, her voice cracking with disbelief. 'Are you sure? I mean, where is he? Have you seen him? Perhaps there's been a mistake of some kind.' Her words came out sharply, like a series of volleys from a cannon.

Max was still keeping his voice much lower, for his reply was still inaudible to everyone who was now unashamedly straining to hear what he was saying. Once again, though, it didn't seem to matter much, since Erica's replies were given at full volume.

'Well, there you are then! What does that dozy old man know? It's not as if he's a doctor or anything! So what if Tris is sprawled out around the back here? Good grief, Max, you know what he's like,' she carried on, sounding more exasperated now than concerned. 'He's probably just passed out — he's had too much to drink, and went around the back to sleep it off, I imagine,' she added scornfully. 'That would be just like him, and typical of the inconsiderate little shit! Or maybe he tripped and fell and has just knocked himself out,' she added, sounding a little less sure of herself now. 'I hope someone's called a doctor,' she finally snapped, somewhat belatedly aware that she was hardly coming across as a concerned parent. One ballet-shoed foot tapped impatiently on the ground as she crossed her arms defensively around her chest, as if sensing the censure wafting her way from the silent but restive crowd.

Max murmured something else.

'Police?' Erica's voice again rose to a scandalized squeak, and her arms uncrossed and went straight down by her sides. 'What on earth do we want the police for?' By now, you could have heard the proverbial pin drop, and Caroline Majors shot her friend Ettie a speaking look. Jenny put aside her plate, abruptly losing her appetite.

The travelling cook was not liking the sound of this. Not one little bit.

Both Caroline and Ettie began to approach the pair cautiously, shuffling tiny steps at a time, as if sensing that the Lord of the Manor's wife might, like her stricken husband outside, soon be in need of succour and support. But since Erica was not popular, and neither woman was quite certain how she'd respond to their offers of kindness, neither one could quite pluck up the courage to make the first overture. The result of which meant that they simply hovered close by, looking helpless. Or, if you were of an unkind disposition, quite useless.

Jenny, after a moment's thought, quietly left her chair and went through to the kitchen, where she hesitated for a moment, before walking cautiously over to the French windows. Once there, she replayed the past hour or so in her mind, going over what she could remember of the sequence of events so far, and then gave a mental nod. Taking a deep breath, she then reached out for the handles on the iron-framed doors, and pressed firmly down.

They were still firmly locked, as she'd been hoping and praying they were, and she felt the tension, which she hadn't until then been aware of, seep quickly out of her shoulders. Without a doubt, the fact that the French doors were still firmly locked would be very good for her, once the police came making their inquiries. It meant that she wouldn't have been able to sneak out the back at any time for any reason.

She couldn't help but feel slightly heartless to be thinking about her own safety first and foremost, but she knew, from some considerable experience, just how the police thought. And being a viable suspect in what might well turn out to be a murder inquiry would be no picnic. And one she would far rather avoid, thank you very much.

And so, being only human, she breathed a sigh of relief, and then stared at the French doors thoughtfully. Of course, she had been pretty sure that the doors must still be locked, and only James Cluley had the key to them anyway. *Or so he'd said.*

And since she'd been in and out of this room all the time, it was highly unlikely that anybody could have sneaked past her to get out and around to the back of the pavilion this way. Even if they had managed to obtain a set of the keys somehow.

So that settled *that.*

Now there was something else that had to be done. Something that she was not looking forward to one little bit. Jenny nodded, closed her eyes briefly, took a deep, reluctant breath, girded her impressive loins, and then stepped as close to the windows as she could get. Once there, she looked to the right, where she could see the chain-link fence, and inside of it, a narrow stretch of recently mown grass.

She took another deep breath and looked as far to the left as her neck would stretch.

And instantly saw him.

Dressed in his cricket whites, Tristan Jones was lying face down, his limbs sprawled around him in a slightly clumsy and graceless fashion. And before she could stop it, the thought came unbidden to her mind that, in life, he'd never have allowed himself to look so inelegant.

Beside him on the ground lay what looked like an old cricket bat.

A little further past him, where the building ended, Jenny noticed movement, and saw that James Cluley was standing in the gap, apparently blocking anyone from going back there.

Jenny nodded in silent approval at this forethought. The police would be pleased with that. It would preserve any forensic evidence, and limit any contamination of the crime scene. She only hoped that the groundsman had had the common sense to position someone at the other end too.

The last thing anyone needed was for ghoulish sightseers to come along, leaving trace evidence behind.

She drew back, and set about making herself a cup of tea, with hands that were not entirely steady. She added a spoonful or two more sugar than she would normally have done. She was feeling a little shaky, and hoped that the age-old remedy of hot sweet tea would stave off the effects of shock.

For although she hadn't really known the man, and the little she'd seen of him had left her with the distinct impression that he was rather too fond of himself, conceit hardly seemed to merit a death sentence. And if selfishness and a lack of sexual discernment was to be judged a good enough reason to murder someone, then the death rate would surely sky-rocket.

Besides, Jenny Starling didn't approve of murder, full stop. And it mattered not a whit whether the victim was a near saint who was beloved by all, or someone who would scarcely be mourned, and had been without a friend in the world.

And now she knew all too well what was going to happen next. The police would come, and the questions would start. And then they'd all be under suspicion.

Even worse, she wouldn't be allowed to continue her cooking for the buffet supper!

CHAPTER FIVE

Detective Inspector Laurence Causon sighed as his sergeant pulled up behind a stationary ambulance in the small car park. He looked around carefully, but there was no sign of any medical personnel in sight, and in fact, the whole scene looked quiet and deserted. One patrol car, likewise unmanned, was parked discreetly by a tall hedge a few yards away. The only sound was the sound of birdsong, and the tick, tick, ticking of the car's engine as it started to cool.

'Doesn't look like there's any sense of urgency about the proceedings, does it, sir?' Sergeant Graham Lane said thoughtfully. And such was their combined experience that he didn't need to add anything. Because they both knew that if the victim had still been alive, there'd be a lot more frenzied activity going on than this.

He sighed somewhat wearily, but also felt an undeniable little frisson of excitement. The call they'd received to Much Rousham had been rather vague as to what exactly it was that they might expect when they arrived. Contrary to the general public's belief, almost any unexpected death had to be classified or treated as suspicious until proved otherwise. This included suicides, accidents, and what might eventually be ruled as death due to natural causes. And although the sergeant wasn't feeling sanguine that his afternoon was going to be particularly exciting, nevertheless, the chance was there. Although he was not a heartless man, the sergeant *was* only human, and he'd been involved in only two other murder investigations so far in his career. So he could, perhaps, be forgiven for hoping that things might become interesting.

But in this heat, he mused, more prosaically, it would probably turn out to be a case of some poor old soul dying of heat exhaustion.

He reached out and retrieved a pair of sunglasses from the dashboard, then withdrew the ignition keys and pocketed them. The sunglasses he slipped into the top pocket of his jacket, knowing that his superior officer wasn't a fan of them, and wondering, with a slight twist of his lips, if he'd work up the courage to actually put them on.

Graham Lane was a slightly built man of thirty or so, with thinning, sandy-coloured hair and eyebrows, and who had just managed to squeeze into the police force when the height regulations had been lowered. Now he climbed lithely out of the car, and glanced around with appreciation. Having been born and bred in a large city in the Midlands, he'd quickly come to appreciate the more bucolic delights that the Thames Valley had to offer. And on a day like today, with the sun blazing down, it was good to get out of the office. Even so, he felt the heat of the day hit him like a hammer blow, and wished that he could ditch his jacket. Surreptitiously, he loosened his tie and glanced hopefully across at his boss. Perhaps the old man would loosen up and allow them to strip down to shirtsleeves?

Inspector Causon, in contrast to his lithe and fit junior officer, heaved his considerable bulk out of the car without any outward signs of contentment, and instantly began to sweat. Not a sun-worshipper by nature, he inwardly cursed the heatwave that they were enduring and briefly thought back nostalgically to the days when good old British summers could be relied upon to be both wet and miserable. He sneered at some perfectly inoffensive moon daisies that were going about their business, innocuously blooming on the roadside verge opposite him, and set off heavily towards the open field clearly visible through a wide set of pale grey iron gates.

The call out had stated only that a member of the public at the sports ground had reported finding a dead body, and like his sergeant, he didn't have any high expectations that he'd be faced with anything too taxing. And the moment that he stepped onto the field, and saw that all the action was centred around an attractive wooden pavilion, he sighed wearily. He might have known. A bloody cricket match.

'What are the odds that some poor sod has had his head bashed in by a cricket ball?' he said grumpily to his sergeant, who merely shrugged, but didn't comment.

Graham Lane was wise to keep silent, since he knew that the inspector loathed sport of all kinds. And was perfectly capable of letting his feelings be known, in no uncertain terms, whenever the mood took him.

As they approached the main area of activity, a man dressed in expensive leisurewear, with silvering hair and an imperious manner, strode out aggressively to greet them. He was white-faced and clearly anxious, and his lips were held so stiffly tight that he could only be holding back some pretty primordial emotions. Grief maybe. Anger certainly. And with a connoisseur's appreciation of human nature, Inspector Causon watched him closely, wondering what his opening gambit would be.

Beside him he felt his sergeant quiver with the alert attention of a whippet spotting a rabbit.

The inspector, who'd worked with the sergeant for several years now, still couldn't quite bring himself to approve of the younger man's obvious enthusiasm. But since Graham Lane was about to become a father for the first time, DI Causon rather cynically (if accurately) suspected that he wouldn't have to put up with such vim and vigour for too much longer. After a few months of interrupted sleep and changing nappies, even Lane's seemingly limitless energy would surely fizzle out.

The thought cheered him up immensely.

'Are you the man in charge?' The man approaching them addressed the inspector abruptly.

The gaze he swept over the elder police officer seemed distinctly less than impressed. Apart from his bulk, Laurence Causon displayed a very thinning head of mouse-coloured hair, a jaw that looked as if it could perpetually do with another shave, and a pair of flat, curiously colourless eyes. Wrapped in a wrinkled and baggy grey suit that had clearly seen much better days, and a pair of scuffed Oxfords on unashamedly size twelve feet, it was perhaps not altogether surprising, since he hardly seemed to represent the modern police force at all its go-getting best.

'Yes, sir. I'm Detective Inspector Causon,' he replied pleasantly enough, if a little heavily. 'And you are?' The inspector's voice had the gravelly undertones of an ex-smoker, but no discernible accent. And for some reason that he later wouldn't have been able to adequately explain, Sir Robert Jones felt some of his anger and dismay slowly evaporate. His first impression of the man might not have been promising, and yet, overlaying that, the agitated stockbroker sensed competence here — and an uncompromising competence, at that.

'I'm Sir Robert Jones,' he introduced himself distractedly, using his full title without even realizing it. 'It's my son who's . . . who's . . .' Sir Robert took a deep breath, but still clearly couldn't bring himself to say the actual words, so he said instead, and somewhat inconsequentially, 'They won't even let me see him.'

He looked more bewildered than anything else now, and although his words could have been mistaken for petty whining, the inspector didn't think that that was the actual case. For all his title and bluster, the man was clearly feeling off balance and brittle.

'Take a deep breath, sir,' he advised neutrally, reminding himself grimly, and with an increasingly heavy heart that, whatever the merits of the situation, it was clearly a tragedy for someone.

Then he saw a uniformed officer rapidly approaching them, one of the two who must have got here before him.

To the victim's father, who was quite clearly in the first stages of shock, he said quietly, 'Perhaps if you'd go and sit down, sir, I'll be able to speak to you in a moment.' He spoke not without sympathy, but with a firmness that brooked no further argument.

Sir Robert looked at him and opened his mouth abruptly, clearly intent on blasting him for his impertinence. But once again, on meeting the inspector's unwavering gaze, he found it impossible to maintain his anger and bluster, and they slowly subsided. Instead, he gave a vague and defeated kind of grunt, before turning away, his shoulders slumping.

'Sir,' the constable said smartly to Causon, and once the civilian was out of earshot, began to fill him in on the basic details of the situation, whilst at the same time leading them towards the back of the pavilion.

'The groundsman here, a Mr James Cluley, was standing guard at this end of the building when we arrived, and one of the other players was at the other end,' the constable concluded his preliminary report, whilst still consulting his notebook. 'He says that they were in place within a few minutes of the body being found, so hopefully they managed to prevent too much contamination of the crime scene,' he finished, with some satisfaction.

Causon nodded. Surprisingly, he made no attempt to step into the narrow space and thus get closer to the body, but squatted down instead where he was, a slightly awkward manoeuvre, given his girth. He looked thoughtfully along the neatly mown grass towards Tristan Jones, whose body was lying about eight feet or so away.

To one side of him was the painted green wooden length of the back end of the pavilion, and the policeman noted that the expanse of green-painted planks was broken only by a single set of windows — which were closed. From here it was hard to be sure, but they looked dusty and neglected. He doubted that, unlike the windows that faced the front, they were often opened or used. On the other side of the sprawled body was a chain-link fence, about nine or ten feet tall, he estimated. On the far side of this, hawthorn hedges had also grown haphazardly against the wire, creating a double barrier. Clearly nobody would have been able to climb over these two barriers from the field on the other side — not without a ladder, and even then, they would have been likely to be scratched and lacerated by the thick, thorny hedge. So whoever had met the deceased in this enclosed and private little space, the inspector reasoned, must have come around here from the sports field side. And hopefully, with all the spectators about, they would have been spotted.

Which all seemed clear enough, and boded well.

'And the medics are sure that he's dead, and not just unconscious?' he asked the constable, more for something to say whilst he gathered his thoughts than anything else.

'Oh yes, sir. That is, the ambulance attendants who were called out declared him dead,' the PC clarified carefully. He knew Inspector Causon by sight, and like the rest of the station house, knew that he had something of a reputation for being a stickler for accuracy and for not allowing slipshod methods to pass muster in anybody that he worked with. So he was careful to be precise in what he said. 'No police surgeon or doctor has arrived on the scene yet to give an official notification of death. But we can take it that he *is* dead, sir. I mean, the ambulance people should know, shouldn't they?' he added, a little uncertainly now.

Causon hid a smile and nodded solemnly. 'One would hope so, Constable,' he agreed dryly. 'That a cricket bat beside the body?'

'Yes, sir. I made sure that none of the medics touched it, but I did have a quick look at it when I first arrived, sir, and it looked to me like it was an old bat. I mean, not one that they would have been likely to play with in their match today, sir,' he clarified. Like Lane, he also knew that Causon was known to abhor all sport, although he himself had played both football and tennis at school, and even a little cricket, so he was careful to explain his reasoning. 'The wood of the bat hadn't been oiled recently with any linseed, so it was too dry, and it had a very faded strapping around the handle, not to mention a bit of a crack in the bat itself. But I suppose the crack might have only just occurred, when it was used in the attack, sir. It would be hard to say without examining it more closely, but that will have to wait for the forensic people.' He paused and then admitted, 'I haven't had a chance yet to account for all the individual cricketers, to see if anyone is missing a bat. But the one lying beside the deceased had just a very little dark red tissue and what looked like a few dark hairs on the business end of it, sir,' he concluded briskly. 'The blow or blows may have broken the skin of the scalp, sir, but that was all, I'd say.'

Causon grunted. He could see for himself that there was very little blood evident on the body, but he didn't like to spoil the youngster's fun. No doubt this was his first call out to a murder scene, and if he wanted to show off his skills of observation to the brass, why not?

'You've called in SOCO?' he asked.

'Yes, sir, they're about fifteen minutes out,' the young PC confirmed proudly, and then rather ruined it by looking suddenly distinctly nervous. 'I'm sorry, sir, but when I radioed back and requested that some more manpower be sent over right away, HQ informed me that there's been a massive pile-up on the motorway just a few miles north of here. And apparently it's taken up a lot of our personnel.' He clearly didn't like being the bearer of bad news, and his eyes darted towards the sergeant in an unconscious appeal for support.

'So? We'll still need at least half a dozen more uniforms here, if not more. They'll just have to pull their finger out,' Causon said shortly.

The poor constable gulped. 'Yes, sir, I know. But unfortunately, there's also the big football match on,' he proffered tentatively. And when the inspector simply carried on scowling wordlessly, he added helplessly, 'It's a grudge match, sir, a local derby, and they're expecting a lot of trouble from the fans. So nearly all our extra men are up there. And what with the two major incidents, we're very short-staffed.'

Causon said something extremely unprintable about football hooligans, and followed it up with something less than complimentary about football in general. Then he vented his spleen on bad drivers, but clearly his heart wasn't in that so much. Like nearly every copper who'd come up the hard way, he'd had his fair share of attending road traffic accidents. And they always broke his heart.

'Yes, sir, it's the fans that drink before going to a match that cause all the trouble,' the constable wisely agreed. 'But HQ have already had to ask some of the neighbouring counties to lend us some help, since we're so seriously short of manpower. So the upshot is, sir, they say they're really up against it, and that they can't possibly get any more than a handful of other officers here for a couple of hours or so yet.'

Causon rolled his eyes heavenward. 'Bloody budget cuts,' he snorted. 'Before long, they'll be expecting us to secure crime scenes with volunteer support staff. Or police dogs.'

The constable, very wisely, pretended not to hear this. Graham Lane winked at him.

'Right. Well then, we'll just have to try and manage with the few men that we've got until help finally does arrive. Not your fault, son, you've done just fine,' he said matter-of-factly, pretending not to notice when the youngster let out a long, slow breath of relief. 'Well, there's nothing more we can do here until a doc's officially pronounced him dead,' he added glumly, nodding towards Tristan Jones's body.

He got laboriously back to his feet, and then glanced down at his watch thoughtfully. It was not quite quarter past six. And there goes the rest of my Saturday night, he thought philosophically. He'd been looking forward to downing a couple of cold pints at his local, too. But he knew there would be hours of work in front of him yet before he could even get the body taken away. The photographer alone would probably want half an hour or more, snapping away. Then there would be the seemingly never-ending round of interviews to be got through, the collecting and logging of evidence, and the hundred and one other things that denoted the start of an official murder investigation.

For there could be no doubt that this was murder. He'd never yet come across anyone who'd successfully committed suicide by hitting themselves over the back of their own head with a cricket bat. And since the body was lying behind the pavilion and was not out on the pitch, it could hardly be a case of a sporting accident, either. The unfortunate young man in front of him clearly hadn't received the injury whilst going about his sporting activity on the pitch.

'OK, Constable. I know you haven't been here long, but give me what you've managed to come up with so far. Let's hear what you've been able to piece together of the timeline.'

'Sir.' The constable succinctly related the gist of what he'd managed to learn, concluding crisply with, 'The 999 call was logged at five thirty-two.'

Causon sighed. 'And I take it that nobody has come forward to say that they saw the victim go around to the back of the pavilion after finishing his tea? Or saw anyone else go behind there with him, or just after, for that matter?'

'No, sir. Everybody seems to have been watching the match, or so they say,' the constable confirmed.

Yes, they all would be, wouldn't they, Causon fumed morosely. So much for his earlier hope that the murderer must have been seen by somebody paying proper attention.

'Bloody cricket,' he muttered. 'When you arrived, who first greeted you? The boy's father?'

'No, sir. It was . . .' he hastily consulted his notes, 'one Mr Max Wilson. He introduced himself as the individual who made the initial 999 call.'

'Did he now?' Causon sighed. 'Was he a friend of the victim?' he shot out.

'Er, more of an acquaintance, he said, sir. He lives in the village, and knew the boy's father, Sir Robert Jones, more than his son, apparently. But since the victim regularly visited his parents, Mr Wilson knew him from round and about.

He'd say hello, maybe share a pint in the local pub if they happened to be in at the same time, that sort of thing, sir. And, of course, they played cricket together, whenever the victim wasn't in London and they had a match on.'

'Fair enough. OK. Set up the scene-of-crime tape around the back of the building, and wait for SOCO. Sergeant Lane and myself will be taking down some preliminary statements,' Causon ordered.

'Yes, sir.'

* * *

Marie Rawley walked openly through the front entrance to the playing fields. They could hardly be called the main gates, since the gap in the low stone wall that fronted just twenty yards or so of the grounds was guarded by little more than a four-foot-high wrought-iron gate, similar to a garden gate. Furthermore it was never locked, and had stood open for so long that couch grass and stinging nettles growing around the rusting posts would probably make it impossible to close and latch it, should anyone attempt to do so.

But she wanted to give the impression that she had nothing to hide, so she strolled openly through the entrance and into the field beyond, dressed in a pair of thin, loose-fitting black trousers and a red and black patterned top. But she kept one hand clenched tightly on the large casual bag that she carried across one shoulder, and when she looked around, she was surprised to note that there was hardly anybody about at that end of the field. Most people, including, confusingly, the cricket players as well as the spectators, seemed to be congregating down the bottom end of the field, near the pavilion.

Which was odd, when she thought about it. Why wasn't the match in full swing again? Tea time must have come and gone by now, surely.

She paused, frowning slightly, then slowly moved forward. She spotted one of her neighbours, a woman whose husband was supposed to be fielding that day, and considered going over to ask her what was going on, but decided against it. Like her son before her, she didn't want to draw undue attention to her presence. So instead, and with a certain sense of déjà vu, she made her way slowly to the bottom of the field, working her way around the edge of the crowd. And was shocked and scared to see that a couple of uniformed police officers were standing by the back of the pavilion.

What on earth was going on?

Her heart lurched in panic and dread. Surely nothing bad could have happened already? She felt a little sick, but took comfort in the fact that Mark was safely back at home. So whatever had happened couldn't involve him.

Perhaps something had been stolen? Somebody's pocket had been picked, perhaps?

But then she spotted the second man that she wanted to confront that day, and moved a little to one side, edging into his line of sight. And, as if sensing her presence, Lorcan Greeves turned from his position on the outer edge of the cricket players and saw her.

He immediately began to look uneasy, Marie noticed, and smiled grimly.

Soon he would be looking even more so, if she had her way.

Her hand clenched on the strap of her shoulder bag, and for the first time, she felt a brief flare of real misgiving.

She wasn't much of an actress, she knew. And she would have sworn that she didn't have a violent bone in her body. When she read in the newspapers about the elderly being mugged, or gang members getting stabbed, or about the riots that sometimes took place even in England's cities, she couldn't understand what could possibly bring people to hurt others.

But now she thought she understood that a bit better. Because, to protect her son, she was fast discovering that she herself would be willing to do anything, anything at all. And that, set against her instinctive pacifism, a fierce maternal instinct won hands down.

Fixing Lorcan Greeves with a hard stare, she jerked her head towards the car park. She saw him flinch and look stalwartly away.

Her lips thinned.

If he thought he was simply going to be able to ignore her then he had another think coming.

She moved a little closer, and when his furtive glance once again sought her out, she again jerked her head, more imperiously than ever, towards the car park, her jaw jutting out pugnaciously.

She knew that he wouldn't want to talk to her, but human nature being what it was, she also knew that, in the end, he wouldn't be able to resist her silent summons. Even if you knew the news wasn't going to be good, not knowing was even worse. And it was far better to get unpleasant things over and done with, rather than have to fret about them.

And so, after another minute or so of the silent battle raging between them, she saw his shoulders eventually stoop in defeat, and watched him shuffle back from the others and head towards the small car park.

Here, she was a little disconcerted to see that two police cars were parked, along with an ambulance. A constable guarded the entrance at the bottom, where a wider set of gates allowed vehicular access. So she headed for the far side of the concrete area, near the hedge, where a slight bend in the greenery would hide them from the sight of both the constable at the gates, and the majority of the rest of the people in the field. Here, a large white transit van had been parked, and Marie took full advantage of it to slip behind it, yet further out of sight of prying eyes.

A moment or two later, Lorcan tentatively joined her. He looked nervous, and was visibly sweating, and Marie had to quickly hide a grimace of distaste. He really was a pitiful specimen of manhood. It was no wonder that his first wife had left him, and that his fiancée had so easily fallen for Tris Jones's more robust charms.

'What on earth are you doing here, Mrs Rawley?' Lorcan asked, trying to sound jaunty and puzzled, but only succeeding in sounding nervous.

'I want to know what's going on between you and my son,' Marie demanded, wasting no time and going straight to the heart of the matter. If he thought that she was going to allow him to take control of this meeting, and turn it into nothing more than a pleasant and civilized little chat, she needed to gain the upper hand now.

She saw his small grey eyes flicker about uneasily, and ignored the slightly sickly grin that twisted his lips.

'Between me and Mark?' he echoed, wondering frantically just what the lad might have told her. Didn't he know enough to keep schtum? And then he realized that of course he did — the woman in front of him was merely fishing. She had to be. 'I can assure you, Mrs Rawley . . .' he began jovially, but already Marie was moving.

She took two quick steps closer to him, her face tight and white with anger and tension. Without thinking about it, Lorcan took a rapid step back, which brought him up against the prickly hawthorn hedge. He felt the small twigs sticking into his back, making him want to scratch.

'Don't bother coming up with some lie,' Marie warned him. 'I know when something's going on. What have you got him doing? That's what I want to know.'

Lorcan blinked, searching desperately for something to say that might pacify her without giving anything away, but, to his dismay, found his normally quick brain going blank.

'Nothing,' he muttered miserably. 'He's just doing some research for me, that's all.' It was a pitiful excuse, and he knew it the moment it left his lips, but it was the first thing he'd been able to come up with.

Marie gave a rather inelegant snort. 'Research, my eye! You're a stockbroker, working in a London firm. I may not know much about such things, but I'm pretty damned sure that you don't ask teenage boys still in school to do research. You lot have trained lackeys for that.'

Lorcan blinked. 'Not always, Mrs Rawley. Sometimes we have to be ultra discreet, you know. If we think stocks are—'

'Oh shut up,' Marie hissed, sensing that he was about to try and baffle her with science or economics or some such thing.

She might have left school at sixteen, and worked in a garden nursery all her working life, but that didn't make her stupid. Or naïve.

'You're dragging him in to your vendetta with Tris, and I'm not having it,' Marie said, all but stomping her foot in frustration.

And when she saw the man in front of her open his mouth in another attempt to bamboozle her, she decided desperately that it was now or never. She had to take control, before he had time to get the upper hand. Before she had time to get cold feet.

It was time for her to go into her act.

And the fact that Lorcan Greeves was still pressed so ridiculously up against the prickly hedge, looking so pathetic and easily intimidated, spurred her on.

She could do this! She could.

Marie reached a little clumsily into her bag, suddenly dry-mouthed and sick with nervous tension. Her whole body was beginning to shake, but she managed to curl her fingers around the small, sharp knife that she'd slipped inside the bag before coming out of her house. It was a black-handled kitchen knife that she usually used to peel potatoes, but it looked sharp and impressive enough.

She drew it out and waved it with a triumphant flourish in front of his face, the blade glinting obligingly in the sun. She only hoped that he wouldn't notice just how badly her hands were shaking.

Lorcan went utterly white, and bleated out something incomprehensible.

'You j-just leave him alone,' Marie Rawley said. 'I'm warning you. I'm at the end of my tether and I w-won't stand for it. Do you hear?' Her voice came out a little squeaky, but she didn't mind. She was trying her best to look like a neurotic woman, and one who was capable of anything. Wasn't that what was supposed to scare men more than anything? An armed woman who wasn't quite in her right mind?

Because, like so many before her, Marie had always regarded Lorcan as a bit of a nothing and a nobody. The kind of man to be ignored, or taken for granted. His mother had always treated him like it, and his wives and girlfriends, apparently, had taken their cue from her. As had his so-called best friend. They all got what they wanted from him, because they all knew that he was the sort of man who never stood up for himself. He was one of life's born victims, and everyone knew it. Including Lorcan himself. So why should she treat him any differently?

So all she had to do, she'd reasoned out beforehand, was to act like an overbearing woman making demands, and he'd be bound to fold, just like he always did. He'd buckle down and give in to the stronger force and meekly do as he was told, because that's the way that men like him always acted.

Wasn't it?

So what Lorcan Greeves did next took her completely by surprise. It clearly took Lorcan by surprise, too, because after a shockingly brief moment of action and reaction, when the blood quickly started to flow, he looked as shocked as Marie Rawley.

* * *

Erica Jones was standing pensively beside her husband, who had taken her place in the deckchair just inside the cricket pavilion door. She had a hand resting comfortingly on his shoulder, but her eyes were like lasers on the two men approaching them, and she looked tense.

Graham Lane eyed up the elegant red-haired woman thoughtfully and gave a low, near-silent whistle under his breath.

'Blimey. That outfit she's wearing must have cost a mint, sir,' he said, and when his chief's eyebrows rose questioningly, he grinned a trifle shamefaced. 'The wife,' he added succinctly. 'She's a bit of a fashion aficionado and can cost down to the last penny any outfit that any woman is wearing from a distance of ten paces, and the knack's sort of rubbed off on me. I reckon everything that redhead's got on has an Italian designer label on it that'd make your head spin. And I bet that very chic hairdo has to be the result of work done in some swanky salon down in London somewhere — the local hairdresser wouldn't be good enough for that cut. And those pumps she's wearing are Jimmy Choos, or I'm a monkey's granddad. Jewellery's discreet, I'll give her that, but it cost a packet too, I'd say.'

'Thank you, *Marie Claire*,' Causon said caustically. 'If police work ever fails to live up to your expectations, I suggest you apply for a job on *Vogue*.'

Graham Lane grinned, showing a flash of perfect white teeth along with the fact that he'd clearly not taken any offence from his boss's habitual sarcasm.

As they approached the couple in the doorway, however, the policemen's manner became more grave.

'Inspector?' Erica coolly greeted the older, heavier man, having instantly clocked him as the man in charge. She held out one hand firmly as they reached her, forcing the initiative. Obligingly, he shook her hand briefly. She wore just a plain gold wedding band, but the inspector felt, rather than saw, Graham Lane notice her long, professionally manicured red nails, and he couldn't help but raise a speculative eyebrow. No doubt, Causon mused sarcastically, with carefully concealed amusement, his sergeant could have informed him of the name of the shade of nail varnish, and where the lady's manicurist had probably purchased it. Exclusively at Harrods, perhaps? Or would that be Selfridges?

'I'm Lady Jones, Robert's wife,' Erica continued crisply, as the inspector carefully released her hand, having made sure that he hadn't gripped it too hard. His wife was always complaining that he had a crushing grip and warning him to be careful. 'I'm Tris's stepmother. Can you tell us, please, exactly what's happening? Nobody will tell us anything. It's very distressing, and I'm sure, totally unnecessary. We are Tris's parents, after all.'

Causon looked her very slowly up and down before allowing one rather shaggy, mousy-coloured eyebrow to rise. 'There's very little as of yet that we can tell you, Lady Jones,' he said repressively. 'As you can see, I've only just arrived. Now, I have a few questions for you, if you feel up to it, of course.'

Or even if you don't, he might just as well have added out loud, for all the trouble that he took to be tactful about it. Clearly, he didn't like having his interviews hijacked, and anyone who thought that they could get the upper hand of him, especially via the very specious route of being in a higher social class, very quickly learned differently.

Erica's patrician face flushed slightly at the none-too-subtle reprimand, and she took a deep breath. Uncouth lout, she might just as well have said out loud in return. And for a moment, the police inspector and the Lady of the Manor eyed each other in perfect understanding. Not to mention mutual antipathy.

'When was the last time you saw your son, Sir Robert?' the inspector asked, turning pointedly to the boy's father, who had been staring rather vacantly down at his feet, and had clearly missed the little interplay between his wife and the investigating officer.

Inside the pavilion, everyone pretended not to be watching or listening. Outside, people pretended the same.

'What?' Sir Robert said blankly, and then clearly made an effort to pay attention. 'I'm sorry. Er . . . let me think. I'm not quite sure. Sorry, I don't know what's wrong with me. It, er . . . yes, it was during tea, I think. Yes, we were having some of that wonderful gateau. And Tris came in late. The boy was always late,' Sir Robert said, his voice catching for a moment. Then he recovered, and made a concerted effort to bring himself back under control. He cleared his throat. 'Tea was nearly over, so he started stuffing himself with cake.

I went outside, to get a good spot for when play resumed. I don't think I noticed him again after that,' he lied smoothly.

No way was he going to admit to this bluff and implacable man that his last words to his son had been so acrimonious and lacking in affection. The businessman blinked rapidly, as he suddenly realized that that last meeting would be his enduring memory of the last time he saw his son alive.

He swallowed hard. Would it really have hurt him to be a little less hard on his son? If only he could take it all back and start again.

'I see, sir,' Causon said, not without sympathy. 'And you, Lady Jones?' He turned with some reluctance to the boy's stepmother.

'Me?' Erica said. 'Oh. I'm not sure. Oh wait, yes I am. It was in here.' She waved a hand vaguely around at the interior of the pavilion. 'Max was heading out to bat. Everyone else was already outside. Tris was eating something — a scone, I think. I saw him chatting to the cook, briefly, at some point.' She dismissed this with another vague wave. 'Anyway. Then he left, passing me by as I sat here, where Robert's sitting now.'

Behind her, standing in the doorway to the kitchen, Jenny Starling had a brief but vivid flash back to that moment. Tristan, blowing his stepmother that mocking kiss. But the fact that Erica didn't mention *that* little episode didn't surprise her in the least. Inspector Causon didn't seem to be the kind of man to inspire such confidences, even if it hadn't clearly been a case of loathing at first sight for the both of them.

'I stayed in here after that — I don't do well in the sun, you see,' Erica carried on, indicating her fair skin with a shrug. 'I burn very quickly and easily. In fact, I never left this building, I don't think. And the next thing I heard about Tris was when Max came in to say that he'd been found . . . behind the pavilion.'

Her hand clenched compulsively on her husband's shoulder as she recited this last bit, but Sir Robert didn't seem to notice.

Jenny shifted a little uncomfortably from one foot to the other. Was it just her, or had Erica Jones been just a little too keen to stress the fact that she'd never left the pavilion? Not that she had, as far as Jenny could remember. But it did seem a little off that she was so keen to give herself an alibi.

Then the cook had to concede, in all fairness, that she was hardly in any position to judge Erica for that, for hadn't she done just the same when she'd checked the French doors were still locked, thus ensuring that her own alibi was safe?

We're all human after all, Jenny Starling thought sadly. And our first thought, ignoble though it might be, is nearly always to look out for our own precious skin.

Besides which, no doubt the Lady of the Manor felt that she needed to be especially careful, since she had clearly rubbed the senior investigating officer up the wrong way right from the start. Yes, Jenny thought with a wry smile, perhaps it was only natural that Erica was feeling just a little bit overly defensive.

And besides all of that, Erica was clearly no empty-headed bimbo, and she must have seen at once that she, along with everyone else who'd known Tris well, had to be a prime suspect for his murder. And given that Causon clearly didn't like her, it stood to reason that she felt the need to get herself out of the frame as quickly as possible.

'I see,' Causon said, still eyeing Erica with a flat, gimlet stare. 'And is there anyone here who can corroborate this?' he asked, turning to glance at the handful of inhabitants inside the pavilion.

'Oh yes, Inspector,' Caroline Majors spoke up at once, if a little diffidently. She gave her name, and nodded towards her friend, 'And this is Ettie.' The two women drew together, as if seeking an alliance against the unknown quantity that was DI Causon. 'Erica was sitting right there, where her husband is now, all afternoon. Wasn't she, Ettie?'

Ettie agreed that she was. 'And it's true, she never did step outside the building. We would have noticed. Wouldn't we, Caroline?'

Causon sighed, but gave no indication what credence he gave the two women's statements, although Jenny couldn't see why he should doubt either of them. Instead he turned back once more to Sir Robert.

'And you, Sir Robert? Were you talking to anyone outside after tea, someone who can confirm your statement?'

'Of course I was,' Sir Robert said, after the merest hesitation. 'I had the vicar on one side of me, and that local historian chap on the other. He could bore for England. I didn't leave my chair until Max was caught LBW and nobody knew where Tris had gone. Anyone can tell you that,' he added rather impatiently.

Causon nodded to Graham Lane without speaking, but his message was clear. The sergeant scribbled a reminder in his notebook to track down these two luminaries and check out Sir Robert's alibi, but almost everyone in earshot was thinking the same thing. Why would he lie about something that could so easily be checked?

So, Jenny thought fatalistically. That was two suspects down, and how many more were yet to go?

And the next person of interest to be cleared, it very quickly transpired, was the captain of Much Rousham's cricket team himself.

'And who was it who opened the batting after tea, please?' Inspector Causon raised his voice to cut across the general hubbub, putting the question equally to all those around him.

There was a general hum and a slight swaying of movement as people began to look around and whisper amongst themselves, as they came to a consensus. The policeman's eyes swept around quickly to take in everyone in the changing room of the pavilion, then quickly pivoted to look behind him when a voice, somewhat reluctantly, hailed him from outside.

Max Wilson, standing on the edge of the cricket pitch boundary, began to make his way forward.

Jenny, when she'd realized that the policeman's eyes were sweeping over her without any apparent recognition, found herself wilting with relief, and letting out a long, anxious sigh. In her experience, police officers tended to look askance at members of the public who made it a habit of helping them uncover murderers. Not that she'd ever willingly set out to do anything of the kind, of course. It just seemed to happen that way, whether she liked it or not.

But she was well aware that trying to explain that to the DI would not exactly endear her to him, and she was not anxious to make herself known now. Perhaps, with a bit of luck this time, she could just remain a face in the crowd, a witness and nothing more. If she kept her head down, and restricted her statement to what she herself had seen and witnessed, surely that was possible?

Or were her hopes just so much pie in the sky?

Her somewhat sombre thoughts were interrupted when a male voice responded to DI Causon's raised voice.

'I did. I was the first to bat.'

The man who stepped forward in response to the inspector's interested look instantly made Graham Lane's hackles rise. He was simply too good-looking, too smooth, and probably — unless he missed his disgruntled guess — too well-heeled for his liking. Men such as this tended to get on the sergeant's wick as a matter of principle. They seemed to cruise through life as if someone had given them a free pass, Lane had always felt.

But nothing of his thoughts showed on his face as Max Wilson came back up the steps and confidently thrust out his hand to Causon. The inspector, after a moment's hesitation, shook it politely. This time he made no effort to hold back on the natural strength of his grip, and Graham Lane hid a gratified grin as he saw the matinee-idol cricketer hide a slight wince as his fingers got mangled.

'I'm Max Wilson, Inspector. I'm also the captain of the home side.'

'Yes, sir.' Causon, who couldn't have cared less about what position he played, smiled briefly. 'Tell me, was it pre-arranged that you should bat first?' he asked, instantly getting down to the point. 'Did everyone know the order of play?'

'Oh yes,' Max said easily. Then frowned slightly. 'Well, to be strictly accurate, no. What I mean is, that's the way we usually do it, and we never discussed changing the form. So I imagine everyone was expecting it to be business as usual, if you see what I mean? I open, and Tris, who is our best hitter, takes over from me. That way, when he's run out, we've got a much better idea of how much work we still have to do, if any, to win the match, and thus we can decide on our batting strategy from there. We usually put in a couple of our weaker batsmen, and then leave our third-best hitter for last.'

Causon stopped himself just in time from saying something rude about cricket and kept his mind firmly on the job. 'So everyone would have a rough idea of when to expect Mr Jones to be on the pitch? And Mr Jones himself would know that he could be called on to bat at any time after you, and thus wouldn't be likely to take himself off somewhere and be unavailable?' he pressed.

Jenny nodded to herself, instantly understanding the DI's need for clarification, and exactly what he was sorting out in his mind. If the crime had been premeditated, then the killer would've had to have some idea of the best time to tackle Tris.

And if it wasn't premeditated then . . . Jenny frowned. Well, then, somebody had been very lucky. Or unlucky. Depending on your point of view.

Max managed a weak smile and shrugged. 'Well, personally speaking, I'd hope that he wouldn't have expected to be called in to play *particularly* quickly, Inspector,' he said ruefully. 'With all due modesty, I'm usually good for fifty runs or so.'

Graham Lane had to hide another quick smirk. Old man Causon had certainly hit his witness in the old ego there, he thought with some satisfaction. Even if he hadn't meant to.

'Yes, of course, sir,' the inspector said flatly. 'Let's stick to the facts, shall we? You yourself came in and had tea with all the rest, I take it?'

'Oh yes, rather,' Max said. 'Because it's our centenary you see, and the committee pushed the boat out and brought in this fabulous caterer. The food was out of this world. In fact, I'm sure I probably ate more than I should have,' he said, again with a rueful smile that no doubt many would have considered charming.

Jenny, who was torn between preening under the praise and hoping that the inspector didn't demand then and there to be introduced to this wonder cook, ducked back a little further into the recess of her kitchen. She still wasn't too sure of the reception she'd get when the inspector realized just who she was. If he did, that is. Maybe, for once, her fame (at least in constabulary circles) wouldn't have gone before her?

Not that she needed to worry for the moment. Causon was obviously a one-thing-at-a-time sort of man, for he didn't let himself be distracted by this culinary side issue.

'I'm sure the food was delicious, sir,' he said dismissively. 'So, did you see Mr Jones inside the pavilion whilst you were eating?'

'Did I?' Max said, cocking his head slightly to one side as he made a show of casting his mind back, causing Sergeant Lane to shuffle impatiently at the theatrics. 'No, I don't think I did, you know, now I come to think about it. Like Sir Robert said, I think Tris was late in. I was just telling everyone that it was time to get a move on and to eat up, when he came in through the door. At that point, I went out and made sure that the state of the pitch was all right, and checked the bales and whatnot. Then, when I judged that everyone was ready, the umpire called play, and I started batting.'

'And you didn't see Mr Jones come out of the pavilion?'

'I was batting, Inspector,' Max repeated cordially, but with a tight smile. 'The only thing I was watching was the ball.'

Causon grunted. And with the man in full view of everyone, he had the whole cricket field as his alibi. Unless . . .

'So when you were run out—'

'I was caught LBW, I'm ashamed to say,' Max put in, with the inevitable rueful grin.

'. . . you left the field,' Causon ignored the interruption as if it had never occurred, 'and then what? When you realized that Tristan Jones wasn't ready to take over, did you all split up and search for him?'

In which case, Causon thought with a slight quiver of excitement, whoever had found him first might also have been the one to kill him.

'Oh no. I mean, there wasn't much of a search needed,' Max explained. 'Someone offered to check the toilets, but he wasn't there, and you could see just by looking around that he wasn't amongst the spectators. Then the groundsman offered to check behind the pavilion, as that was the only other place where he could possibly be hiding, I suppose, and well, that was that.'

Max finished with a graphic shrug.

Causon nodded, but his mind was racing. Hiding? Now that was a curious way of putting it, he thought. Why exactly would their victim have been hiding? It was something he'd have to bring up with Wilson later, at a formal interview. 'And you were out here,' he indicated the area in front of the pavilion, 'that whole time?'

'Yes, speaking to Sir Robert mostly,' Max confirmed.

'I see,' Causon said heavily.

And scratch three, Jenny added silently to herself, no doubt echoing the policeman's own mental tally. Because whilst Max might have the best motive of anyone for killing the man who was so clearly having an affair with his wife, he also had by far the best alibi of all.

Jenny sighed. Things were beginning to look distinctly tricky.

'And you talked to no one else during this time?' Causon asked Max, proceeding to cross every T and dot every I with his usual pedantic thoroughness.

Graham Lane, who sometimes found his superior's methods frustrating and slow, had to admit that they were usually effective, and tried to stay patient.

'Only to my wife, Inspector,' the captain of the cricket team said easily. And, to Jenny's alert ears at least, without any apparent sign of strain or subterfuge. 'When I realized we'd be held up by Tris, I went to chat with her.'

Jenny looked at Max Wilson thoughtfully. The man was a good actor, she had to give him that. If she hadn't already seen and heard for herself just how things really were between the married couple, she'd never have been able to guess it from Max's demeanour. But she had a shrewd idea that DI Causon would soon uncover all that for himself. He looked the thoroughly competent sort.

And thinking of the married couple, Jenny mused, her interest perking up, just what *had* the other woman in the eternal triangle been doing all that time?

And as if reading her mind, Causon asked briskly, 'And your wife was where, sir?'

Max smiled and turned to look off to his left. 'I'll go and get her, shall I?' he offered, and before either of the two policemen could object — had they wanted to — Max moved abruptly away, and came back a moment or so later with an attractive blonde woman, who looked, at that moment, both sick and pale.

Jenny, who rather thought that Max was deliberately punishing her by making her the focus of police attention so soon, thinned her lips in disapproval. If Max knew about their affair (and she'd bet her last custard slice that he did) then he was obviously feeling vindictive about it. And if he could take it out on his wife with acts of petty revenge such as this, then what might he have done to Tris?

Except, of course, he'd been in full view of everyone when Tris had been killed. And unless she could think of a way that he might somehow have miraculously got around that, it was no good thinking of him as the killer. She supposed that he could have paid someone else to kill him. But she had never been much of a conspiracy theorist. Besides, hiring a killer opened you up to blackmail, and she couldn't see someone as canny as Max Wilson doing that. And wasn't that method over the top anyway?

Jenny sighed wearily and rubbed her forehead. What with the heat and the tension, she was getting a mammoth headache. If it kept up, she'd have to take some aspirin.

'My wife, Michelle, Inspector,' Max introduced his wife, sounding almost cheerful. 'Shelly, the policeman would like to talk to you about Tris,' he added pleasantly. From his manner, Sergeant Lane thought with disgust, you'd think they were at some social soirée, instead of at a crime scene.

Michelle Wilson managed to smile tremulously at the two police officers. But she was clearly feeling a terrible strain, and Jenny, for one, simply had to look away. She found it impossible not to feel sorry for the woman. She couldn't imagine what she must be thinking, or feeling.

If she'd genuinely been in love with Tris Jones, then she must be in hell right now, unable to admit to her grief, let alone give way to it. And even if the affair hadn't been that serious, losing someone you had been intimate with to violent death would still be more than enough to shake anyone to their core.

The blonde woman licked her lips tensely. 'How can I help, Inspector?' Michelle asked, her voice faint and not quite steady.

Causon, who was obviously nobody's fool, sensed instantly that something odd was going on here. The husband was smiling a little too much like the cat that had dined on a canary soufflé, and the woman beside him flinched as he put a protective arm across her shoulders.

His eyes instantly sharpened on her. 'Did you see the victim at all today, Mrs Wilson?' he demanded abruptly.

'Only in passing,' Michelle said, obviously rallying just a little. Evidently she was the sort of woman who didn't like to be bullied. Which was probably just as well, Jenny mused, married to a man like Max.

'You knew him well?' Causon persisted.

'Tris didn't live in the village, Inspector, he had a place in London,' she prevaricated. 'He only came up sometimes at the weekends to visit his parents. We've had the Joneses over to dine with us a number of times, but that's all,' Michelle went on cleverly. Clearly, she was going to admit to nothing. And her voice was slowly getting stronger.

No doubt, Jenny thought, it had finally occurred to her that she herself might be in some danger now, and she was clearly stiffening her spine in order to face the challenge. 'Sir Robert and Erica are more our friends than Tristan,' she added more firmly.

Beside her, Max continued to look matinee-idol handsome and perfectly bland.

'I see,' Causon said. And believed that he did. He hadn't thought to ask the constable, but he suspected that the victim had been a good-looking young bloke. He'd been lying face down the only time that Causon had seen him, but it made sense. And he'd bet his next month's salary that their victim was known to be a bit of a one for the ladies, as well.

'But did you have a chance to talk to Mr Tristan Jones today?' he pressed Michelle remorselessly, intent on pinning her down to some definitive answers.

'No, Inspector. I was sitting out on one of the deckchairs sunbathing nearly all day. I came in for a cold drink and a sandwich at teatime, but I never saw Tris. And I was back in my seat before our team started to bat,' Michelle said, a little colour returning to her cheeks now. She seemed to be feeling on much firmer ground, and Jenny couldn't help but think that she was probably telling the truth.

Unless she was as good an actor as her husband?

What's more, Jenny got the odd but definite feeling that Michelle was talking for somebody else's benefit, as well as the inspector's. As if she was trying to get a message across to another person, listening in.

'You didn't see Tristan Jones leave the pavilion then?' Causon carried on.

'I don't think so. I was talking to Mavis Dalton, I think. She was telling me all about the birth of her latest grandson. You can ask her,' she added defiantly.

And again, Jenny felt sure that she was telling the truth. And, once again, telegraphing some triumphant or belligerent message to someone other than the man she was talking to.

Jenny's eyes went quickly to Michelle's husband.

Max Wilson's smile was fixed on his face, and his eyes very carefully avoided looking at his wife directly.

Causon again nodded almost imperceptibly to his sergeant, but Graham Lane caught it and interpreted it instantly with a brief nod. Oh yes, he would most definitely be talking to this Mavis Dalton lady.

But even the sergeant suspected that the proud grandmother would probably end up corroborating the witness's story in every detail. For it would be foolish indeed for Michelle Wilson to lie about something that could so easily be disproved. Besides, if she *had* been seen leaving her seat and wandering around to the back of the pavilion, he was sure that they would all have known about it long before now.

He knew how villages and their grapevines worked. Someone (and probably more than just one) would have been only too eager to tell one of the uniforms all about it. People did so like to be at the centre of a drama.

No, Graham Lane thought to himself with some satisfaction. On the whole, he was convinced that here was yet another one they could eliminate from the pool of suspects. And at this rate, they'd be zeroing in on the killer in no time, by the simple process of elimination if nothing else.

'All right, that's all for now, thank you, Mrs Wilson,' Causon said with a brief smile.

But without a doubt, he'd be speaking to her later on at some point, when he could get her on her own and safely down to an interview room at the local station, with a recording device firmly in play. Because unless he missed his guess, there was plenty of mileage to be had there, and he wasn't going to be satisfied until he knew what exactly had been going on between the Wilsons and the victim.

'And thank you, too, sir,' Causon nodded a dismissal at Max Wilson, who nodded amiably back, slipped his hand around his wife's waist and said sweetly, 'Come along then, darling.'

Michelle's eyes flickered bleakly, but she moved off with him without a further word.

Jenny watched them go pensively and sighed.

She too could count, and the suspect list was now narrowing very sharply indeed. Her eyes sought out, and found, those of James Cluley, who was standing some little distance away out on the field, and therefore presumably out of earshot of what was happening.

He looked a lonely and forlorn figure, and her heart contracted with a slight pang.

She hadn't forgotten seeing young Mark Rawley passing behind the back of the pavilion shortly before tea. And she knew that she had a duty to tell the inspector what she'd seen then — and also what she'd seen and heard for herself earlier in the day, about the state of their family's finances.

Although it made her feel like a bit of a rat to have to do it. What's more, she was sure that Inspector Causon would have filed away the fact that, of all the people who'd wondered where Tris might have been, it had been the old man who'd thought of looking for him behind the pavilion.

And that in itself surely raised some serious questions.

So, before she could chicken out, she forced herself to step out of the doorway to the kitchen and moved a little closer to the two policemen just inside the main room. There was no point putting the evil moment off, she tried to console herself. It simply had to be done.

She caught the slighter, fair-haired police officer's attention first. His eyes met hers, were about to move away again, then came back as she made a slight movement with her hand, raising it just a little. She then nudged her head towards the interior of the kitchen, looked pointedly at his superior, and then turned and walked inside.

Several people saw the sergeant step up to his chief and say something quietly in his ear, but none caught what he said. And the inspector's face didn't change.

Just then, one of the PCs came back. 'Sir, SOCO is here, but no sign of the pathologist yet.'

'OK. Any sign of any other reinforcements yet? A couple more uniforms at least?'

'I'm afraid not, sir. Not yet. But I rang the station and asked if they could call in anyone off duty, and they said two more PCs were on their way over. They should be here any minute.'

Causon grunted in disgust. It was better than nothing, he supposed, but this was no way to be forced to run an investigation. Until he had more men on the ground, he was severely restricted in what he could do.

'Right then. Constable, direct SOCO to the scene. Lane, I want you to organize what uniforms we do have. We need the names and addresses and a brief preliminary statement from everyone here. Concentrate on those who saw Tristan Jones, or spoke to him, obviously. But I also want to know if anyone saw or noticed anything else in the least out of the ordinary — whether it concerned the victim or not.'

'Yes, sir.'

Causon nodded, and disappeared further into the pavilion.

Caroline Majors and her friend Ettie watched him avidly to see where he was going, but just then, Graham Lane ushered them outside, to be corralled with the others to give their statements.

Jenny was standing with her back to the kitchen door, looking pensively out of the French windows when Causon stepped into the room. He closed the door firmly behind him.

'I wondered just when you were going to speak up,' he said.

Jenny jumped guiltily, turned around, and then told herself off for feeling so wrong-footed. It was not, after all, as if she'd done anything wrong.

'Oh. You know who I am then?' she said, her shoulders slumping a little. So much for hoping to fly under the radar.

'I recognized you the moment I set eyes on you,' Causon agreed heavily. 'Our very own Miss Marple. Every copper in a fifty-mile radius knows all about you, Miss Starling,' he assured her.

His tone was not particularly complimentary.

Jenny shot him a glance. 'Now really, Inspector. Do I look like a fluffy little old lady?' she snapped.

The inspector's lips twitched briefly as his eyes roved over her ample, voluptuous figure. 'Not hardly,' he agreed sourly. 'But I don't like people who meddle in police investigations.'

'Neither would I, in your shoes,' Jenny responded coolly. 'And if you really knew all about me, then you'd know that I've never meddled with the police in my life. It's not as if I *ask* to get caught up in stuff like this,' she added, genuinely aggrieved.

Causon sighed, and held out his hands in a brief conciliatory gesture. 'Look, let's not get into semantics, OK? Let's just say that I'll freely admit that you've proved yourself to be a useful witness in times past. Now, do you have anything for me, or don't you?'

Jenny sighed and sat down. 'I suppose I do.'

And she proceeded to tell him all that she knew about James Cluley, his financial predicament, and the movements of his angry grandson, Mark Rawley.

CHAPTER SIX

'And you saw the boy when exactly?' the inspector asked, when she'd finished her account.

Jenny sighed, immediately feeling foolish. She'd known that that was bound to be one of the first questions that he'd ask, of course, and she'd been trying to pinpoint the time now for some while, and had totally failed. She felt curiously ashamed of this, as if she should have been able to do better. After all, given all her previous experience with police cases, she wasn't exactly new to this.

But at the time, she'd had no reason to pay particular attention, and she was regretting it now.

'I'm sorry, Inspector, really I am,' she said humbly. 'Especially in light of what you've just said about me being such a reliable witness and all, but I really can't give you an accurate time,' she admitted wryly. 'In my defence, I can only say that I *have* been working flat out all day, what with only having the one oven, and so much baking to get done, which meant that I haven't really had a chance to catch my breath and . . . Oh, never mind.' Now she was just making excuses, she thought crossly, and if there was one thing she hated, it was a whiner. So she firmed her shoulders and forced herself to concentrate on what really mattered. 'I *think* it was just before teatime,' she said, still feeling all kinds of a fool for not being sure. 'Now that was *due* to start at four, but I'm sure it started a little before that, because I can remember Caroline saying that the other team were all out, or over, or dismissed, or whatever it is, early. So, say at a rough estimate, it should have been sometime between three twenty and three forty? Er . . . but I really would like to point out that it can only be regarded as my best guess. I wouldn't rely on it without some other form of confirmation, if I were you,' she added lamely.

Causon sighed, piling on her sense of failure. 'And you saw him go by the French windows, over there, you say?' He indicated the double set of glass doors at the back of the room with a cursory wave of his hand. 'He never came into the pavilion, for instance? To eat, maybe? A young lad, free food and all that?'

'No, I'm positive I never saw him hanging around. I only happened to notice him at all because you know how it is when something moves past you in the corner of your eye, it attracts your attention.'

Causon nodded. 'Yes — it distracts you.'

'Yes, exactly. So I just looked up from whatever it was I was doing, saw him walk past outside and thought nothing more about it. But if I'd seen him inside the pavilion, I would have remembered. And I'm sure that I didn't. Mind you, I was in and out of the kitchen all of the time, and if he'd made a fleeting visit — to filch some cakes or whatever and then amscray with them — I might not necessarily have been aware of that. You'd have to ask Caroline, or her friend Ettie. I'm not so sure whether Erica would have noticed him,' she added with a slight smile. She rather thought that the local peasantry might not have registered on the Lady of the Manor's radar.

'Right,' the inspector grunted, no doubt thinking much the same thing. Causon reached into his pocket, withdrew his mobile and pressed a speed-dial number — obviously his sergeant's. 'Yes, Lane? I want you to find out the address of one Mark Rawley, the grandson of James Cluley. It's almost certainly somewhere in the village here. Then I want you to go and fetch him down here. Yes, here.' He paused, then sighed. 'I know it's not procedure. But I want the lad on the scene. I want to see how it affects him.' Again he paused and listened, then grunted. 'No, bring him through into the kitchen. And, Lane — I want you to make sure that his granddad sees you bringing him in here. Got that? Right.'

Jenny winced as she quickly ran over the ramifications of the senior policeman's orders. Poor old James, she thought. No doubt about it, Causon had him firmly in his sights by the looks of it. And there were no flies on the inspector, Jenny thought, with both admiration and just a smidgen of apprehension.

'Sir!' Both Jenny and the inspector jumped a little as a police constable suddenly pushed open the door and stuck his head in. Causon shot him a sour look, but mercifully refrained from telling him just what he thought about idiots who nearly gave their superior officers heart attacks. 'Sir, I thought you'd like to know.' The constable, unaware of his lucky escape, was too keen to impart his news to even notice Jenny's presence. 'One of the witnesses I've been talking to says that he saw something which struck him as odd. But it was nothing to do with the victim, though.'

'Well, spit it out, man,' Causon said, ignoring the way the young constable finally looked at Jenny a shade questioningly, and, rather late in the day, became unsure whether or not he should be discussing police business in front of a member of the public.

He shot the inspector a slightly shamefaced look, and seemed braced for impact, but Causon, after a moment's deliberation, decided to let it pass. Although he knew himself to be many things (and short-tempered may have been one of them), he was not a hypocrite, and since he too had decided to work with rather than against the travelling cook, he didn't feel comfortable lecturing others for committing the same sin.

'Yes, sir.' The lad flushed at the older man's gruff tone, and carried on quickly. 'He says that just before play began for the second time, that is just after tea, he saw one of the Much Rousham cricketers called Lorcan Greeves re-enter the playing field and sit down just outside the pavilion. He thought nothing much of it, except for the fact that Mr Greeves had just been talking to a young lad, and that he, Mr Greeves that is, looked "sort of furtive" about it.' The PC, consulting his notebook, shrugged defensively. 'I know that witnesses can start imagining all sorts of things during situations like this, so when I pressed him a little, he couldn't really back up why he thought this Mr Greeves person was being furtive. He just thought that perhaps it was because of the way this Mr Greeves looked all around before coming back to the pavilion, as if checking to see if anybody was watching him.'

The young police constable paused to take a much-needed breath of air, and glanced nervously at his superior officer. 'You did say that you wanted a note to be made of anything out of the ordinary, sir,' he reminded him diffidently.

Causon nodded a touch impatiently. 'Yes, yes, you did the right thing. Keep at it, son. And I'll be wanting a word with this witness later.' Especially since, according to that fount of all knowledge, Jenny Starling, this Lorcan Greeves creature might very well be another man with a good motive for wanting Tristan Jones put out of the way. 'I don't suppose this witness of yours said who the lad that Greeves was talking to might be, did he?'

'No, sir. My witness is one of the Steeple Clinton lot. He knew Lorcan because they'd played against each other before, but he didn't know the lad.'

'OK,' Causon acknowledged heavily. But since they were already about to interview a local lad who was already very much of interest to them, he didn't much like the coincidence surrounding this encounter between Greeves and yet another young lad. The chances had to be fair to good that they were talking about the same individual. 'Make sure Greeves doesn't leave before I've had a word with him, will you?' he reiterated.

'Yes, sir,' the constable said, and after another slightly puzzled look at Jenny, promptly left.

The cook glanced once at Causon and then quickly away again. Then, after a moment's quiet reflection, she said tentatively, 'Are you thinking that Mark Rawley is the one Lorcan was talking to?'

'Perhaps. But it could be another lad altogether. Just because Rawley's already become a person of interest, doesn't necessarily mean that he was the one who had to be having a little chinwag with this Greeves character.' Then Causon scratched his chin and grinned a crocodile smile. 'But it's certainly suggestive, isn't it?'

Jenny supposed, fairly, that it was.

'So, any other insights you might have for me?' the inspector carried on wryly. And was that just another hint of a crocodile smile on his lips? Although she wouldn't have been rash enough to bet money on it, Jenny was beginning to suspect that the old duffer might actually be warming up to her.

She shrugged fatalistically. 'You've probably already guessed that Tris was a bit of a heartbreaker?' She went on to describe all over again the other people that she'd met in the course of the day, most of whom had confirmed Tris's Lothario credentials one way or another. And she finished wearily with, 'And you probably saw for yourself just how the land lay between Tris and Michelle Wilson?'

'You think Tristan Jones was the reason the Wilson marriage was in so much trouble?' he asked sharply. He had, in fact, come to pretty much the same conclusion himself, but it didn't hurt to have confirmation.

'One of them, probably,' Jenny said cautiously. 'Though if I was married to the unctuous Max, I'd probably be panting for a divorce anyway.'

Causon smiled grimly. For try as he might, he could not, under any circumstances, imagine this redoubtable woman falling for the rather suspect charms of a man like Wilson. And certainly not going so far as to compound the mistake by actually marrying the man.

'No doubt,' he said, with a definite twinkle in his eye now. 'Anything else?'

'Yes. His stepmother,' Jenny said.

Causon stirred. He was aware that he'd taken an instant dislike to Lady Erica Jones, and as such, knew he had to be careful when dealing with her. Consequently, he wasn't, perhaps, quite as quick on the uptake as he should have been, when he said abruptly, 'Well? What about his stepmother?'

Jenny just continued to look at him, until she saw the penny finally drop.

'Ah,' the inspector said, pursing his lips in a long, slow, silent whistle. Well, well, he thought, with a certain amount of glee. 'Like that, is it?' Then he thought about it some more, and finally shrugged. 'Well, there's no reason why they shouldn't have been having an affair, I suppose — they're not related by blood or anything. And even if they were at it, there may not be anything in it for us. Nothing that relates to the matter in hand, that is. Was it recent, do you reckon?'

'Recent enough, I'd have said,' Jenny responded, and not at all sure that she agreed with the policeman about it not providing an adequate motive for murder. In her experience, a woman scorned might be one of the oldest clichés in the book, but that didn't necessarily mean that she shouldn't be taken seriously. And from what she'd observed of the fiery redhead, Erica Jones had a very healthy ego indeed, and wouldn't have taken to being messed about with much equanimity.

'Anyway, I'd be prepared to bet my last doughnut that she was jealous of Michelle,' she insisted, 'which suggests that the other woman had only just taken her place, so to speak. And I also think that they'd only very recently just argued about something — Tris and his stepmother, I mean.'

At the inspector's interested look, Jenny then went on to describe the cross words they'd had with each other, which had been mostly about Robert Jones. And which one of them the Lord of the Manor would believe if they started telling tales on each other. She also described the way that Tris had mockingly blown her a kiss on leaving the pavilion.

'It really wasn't very nice to watch,' Jenny said, in mild understatement, 'since it seemed so petty and somehow spiteful. And I'm pretty sure he did it just to rile her,' she finished. 'Well, that, and to indulge his rather sardonic nature.'

'Hmm. This victim of ours is definitely beginning to come across as being a bit of a lad, isn't he?' the policeman mused without humour. 'Perhaps it's no big surprise that someone walloped him over the head with a cricket bat.' In point of fact, he was pretty sure, from all he'd heard and seen so far, that he'd probably have felt like doing it himself, if he'd ever actually met the man. Know-it-all chancers and Lotharios were well up there on Laurence Causon's list of people that he didn't much like.

Jenny flinched at the inspector's rather harsh judgement. Tact, clearly, wasn't one of the man's strong suits. Still, it wasn't her place to point it out.

'And speaking of people who might have wanted to introduce our victim's head to some seasoned willow . . .' Causon mused quietly, startling her even more, until she realized that he was looking just beyond her right shoulder.

Jenny looked around and saw that the door was opening, and that Graham Lane was entering. Only he was clearly alone. Causon's sharp gaze looked pointedly behind his sergeant's lean form, but when nobody else appeared in his wake, he transferred his gaze back to his junior officer.

'I thought I told you—' he began ominously, his bullish neck turning a shade of red.

'To bring the boy here, sir. Yes, I know,' the younger man rushed in, before his boss could work up a proper head of steam. 'And I tried to, but I ran into a bit of a problem. Well, actually quite a large problem, in point of fact,' Lane admitted, looking abashed now.

'Oh? Gave you the slip, did he?' Causon jibed. 'Did a runner? What's up — wasn't your sprinting up to the challenge of a teenager, Sergeant? Tut-tut. What would the chief super say about that? You know how he's always going on about fitness.'

Graham Lane sighed heavily. He hated it when superior officers got like this. And as if Causon was in any position to lecture anyone about physical fitness!

'No, sir. That is, there was no running involved.'

'Then perhaps you'd better tell me exactly what *was* involved then, seeing as you seem incapable of following a simple order. So, Sergeant Lane, what mammoth problem prevented you from doing your duty?' Causon said, crossing his massive arms across his chest, stroking his chin with a couple of sausage-like fingers and watching the younger man with an expression of exaggerated interest.

Graham Lane's lips twitched briefly, showing that whatever else he lacked, it certainly wasn't a sense of humour. He looked at Jenny, then back at his superior to check that he could speak freely. Of course, he'd recognised the infamous Jenny Starling right away, and suspected his boss had been making use of her 'insights' while he'd been gone.

'Yes, it's OK, go on,' Causon urged impatiently.

'The boy's mother, sir,' he said blandly. He paused, waiting to watch as Causon blew out his cheeks like a bullfrog. But before he could let out the breath again and indulge his obvious bad temper further, Lane slipped in smoothly, 'The boy's mother, one Marie Rawley, answered the door, and when she saw my ID, refused me admittance. Which, as you know, sir, without a properly authorized warrant, she had every right to do. And when I told her that I just wanted to speak to her son, she pointed out that the lad was only seventeen and couldn't be questioned without an adult.'

'That's not . . .' Causon began to roar, then caught the glimmer of amusement in the younger man's eye, and suddenly subsided.

Whilst he obviously liked to vent his spleen from time to time, Jenny noted with interest, it was clear that the inspector also knew when to be still, and to actually listen. And he recognized the fact that his sergeant seemed to be on to something, for after he'd thought about it for a moment, he said softly, and in a much more reconciliatory way, 'Something about the situation tweak your radar, did it, Lane?'

Graham smiled. He knew the old man would get it sooner rather than later.

'Oh yes, sir. So many "somethings," it's hard to know where to start. To begin with, when Mrs Rawley first opened the door, she was clearly agitated and under some considerable stress. She was as pale as milk, and her hands were distinctly unsteady.'

'Booze?' Causon hazarded abruptly.

Alcoholic mothers and bored housewives were hardly unheard of. But not in this case, it seemed, for his sergeant was already shaking his head.

'Oh no, sir. Not a whiff of it. And her speech was fine, not slurred. No, I'd say that she was far more likely to be suffering from shock or something of that nature,' the younger man said. 'She had her hands under her armpits, too, like her hands were very cold and needed warming up.'

Causon's eyes narrowed thoughtfully. 'Did she now?' he asked softly.

Now that *was* interesting. And he didn't doubt his sergeant's assessment.

Like many coppers, Lane had cut his teeth on the streets, and he'd attended his fair share of RTAs and violent domestics. And if anyone quickly learned how to read the signs of shock or stress in a witness or suspect, it was a copper like Lane.

'And another thing that struck me as distinctly odd, sir,' Lane continued, 'was the fact that she didn't look all that surprised to see me.'

Causon grunted but took the hint. Most respectable middle-aged ladies, living a respectable lower middle-class life, found the police turning up on their doorstep to be a little out of the ordinary at least.

'Does she have form?' he asked, getting to the crux of the matter with just four simple words.

'No, sir. I asked HQ for a background check on her as soon as I left,' Lane confirmed. 'She doesn't have so much as an outstanding parking ticket or traffic fine to her name.'

'Hmm.' Causon rubbed his chin thoughtfully, and this time he did so without any of his earlier sarcastic dramatics. 'We'll have to ask the uniforms — when we finally get some more bloody men here — to make it a priority when questioning that lot outside to see if there's any history between our victim and Mrs Rawley. I was just telling Miss Starling here that I'm getting the picture that he was a bit of a ladies' man, our Mr Jones. Perhaps this is a simple enough case of him messing about with the wrong woman. Nice-looking is she, this Mrs Rawley?'

Graham Lane shrugged noncommittally. 'She's tall, dark-haired, dark eyes. Slim. Has a nice enough face, but I'd hardly class her as a femme fatale, sir.'

'Still, it needs to be checked,' Causon insisted.

'Yes, sir,' Lane said diplomatically.

As if he wouldn't have, anyway! He could, at that point, have mentioned something about grandmothers and egg-sucking, but decided discretion was probably the way to go.

'Well, don't just stand there imitating a statue, man.' The inspector, who clearly knew his sergeant very well indeed, glowered at him. 'What else happened to bring you back here with your tail between your legs?'

'Like I said, sir, when I told her that I needed to question her son, she point-blank refused. She told me that he'd been in the house all day, as had she, and that there was no way I was going to come in and question him without a warrant.'

'Did she just?' Causon said. Now *that* smacked of someone who'd had dealings with the law before. It sounded as if she was making a point of giving both herself and her nearest and dearest an alibi, whilst at the same time giving the sergeant his marching orders. Most members of the public didn't have the nerve to do that, without some prior experience of having to deal with people in law and order. 'And?' he went on impatiently.

'And it's my opinion, sir, that she was lying through her teeth,' Lane said succinctly.

'About the boy being inside all day? Or about herself being inside all day?' Causon shot back briskly.

Lane opened his mouth to respond instantly, then quite visibly paused to think about it more carefully for a moment. And then opined cautiously, 'If I was a betting man, sir, I'd say both.'

'Right. Well, no doubt if we had more men here, we'd probably already know by now whether or not Mrs Rawley had also been seen hanging around. There are certainly enough witnesses to have spotted her, if she has been telling porkies. But since, as it is, we've barely begun to gather in the preliminary statements, we'll just have to wait a bit. But we know for sure that Mark Rawley *was* here, at least on one occasion. We have a reliable witness for that.' He sighed. 'Well then, if the mountain won't come to whoever it was, then we'll just have to go to him. It. Whatever. But first, I want to have another word with the chap who found the body. Fetch him in, will you, Sergeant?'

'Sir.'

Jenny made herself look busy, trying to remain as inconspicuous as possible, so that when the groundsman joined them a few minutes later, he hardly seemed to register her presence. Perhaps that was not so surprising, since the old man had eyes only for the police officers. And his eyes, both Jenny and Causon could quite clearly see, were very frightened eyes indeed.

'Ah, Mr Cluley. Come on in, have a seat. I just have a few questions for you. About Tristan Jones, obviously,' Causon began casually enough. 'Your grandson was heard to argue with him earlier on today. Behind this building in fact. Do you know what that was all about?'

James Cluley paled a little bit, but managed to shrug one bony shoulder. 'Sorry, but this is the first I've heard about it,' the old man said, slumping down wearily onto a folding chair. 'Who was this witness then?'

Causon ignored the question.

'What can you tell me about your daughter, Mr Cluley?' he said instead, the abrupt change in subject clearly unsettling the older man. As it was probably meant to. Over in her corner, Jenny shifted a little restlessly. She never had liked to see people bullied, and especially not the elderly or the young.

But she could hardly leap to James's defence, even though she felt as if she should. Besides, Causon had a job to do, and if she didn't let him do it, he might eject her from the proceedings. And, in spite of herself, she was becoming rather interested in finding out who had killed Tris Jones.

She might not have liked him exactly, but he'd been young and so very vital and full of life. And people just couldn't go around killing other people.

'My Marie? What's she got to do with any of this?' James Cluley asked, sounding genuinely puzzled — as well as a little aggressive. But this was something Causon was inclined to take for granted. Parents tended to feel protective of their children, no matter whether they were three years old or forty-three.

'Was your daughter having a relationship with Mr Jones? I hear the young man was a good-looking one, and had something of a reputation with the ladies,' Causon carried on smoothly.

'What? Are you mad?' James Cluley yelped. And again, his outrage seemed genuine enough. 'My Marie wouldn't look twice at a chancer like that w— like Tris.'

He'd obviously been about to use much stronger language, but had realized, just in time, that showing how he really felt about a newly discovered murder victim probably wouldn't be very smart. He cast a quick eye up at Jenny to see if she'd registered his outburst, but she was studiously wiping down the work surfaces.

'They were not on good terms then?' Causon immediately pounced. 'Had an argument recently, had they?'

'No! Here, what are you implying?' James said angrily. 'Why are you picking on my Marie all of a sudden?'

'Because, Mr Cluley, she's refusing to co-operate with us. Now why do you suppose that is?' the inspector all but purred. 'Most law-abiding citizens, especially in a serious case such as murder or violent attack, tend to want to help the police. Not obstruct them.'

James clearly looked baffled. He sat there, shuffling his feet a little in front of him, but when Graham Lane offered him a cup of tea, he merely shook his head and continued to shuffle.

'I dunno, do I?' he said at last. 'What's this all about?' he demanded sullenly.

'When my sergeant went to your daughter's address to speak to her son, Mark, she refused to let him in. Any idea why she should be feeling so obstructive, Mr Cluley?' he asked, watching the old man closely.

And right on cue, James Cluley went red, then abruptly white.

He swallowed hard. 'No,' he said. But his eyes wouldn't quite meet those of the inspector.

In her corner, Jenny's heart went out to him. He was obviously a bad liar. And clearly torn between his desire to protect his family and wanting to do the right thing. Unless, of course, Jenny thought unhappily, he was the killer. In which case, his dilemma was even more urgent. Would he sacrifice his family — his daughter and grandson — to save his own neck?

'Don't lie to me,' Causon said warningly. 'Lying to the police is a criminal offence in its own right, and carries severe penalties, especially in a case as serious as a murder investigation. Clearly your daughter is trying to hide something. It'll be easier for everyone concerned if you simply tell us what it is.'

But James Cluley wasn't about to volunteer information. He merely shrugged and waited passively for the next verbal assault.

And in this, the inspector was willing to oblige him. 'All right, Mr Cluley,' he carried on grimly. 'If you're unwilling to talk to us about that, perhaps we can turn our attention back to Tristan Jones. And why it was you, out of all the people present here today, who actually found his body. Something of a coincidence that, don't you think? And you know what they say about coincidences. So, is there something that you have to tell me about *that*?' he asked portentously.

This time, James Cluley slouched further down in the chair. He stared at the back of his hands for a moment, heaved a massive sigh, and then he looked up at the policeman helplessly. It seemed as if he was desperately trying to find the right words, but in the end, he merely shook his head helplessly.

'You won't believe me about that,' he predicted sadly. 'You just plain won't believe me.'

'Try me,' Causon said quietly.

But again the old man shook his head. 'It's no use. You just won't believe me,' he repeated again, shaking his head obstinately. 'Hell, I wouldn't believe it, either, except I know that it happened.'

Jenny stirred. She didn't like the sound of this.

'You knew that Tristan Jones was behind the pavilion all the time, didn't you?' Causon began, carefully steering the old man towards his confession. 'When it first got around that he was missing?'

James sighed and shrugged. 'Yes, I knew,' he admitted quietly. He passed a shaking hand across his forehead, and his shoulders slumped back.

Lane shot his superior a triumphant look, and began to scribble furiously in his notebook. At a nod from Causon, he quickly informed the suspect of his rights, according to PACE. But the old man barely seemed to listen. Instead, he continued twisting his hands about in his lap, and shaking his head in frustration.

Jenny wanted to warn him that he really should shut up and get himself a solicitor, but she knew that Causon wouldn't thank her for interrupting the flow of his interview, let alone giving the old man unsolicited legal advice.

'I saw him go behind there, just as tea was finishing,' the old man admitted now with surprising ease. 'He was eating the last bit of something and he looked around, as if checking to see that he wasn't being watched, and then he slipped behind the back of the building,' James said listlessly.

'And you followed him?' Causon encouraged.

'Oh no. No, the thought never crossed my mind,' James said, with a slight laugh. 'I was sure, knowing Tris, that he'd be meeting up with some floozy or other back there, and I'm no peeping Tom!' He looked up at Causon with a brief flash of rebellion. Then he sighed and shook his head. 'But I'll admit that I *was* sort of curious as to who it was that he was seeing now. So I watched and kept an eye on both ends of the building to see her come out. I thought . . . Never mind what I thought,' James said, flushing a bit.

But Jenny could easily guess. The old man had wanted to know who Tris's latest conquest was, in case there was some way that he could use it to twist Tris's arm into giving him his money back. She doubted that James had even thought of this as blackmail, though. In his mind, it would have been justifiable.

And who was to say that he wasn't right? In a twisted, natural justice sort of way.

'So that's why I know you won't believe me,' James said yet again. It was annoying the policeman, Jenny could see, this constant refrain of his that he wouldn't be believed.

'Believe you about what?' Causon pressed impatiently.

The old man twisted restlessly on his chair. 'Well. I saw Tris go behind the pavilion, right?' he began heavily.

The others nodded.

'And I kept a sharp eye out on the pavilion, all the time that Max was batting. So I knew that neither Tris nor his lady love had left or sneaked off.'

Jenny could see that Causon was becoming red-faced again, and was obviously having trouble keeping his temper and patience intact. She silently urged the old man to get on with it before the inspector said something they'd all regret.

'So when he was needed to bat, I knew just where he must still be,' the groundsman plodded on patiently, oblivious to his audience's angst. 'So I kept watching, expecting him to come out one end, and his bit of stuff to skulk out the other. But he never appeared, see? So eventually I offered to go and fetch him, still keeping an eye out until the last minute to see who might come out. But no one did.'

James turned on his chair to look fully at Causon, who was still staring at him blankly, waiting for him to get to the point, and said tensely, 'Don't you see? Don't you get it yet?'

James Cluley looked over at Jenny, then at Lane, and finally back at the inspector again, beginning to look angry himself now. 'I looked behind the pavilion, and there he was, the poor sod, quite dead. *But nobody else had left the scene.*'

CHAPTER SEVEN

'But that's simply not possible,' Causon said, after a moment's startled thought. He frowned, then eyed the old man cynically. 'Unless you're lying, of course. You do realize that that's by far the most likely interpretation of what you've just said,' he finished heavily.

'I know that — isn't that what I've been saying all along?' James demanded helplessly. 'That's why I was so sure that you wouldn't believe me.'

The frustration was clear in his voice now, and Jenny, for one, was convinced that it was real. The older man sounded both indignantly aggrieved, which was the way you genuinely felt when you were speaking the truth and no one believed you, and at the same time resigned. As if, even before he'd made his case, he knew that it was hopeless. All of which combined to incline the travelling cook to believe him. Either that, or the groundsman was wasted in the world of turf management, and should get himself to a theatre forthwith, where he could give Gielgud, Richardson, and all the others a few pointers.

'That's exactly why I haven't said anything about it before now. Don't you think I know how far-fetched it sounds?' he demanded. 'Even I can see that it's simply not possible. I've been trying to make myself believe I was mistaken. That someone must have slipped out, I dunno, really quickly or something, so that I didn't notice. But I just don't think it happened. I can't really take it all in,' the old man was carrying on despairingly. 'But I'm *not* lying, I know I'm not, even though I also know there's no way on earth I'll be able to convince you. And it stands to reason that you've got no incentive to believe me anyway. A man with a job like yours — you must have people lying to you like troopers all the time.'

James Cluley heaved a massive sigh and rubbed a hand wearily across his chin. 'And you don't have to say it, either, about how bad it looks for me. I ain't blind, nor yet stupid,' he added bitterly. 'But I swear on my dear old mother's grave, I didn't kill him. But again, I have no way of proving it. I can only tell you the truth, and hope . . . somehow . . .' he trailed off, as if once more acknowledging the futility of his cause, and his thin shoulders slumped. But when, after a few moments, he raised his face again, he was looking stoical and oddly calm. 'But the simple fact is,' the old man reiterated, 'I *did* see Tris go behind the pavilion, and I *know* that nobody else came back out again — at either end. And yet, when I went to get him, he was dead. And I didn't do it. Now, make of that what you will, but that's all I can say.'

Exhausted, and finished, he slumped forward, dropping his head into his hands.

Causon opened his mouth to speak, looked at the old man's set shoulders, and then closed it again. In all his years as a policeman, he'd never heard anyone deliver such a preposterous statement with such heartfelt belief before. His sergeant, he noticed, was looking similarly nonplussed.

'But what you're saying simply can't be true, man,' Causon said, beginning to feel both frustrated and deeply affronted. Did this old man take him for a fool? Was he really thinking that he'd be so gullible as to swallow any old tripe? 'Are you trying to cover for someone, is that it?' he asked, seeking out the mostly likely explanation. 'Your daughter, perhaps? Or grandson? I can understand, if that's the case. It's only human to try and protect those you love. Hell, even I'd probably do the same in your position,' he encouraged. But even as he said it, he could see how little sense that made. He didn't need that Vulcan chap in those old *Star Trek* episodes to tell him that he was being illogical. For if James Cluley had seen anything like that happening, why would he make up such a stupid, impossible statement to try and cover for it? Why not just keep quiet and say nothing at all?

He glanced at Jenny Starling, and saw her raise a thoughtful eyebrow. Clearly, she wanted to discuss this latest development with him in private, and he certainly had no objection to tossing things around with her.

Like many police officers before him, he was finding it very useful indeed to have her as a sounding board. She had a clear head, and a no-nonsense way of thinking that could do wonders in helping you see things in their proper perspective.

'Mr Cluley, if you wouldn't mind, I'd like you to leave us for just a short while,' Causon said wearily. 'But don't leave the grounds, sir,' he added quickly, 'we'll want to talk to you again soon, I have no doubt.'

'Yes, of course,' the old man said with obvious relief, and got up quickly from the chair and moved over to the door, where a uniformed officer stood outside and watched him approach. He was still shaking his head in despair.

As he went by, the young constable said to Causon, 'Sir, I just thought you might like to know that two PCs and two other volunteers from Traffic have arrived. I asked the men from Traffic to cover the two other exits, apart from the main one at the car park, and to take a note of anybody either trying to enter or leave. The PCs are helping us collate witness statements. I hope that's all right, sir?'

'Yes, yes, that's good thinking,' Causon said, a touch impatiently. 'Let me know when the medical examiner finally arrives, will you?'

'Sir.'

When they were alone again, Causon turned to Jenny and said flatly, 'OK, Miss Marple, let's have it. What's your take on what's been going on?'

Jenny sighed and glanced idly out of the French window. As she did so, she saw Erica go by, her long-sleeved blouse draped loosely over one arm. She looked pensive — as well she might. And so much for her burning quickly, Jenny thought with a wry twist of her lips. She didn't seem to be that concerned about her precious pale complexion now.

And that the sun was still viciously hot out there was obvious when she saw Sir Robert pass by, going in the opposite direction. He was red-faced and sweating copiously with the heat, and looked, in fact, almost ill. Jenny hoped that he wasn't coming down with heatstroke or something.

She saw husband and wife meet up, talk briefly, and then part company again, with Sir Robert heading back towards the pavilion. Was he hoping to be allowed to see his son's body?

She wondered, with a pang, if the Joneses had been able to offer any sort of comfort to one another, but somehow doubted it. They didn't strike her as being a mutually beneficent couple.

'Miss Starling,' the inspector chivvied, and as she was forced out of her reverie, she felt herself becoming unaccountably grumpy. Here she was, being asked things that she felt utterly unprepared to answer, and it simply wasn't fair, damn it!

'Oh, why ask me?' she answered resentfully. 'You know everything that I do, after all,' she pointed out in exasperation. 'What do *you* think is going on?' She wasn't sure why she was feeling so out of sorts, except for the fact that all she'd wanted from this day was a pleasant stint of baking. And being presented with murder and mayhem instead was making her feel downright crotchety.

She sighed, brushed a lock of long dark hair out of her eyes, and tried to arrange her thoughts in some semblance of order. Then she duly apologized to the two policemen. 'Sorry, I have no right to take things out on you.'

Instead of looking angry himself, however, Laurence Causon shook his head with every appearance of contrition.

It was just so easy to forget, he realized with some surprise, that this woman was only a civilian. She hadn't gone through any training or counselling and perhaps it wasn't fair to take her for granted like this. It was just that she was such a good witness, and clearly had such a good head on her shoulders, that it hadn't occurred to him not to make use of her.

But before he could say any of this, however, Jenny Starling had already got over her wobbly and started to pace back and forth, as she clearly began to employ her brain cells.

'Well, on the face of it, James Cluley must be lying about what he saw. Or says he didn't see, if you understand what I mean. And yet . . . You know, he sounded as if he actually meant what he said,' she added with a puzzled frown.

Causon eyed her curiously. 'Which only means that he's good at lying,' he dismissed at once. 'If you had my job, you wouldn't be at all surprised by the human race's appetite for lies. Who knows, perhaps he's spent years in amateur dramatics, and could give Sir Larry Olivier a few master classes. Then again, maybe he's a bit . . .' And here he placed his forefinger against the side of his temple and made a twirling motion. 'But my bet is that he's covering for someone. Either his daughter or his grandson, or both, most probably. After all, they're the ones he'd have most reason to want to protect.' Here he shot Sergeant Lane a graphic scowl. 'We'll have to go and have a word with that precious pair soon, and see if we can't start getting at the truth about that family once and for all,' he added grimly. 'I want you to go outside and ask someone if they can find anyone who saw Marie Rawley around the cricket ground any time this afternoon.'

'Sir,' Lane said, and slipped out, returning a minute later.

Jenny looked at Causon thoughtfully. 'You have, of course, considered the possibility that James may have been lying about not seeing anyone go behind the pavilion with Tris for a very different kind of reason?' she asked quietly.

Causon smiled grimly at her. 'For strictly financial reasons, you mean?' he said, nodding.

Yes, of course he had immediately thought of that, and he was impressed that this civilian cook had thought of it, too. It was, after all, his job to think the worst of everyone. And years of experience of people behaving very badly indeed had made this very easy for him. But he was still a little taken aback to realize that the cook, who seemed to get on with everyone and seemed so easygoing, was also capable of looking automatically on the black side. And it was even more impressive because he suspected that Jenny Starling rather liked the old man. But evidently that hadn't stopped her from taking a purely sceptical view of the situation.

'Well, we know he's hard up for money,' Jenny said, reluctant to talk like this about James, a man that she had, in fact, rather begun to like, but knowing that the possibility had to be aired. 'And if he saw who killed Tris, it might just have occurred to him that a little blackmail could prove very lucrative indeed.'

Causon again nodded, and mentally began rubbing his hands together in glee. Now this was more like it. Something positive he could get his teeth into. 'Especially if the killer was loaded up with a few of the old readies,' he said, rubbing his fingers together in the universal gesture that denoted the presence of money. 'So who amongst our pool of possible killers would be able to make it worth Cluley's while?' he demanded.

'Sir Robert and his wife must be rolling in it,' Sergeant Lane pointed out instantly.

Jenny grimaced. 'You think Sir Robert would kill his own son?' she asked, a touch scandalized. Then blushed, as she realized how naïve that must have sounded.

Causon grunted. 'I've known parents kill their children for the price of their next fix. And vice versa. And I once arrested a man who'd killed someone because he'd been paid a hundred quid to do it, and a moped thrown in. A bloody moped, I ask you.'

Jenny blinked.

'Right. Well, I imagine a lot of people out there,' and here she waved a floppy hand outside at the playing field, 'aren't exactly short of money. Nowadays, if you can afford to live in a village, you have to be reasonably well off.' She sighed as she considered the injustice of this. Being on the move a lot, she had yet to try and buy a place of her own, but she doubted she'd be able to afford a place in any country village. A smart little semi on the edge of an attractive old market town would probably be the best that she could hope for. And even then, she might be aiming high.

She heard Graham Lane echo her sigh, and she had no doubt that he'd already learned much the same lesson.

'Then again,' she continued prosaically, 'Lorcan Greeves was in business with Sir Robert, and a stockbroker can't be poorly off. Not to mention Max Wilson. I don't know what he does for a living exactly, but I bet he isn't a plumber, or a shelf-stacker at Tesco. From his Sloane Ranger accent, and his duds, and the fancy four-by-four that he arrived in, I would hazard a guess that he'd been born with the proverbial silver spoon in his mouth.'

Causon laughed. 'Not that that means much these days — some so-called aristocrats are so cash poor they live off baked beans. But in our debonair cricket captain's case, he's probably rolling in it. He's probably a banker, or in real estate management, something along those lines would be my guess.' He sighed and rubbed his face wearily. 'No, you're right. The field's wide open when it comes to that. Cluley could blackmail any one of them and confidently expect to put his finances back in the black.'

'Always supposing that *that* was his motive for lying,' Jenny began, but then had to wonder. It just didn't feel right, somehow. 'It is, after all, just pure speculation on our part.'

'You still think he's more likely to be protecting someone?' Causon caught her pensive mood and shrugged. 'Got a soft spot for the old geezer, have you?' he jeered gently. 'Well, you could be right. I'm not saying I'm sold on the blackmail scenario myself. But if so, then that brings his grandson right back into pole position, doesn't it? Or his daughter, maybe. Which reminds me . . . Since Marie Rawley is so anti-police, perhaps you'd like to come along with me when I question her?' Causon asked craftily. 'After all, having another woman there, and one who doesn't have anything to do with the police, might make her talk more freely,' he put in, oh so casually.

Jenny eyed him grimly. Oh yeah? And she was a monkey's uncle.

Causon grinned at her, rightly interpreting her scepticism. But not for the world would he voluntarily admit that he would value her opinion, let alone concede that a second pair of eyes and ears might pick up on something that he missed. Especially when said eyes and ears belonged to someone as sharp as this startling cook. Besides, his wife had often said that it takes a woman to truly know another woman, and he was wise enough to concede that she might just have something there.

Jenny sighed. 'OK, fine,' she mumbled. She might as well give in gracefully, she supposed. It wasn't as if she would get any more cooking done by the looks of it. Unless she could persuade him to relent a bit later on? There was still the possibility that that evening's barbecue could go ahead.

She'd have to give it some thought and think how she might be able to persuade him.

But as for questioning another suspect, she didn't have any real objection to going along. Besides, she had to admit, she was rather curious now to hear just what the Rawleys had to say for themselves.

But, as it turned out, that would have to wait just a little while longer yet.

* * *

Outside, James Cluley paced restlessly along the bottom edge of the field. He could feel the sun beating down on him ferociously, and wished that he'd thought to bring a hat.

His sharp eyes had already noted that a policeman was guarding the double gates by the car park, and that another man was standing by the open, single-gated entrance on the opposite side of the field. And he didn't doubt that if he cut across the pitch and went under the horse chestnut trees, the only other official exit — guarded by a pair of iron bars that didn't meet in the middle, allowing dog walkers and others to zigzag between them — would also be guarded.

Not that he had any intention of trying to leave. That would only get him into more deep water with the police, and that was the last thing he needed right now. You didn't have to be a genius to realize that Inspector Causon hadn't believed a word that he'd said.

For a moment, the old man stopped and wondered what he'd do if he were to be arrested for murder. His poor wife would be beside herself. And he would need a solicitor, even though they could scarcely afford one. And what if the worst came to the worst, and he actually had to go to prison for any length of time? An old man like him . . . Would the other prisoners leave him alone? You heard such horrific stories about life inside. Would he be the target for bullying, maybe even—

But James's frantic thoughts were interrupted when he heard his name being spoken quietly, and sensed someone moving up alongside him.

He turned his head, looking slightly surprised at the identity of his visitor.

'James, I just need to have a quiet word.'

James nodded. 'All right,' he said equably.

* * *

Somebody else intent on having a quiet word — in fact, two people — were Max and Michelle Wilson.

Max had found them a quiet spot a couple of hundred yards or so from the car park, near a separate area where the children's swings and slide were situated. No children played there now, however, having either been called over to their anxious and watchful parents, or because they were too busy gawping at the police as they went about taking down everyone's name and getting their initial statements.

Michelle perched uneasily on the seat provided by the bottom bit of the slide, and she winced as the galvanized steel, heated by a day in the sun, threatened to scorch her thighs through the thin material of her dress.

'So just what the hell did you do?' Max charged straight in, but was nevertheless careful to keep his voice low.

'Funny,' she snapped right back. 'That's just what I was going to ask you!'

Max shoved his hands moodily into the pockets of his white cricket trousers and glanced nervously around. But there was no one within earshot.

'Look, now's not the time for this,' he hissed. 'Before long, we're going to have to make our statements to the police, and we need to make sure that we don't say something we'll regret. Once it's official and down on paper, it becomes a legal matter.'

Michelle gnawed on her lower lip and looked away. Her husband smiled grimly. 'Yes, exactly. It'll do neither of us any good if we contradict the other, or give the cops reason to suspect . . . well, suspect anything.'

Michelle's lips twisted with grim irony. 'You mean suspect that you might have wanted Tris dead, you mean?' She couldn't help but goad him.

'Me?' Max squawked. 'Not just me, sweetheart. You had a motive just as strong as mine,' he pointed out savagely.

'I did not!' Michelle denied vehemently. 'Why would *I* want Tris dead? We were in love with each other.'

Max snorted inelegantly. 'In a pig's eye you were in love. Oh, *you* might have thought it was true love, sweetheart,' he sneered, on seeing her shoot him a hurt, venom-tinged look, 'but you can't seriously be so naïve as to believe that lover boy ever thought the same?' Max laughed harshly. 'The whole world knew he was just a hound. He'd have shagged anything that offered.'

'Don't be so coarse!' his wife said hotly. 'You're just jealous. Just because Tris still had his looks, and you're losing

119

yours. Because Tris was still young, and you're staring fifty right in the face! No wonder you hated him.'

For a moment, Max went quite still. Then he smiled flatly. 'Other than the fact he was sleeping with my wife, you mean? Be that as it may, it doesn't alter the fact that Tris was probably bedding at least a couple of other women besides you.'

This time it was Michelle who went very still.

For a moment, husband and wife regarded each other in immutable, implacable enmity. Then Max let out a long, shuddering sigh.

'Look, this is all going to have to wait for another day. Right now, like I said, we need to get our stories straight before the cops get to us. First things first — it's vital that we say nothing about the divorce.'

Michelle laughed shrilly. 'Well, that was all your idea anyway, wasn't it, *sweetheart*,' she mimicked him savagely. 'Springing it on me like that, just before you swaggered off to take your turn to bat. What did you imagine you looked like? Some hero from a J.D. Salinger novel? It was pathetic.'

Max's hands clenched into fists.

'What?' Michelle snapped, seeing his convulsive movement. 'Did you think you could just thrust a solicitor's letter in my hand and that I'd fall apart? Really, Max, it was laughable,' she mocked, near-hysterically.

Max slowly unclenched his fist. 'Just listen to yourself. Do you wonder why I want out of this marriage?'

Michelle flushed. 'Don't think that you're the only one!'

Max smiled with biting savagery. 'Well, you were the one who was playing away, and with a joke like Tris Jones, of all people. I thought you'd at least have had better taste than to cuckold me with the likes of *him*!'

Michelle's shoulders suddenly slumped. Her golden head bent a little, and her lips trembled. 'Oh, he's dead now. Can't you just leave him alone, even now? What does any of it matter, anyway?'

Max looked abruptly away towards the pavilion, wondering what that policeman, Causon, was doing in there.

Who was he questioning? What was he thinking? *What were people saying?*

He turned back to his weeping wife, and sighed impatiently. He'd have to take it easy on her. The last thing he wanted was for her to bring the attention of the police their way.

'Look, Michelle, you've got to pull yourself together and understand the danger we're in,' he began more reasonably. At this, her head snapped up, her tears instantly drying.

'Danger?'

'From the police. From public opinion. From scandal. Don't you see, you stupid woman,' he hissed, his teeth all but clenched in frustration, '*somebody* killed Tris, and the cops are over there right now, looking for suspects. That's people like you and me, sweetheart. We were both here, right on the spot, and we both had a reason to kill him. And it's vital that we don't offer ourselves up on a silver platter. Neither of us can afford to get arrested. I'll lose my job, and can you just imagine all the shit that goes with that? I could kiss a decent pension goodbye, and I'd never get another position that pays half so well. So we could both say goodbye to the house and the cars and the holidays abroad. And you wouldn't be able to rely on a nice cushy settlement in any divorce court then, would you? And that's not the end of it. You can't doubt that your so-called friends would sell you out to the newspapers in an instant, in order to get their ten minutes of fame and a nice big pay cheque, can you?'

Michelle opened her mouth angrily, and then, after a moment's thought, slowly closed it again. As loath as she was to admit it, her husband was making sense.

'OK, fine,' she said angrily. 'So what do you want me to do about it?'

'Just say nothing to anybody about my giving you the divorce papers,' he said at once. 'And whatever you do, say nothing about your fling with Tris. And I'll play it the same way.'

Michelle smiled grimly. 'What? You think that others won't already be whispering in that grubby little inspector's ear, hinting at things?' She glanced around the field, at her neighbours and, as Max had called them, their so-called friends, and laughed softly. 'You know what it's like in a small village. Everyone knows everyone else's business. And they can't wait to spill the beans. If that man — Causon, is it? If he hasn't already heard the rumours about Tris and me, I'll do a streak at the next match at Lord's.'

Max sucked in a sharp breath. She was right, damn it. The grapevine would already be doing its worst to put them right in the thick of it. But he didn't see that they had any other choice.

'Rumour is one thing. Proving it is another,' he said. But even to his own ears, he sounded as if he was trying to convince himself, as well as her. 'If you and I both firmly deny the rumours, how are they going to prove us wrong? We just have to stick to our guns. Right?' he added aggressively.

Michelle shrugged sluggishly. 'If you say so. Oh all right, fine!' she flared, as he looked set to lambaste her again.

Max's eyes narrowed on her angrily. 'You need to buck your ideas up, my girl. And don't think for one minute that our dear inspector is above arresting *you* for the crime,' he warned her mockingly.

Again, Michelle's head shot up. 'What? Why should he? I never killed Tris,' she said hotly.

Max snorted. 'Says you. But who's to say that you didn't?' His eyes narrowed on her thoughtfully. 'After I gave you the papers, I went straight out to start batting. I wasn't watching you, or lover boy. Did you go straight to him to cry on his shoulder, Michelle?' he asked grimly. 'Did you expect him to be delighted? He probably wouldn't have cared and would've turned you down.'

Michelle gaped up at him, her usually beautiful face rendered almost plain by her shocked expression.

'No! I never even saw him. Not that that's what he would have done anyway,' she insisted. 'Oh, I looked around for him,' she reluctantly admitted, 'but . . . I couldn't see him anywhere.'

Max smiled, feeling smug at catching her out. 'So you did want to run to him and weep on his shoulder?'

'I told you, I never saw him!'

'Which is just as well for both of our sakes,' Max sneered. 'Because if you had sought him out and told him, he'd only have told you not to be such a stupid little tart,' he taunted cruelly. 'And he'd have laughed in your face if you'd been silly enough to suggest that you and he made it official. Is that what happened?' Max demanded. 'Did he tell you to your face not to start getting ideas above your station? As if Tris would ever seriously consider hooking up with you!' Max laughed. 'You're not young enough to suit his criteria for wife material, and what's more, you don't have a rich daddy waiting in the wings. Tris always boasted that he'd marry an heiress, did you know that?'

'Lying bastard,' Michelle said. But whether she was talking to her husband, or talking about Tris, it was hard to say at this point.

'Is that what happened, though?' Max pressed. 'Did you confront him behind that damned pavilion, and when he laughed in your face, did you bash him over the head with his cricket bat?'

'No! I already told you I never even saw him!' Michelle snapped.

She already knew that Tris had been hit over the head with a cricket bat because before the first police had arrived on the scene, a number of people had been ghoulish enough to go and take a look. Oh, the old groundsman had stopped anyone from actually going behind the pavilion, but they'd clearly been able to see Tris's body, and the cricket bat lying beside him. And it didn't take much of a leap of the imagination to guess that he had probably been whacked over the head with it.

And the thought of it made Michelle feel sick. That handsome, fine head of his, beaten . . . She shuddered. It must have taken someone monstrously angry to be able to do that. Someone really angry . . . She looked up at her husband grimly.

'Did you do it?' she asked. 'Did you kill him? Did he wound that monstrous ego of yours to such an extent that you struck out?'

But Max was already shaking his head grimly.

'Oh no, sweetheart. That won't do. You can't pin it on me! I was on the field playing cricket, with dozens of witnesses for my alibi. It's you who's in real trouble on that front. Oh, I know you said you were in your chair, chatting to what's-her-name. But no one knows exactly when Tris died after tea, and you could have left your chair for five minutes or so to go to the loo or something, and she might not have remembered it. No.' Max smiled an unbearably smug smile. 'When it comes to murder, your alibi has to be airtight. Mine is. Yours isn't, I'm afraid.'

He felt savagely satisfied to see her go pale with fear.

'Yes, just think about that for a moment, will you,' he said cruelly. 'And then perhaps you'll realize that what I'm saying about lying to the police makes sense. We have to stick to our story. There was no affair. We know nothing, saw nothing, said nothing. And I didn't show you those divorce papers. Where are they, by the way?'

'In my handbag.'

'Then burn them,' he ordered her peremptorily. 'Just to be safe. And when we give our statements, just remember — there was nothing going on between you and Tris, and no shred of truth in all these foul and slanderous rumours going about that you were having an affair. Agreed?'

And slowly, reluctantly, Michelle Wilson nodded.

* * *

Back in the pavilion, Jenny was just reaching for her handbag when Causon looked up abruptly. They were just about to take a walk into the village to confront the Rawleys, when Graham Lane, who had left them for a time, erupted back into the room.

'Sir!' he yelled.

Causon jumped about a foot in the air and clamped a huge mitt to the middle of his chest.

'What? Don't shout like that!' he shouted in turn. 'You nearly gave me a damned heart attack!'

Lane waved an apologetic hand in the air. 'Sorry, sir. I didn't mean to . . .' He paused, and took a deep calming breath. 'Sir, we've just found another body.'

CHAPTER EIGHT

'*Another* one?' Causon echoed incredulously. 'What do you mean, another one? And why wasn't it found before?' He'd gone slightly pale, and he was staring at his junior officer in frank horror.

Graham Lane swallowed hard and shrugged helplessly. 'We just . . .' But before he could carry on, his superior was already steamrollering over him.

'If we had been given the manpower we needed right from the get-go, an immediate search of the area would have been carried out as a matter of course, and we'd have found another victim right away. Damn it!' The older policeman was going very red in the face by now, and a vein over his temple was throbbing madly.

It was clear to Jenny that this was a major disaster from the professional's point of view, and she could only hope that Inspector Causon wasn't going to be made a scapegoat should there be an internal police investigation. Not that that was anyone's number one priority right now.

'Sir, it's worse than that. Much worse,' Lane said, looking, if possible, even more dreadful than his boss. 'The body wouldn't have been there for us to find.'

Causon's eyes narrowed. Slowly the ruddy colour left his face, leaving him looking rather more grey than anything else. 'What are you talking about, Lane?' he asked hoarsely.

'Sir, I think you'd better just come and see,' his sergeant said.

The younger man looked very bleak now, and Jenny felt a snake of fear slither down her spine. Just what on earth was happening here?

Naturally, Jenny was right on his heels as Causon turned and stepped smartly out of the pavilion.

Jenny could understand why the two policemen were so anxious, of course. Finding a second body only now would reflect badly on them — no matter what the circumstances — and on Causon, as the senior investigating officer, most of all. But she could tell that there was something else worrying the sergeant, besides concerns about how this would look on his CV.

They were headed for the top end of the field, Jenny quickly realized, towards an incline and a stand of majestic horse chestnut trees, which stood in a frothing white and green haze of tall cow parsley.

As they approached the scene, they could see one of the PCs was standing there, with a white-faced spectator beside her. He was an older man, with a shock of white hair and matching caterpillar eyebrows. His shoulders were hunched, as if he was protecting himself from some unseen enemy, and he was visibly shaking as they power-walked past him. Jenny surmised that he'd probably been the one to find the body, and she was glad that the policewoman was there, taking care of him.

Jenny felt a fleeting wave of hot anger shoot over her. This poor old chap had just come out on a hot summer's day to watch his village team play cricket, and now here he was, looking near the point of collapse. No doubt what he'd just seen would be giving him nightmares for years to come.

It just wasn't fair. The cook felt her shoulder blades stiffen mutinously. Whoever was responsible for all this damage was going to have to be caught, and soon. It made her feel ashamed of her own small attack of self-pity earlier on. After all, whilst murder might have blighted her day, for others it had been nothing short of a devastating tragedy.

It made her even more determined than ever to do what she could to help.

The policewoman shot Causon a quick, worried look as they passed, and Jenny saw Sergeant Lane give her a warning shake of his head. Again, Jenny felt the tension ratchet up a notch. But she didn't have too much time to anticipate what disaster lay ahead, because suddenly they were in the welcome shade of the trees, and her eyes took in the scene quickly.

Someone had clearly made a path through the large hollow stems of the cow parsley quite recently. A large area off to one side had been trampled fairly comprehensively, as if someone had loitered there for some time, maybe restlessly shifting about. But a more narrow avenue of flattened flowers and foliage had been created, leading further into the trees, as if whoever had stood there hadn't been satisfied with standing in the one spot and had moved deeper into the nest of wild flowers at some point. The cow parsley itself, Jenny gauged with a quick glance, had to stand at least four and a half feet tall — if not more. And given the deep shadows cast by the trees, it would have been hard for anyone casually glancing this way from the brightly-lit playing field to see anyone standing in here.

'It looks as if only one or two people went through here,' Causon said, looking at the pathway created through the stand of weeds. 'Damn it, we need this photographed before we move in.'

'Sir, SOCO are still with the first victim,' Lane offered. 'Shall I divide their attention?'

'Well, get the photographer up here at any rate. We need to document the crime scene before we go any further in. Is the medical examiner here yet?'

'Not yet, sir. They're all busy with the motorway pile-up, but—'

Causon swore and cut him off. 'Just get the photographer up here, Lane,' he said firmly, then reached for his own phone. When Jenny realized that he was calling his superiors, and was in no uncertain terms outlying the seriousness of the situation and the utter necessity for more men, she wandered away to give him some privacy to vent his spleen. No doubt he would be making it very clear to whoever was unlucky enough to be on the other end of the line just what the consequences of him being so under-staffed had led to.

Taking advantage of having a few minutes on her own to think, she very carefully circumnavigated the stand of trees, and when she'd done an almost 180-degree turn, she paused and eyed the stand of white lacy flowers carefully.

Yes, this is where someone had come back out again. Although the frothy weeds tended to interlock, you could just see where someone had pushed their way through — though the path created wasn't as clear as it was on the other side. Which meant perhaps only one person had used it. Two had gone in, on the other side, but only one had come out this side.

The killer.

Although it was a bakingly hot and dry day, Jenny nevertheless felt as if the atmosphere around her had darkened. It was all psychological hogwash, of course, and she shook off the creepy feeling with a grim little toss of her head.

She glanced around, forcing herself to look at things with a no-nonsense attitude, and found herself nodding. Yes. This made sense — the stand of trees hid you from the vast majority of the playing field below, and behind her was the tall perimeter hawthorn hedge and chain-link fence. Which meant that nobody was likely to be able to sneak up on you unawares — a circumstance, she imagined, much desired by anyone bent on homicide.

A mown, narrow pathway led to the doglegged iron bars that allowed egress to the village lane behind it, but not even that was overlooked by the nearest houses.

Yes, someone could leave just here and expect — or hope — to be unobserved. And the chances had to be fair that they'd get away with it.

Thoughtfully, she continued her circuit, careful where she put her feet, since the last thing she wanted to do was interfere or compromise any evidence — but the ground had been baked so hard in the recent heatwave that there were no footprints visible, even in the grassy turf. And there was certainly no soft mud to take a shoe-print impression. And as far as she could see, the killer hadn't been obliging enough to drop any monogrammed handkerchiefs or pieces of jewellery about, let alone any DNA-laden cigarette butts.

When she finally got back to Causon, she saw that the photographer had arrived and was busy snapping away, and that the DI was just thrusting his mobile phone back into his pocket. To Lane, he grunted grimly, 'Well, we're finally going to get a full team dispatched. Better sodding late than never, I suppose,' he added in disgust.

Jenny moved up beside them as the photographer, snapping as he went, led the way through the cow parsley, and to the grim prize in the centre of the weed patch. Over the backs of the three men, she saw the legs and feet of the victim first. Plain white trousers, slightly coloured green from grass stains, and a pair of white trainers. One of the cricket players then, she mused.

Then Causon moved slightly, and Jenny gulped as she found herself looking at an unexpectedly vibrant sea of sodden red. She blinked a couple of times, and her vision became clearer — and she saw a man's chest, soaked in blood. And sticking obscenely up out of the middle of it, the end of a smooth, rounded, pale-coloured piece of wood.

For some reason the object looked both alien and familiar at the same time. It gave her a slightly *Twilight Zone* feeling, and she frowned, not sure at first if her mind, rather than her eyes, was playing a trick on her. Then the eerie moment thankfully passed, and she realized at last just what it was that she was looking at. She had, in fact, seen similar pieces of wood all that morning. On the cricket pitch.

For the murder victim had been stabbed through the heart with a cricket stump.

Jenny glanced away, swallowing hard as her gorge rose. But even as she fought back the nausea, her quick mind was already buzzing.

That wasn't really possible, was it? That was the first thought that her brain threw up at her. A cricket stump was just a blunt piece of wood that had a vague point at one end that you stuck into the ground. Surely you couldn't pierce a human body with an implement like that?

Unless, of course, it had been deliberately sharpened to turn it into a stake.

Jenny put a hand over her mouth and shuddered as every corny vampire film she'd ever seen raced through her mind. What kind of sick individual were they dealing with here?

But then, as if to distract her from the horror of what she was seeing, her quick brain summoned up yet another image. A less lurid and far more relevant and interesting memory — something else that she'd seen that morning, something that now might have vital significance.

She turned, already opening her mouth to tell the inspector what it was, but now the photographer was bending down, taking snapshots, and for the first time, Jenny saw the man's face.

The sightless eyes, staring up at the tree canopy above him. The white hair. His slack-jawed expression of surprise. A face she'd seen not ten minutes ago — very much alive and looking both haunted and aggrieved.

James Cluley.

Jenny felt tears blur her vision and she turned quickly away. She didn't want to see any more.

That poor old man.

Now she understood why Sergeant Lane had been acting so oddly. The killer must have struck only minutes ago. And right under the noses of the police, and everyone else in the playing field too. And that, perhaps more than anything else, would be bound to sit very heavily indeed on the inspector's shoulders. Even though she hadn't known the man that long, she was sure that Causon couldn't help but feel both guilty and responsible for failing to protect the groundsman, even though he couldn't possibly have been expected to predict such a turn of events.

Who would have thought that the killer would strike again — and so soon? She certainly hadn't.

But that being the case . . . what if the killer wasn't finished yet? If they were dealing with someone who was truly mad, or had gone berserk, who might be next? She felt incipient panic take a cold hard grip on the back of her neck, and it took some effort to force herself to stay calm.

Even under-manned, there were now half a dozen police officers here. So even if they were dealing with a homicidal maniac, if he or she attacked again, they would be quickly discovered now and overpowered. Wouldn't they?

Jenny found herself glancing wildly about, trying to spot someone acting oddly.

Of course, no one was, and she rubbed her forearms briskly, in an attempt to smooth down the goose bumps that had risen on her flesh.

Besides, in her heart she knew that they weren't dealing with some random, ravening serial killer, or out-of-control lunatic.

Whoever had killed James Cluley had taken a mighty risk, yes, but they had also been very clever about it. Cold, calculating and ruthlessly clever. And whoever had done it had got away with it, and would now be trying to blend in and go unnoticed. And drawing attention to themselves would be the last thing on their mind.

She tried to concentrate on something else, and became aware that Causon and Sergeant Lane were now conversing quietly just behind her. It was clear that, just as she'd expected, both men felt bad — and guiltily aware that they had failed to protect James Cluley. Even if she were to try and tell them that they couldn't possibly have been expected to predict such a tragedy, it would do no good.

'Well, one thing's for certain, sir,' Lane was saying. 'Whoever killed him must have got blood all over them. There's no way that they could have avoided the arterial blood spatter from a blow such as that.'

'I agree. And by the looks of the angle, they must have been standing right in front of him when they plunged the stump in,' Causon agreed.

So, Jenny found herself thinking automatically, it probably wouldn't have been one of the cricketers then. Dressed all in white, they'd have had no chance of not being spotted the instant the deed was done. But if the killer was dressed in dark clothes, would anyone notice bloodstains? In this heat, clothes would dry quickly anyway, and . . .

'Must have taken a bit of strength, sir,' Lane pointed out. 'To ram a piece of wood into someone . . . I reckon we must be looking for a man.'

'Right. We need to start checking everyone on the field for bloodstains,' Causon said, and then cursed again. 'Damn it, those reinforcements had better get here soon. And I want the cricketers' kit bags checked, too. Whoever killed Cluley could have brought their bag with them to the scene, and changed their clothes right here. He or she wouldn't dare walk away dripping with blood and gore.'

That stark statement made even Graham Lane wince, and Jenny Starling felt a sudden need to be sick in a conveniently placed stand of stinging nettles. However, a few deep breaths and calling on her mettle saved her — just — from such ignominy.

'Sir. We need to search the entire grounds as well — they could have stuffed the bloodied clothes anywhere in these hedges, rather than risk being caught with them in their possession,' Lane pointed out.

'If they haven't already left the field altogether,' Causon growled.

'No, they can't have done that,' Jenny heard herself say, and saw the two policemen both pivot in surprise at the sound of her voice. Finding herself the abrupt focus of their complete attention, she shifted nervously. 'Don't you remember?' she prompted the inspector. 'The last time we saw James, he was leaving the pavilion and you told him not to go anywhere. At the same time, one of your men told you some volunteers had arrived, and he'd set them guarding all the exits. So James must have been killed right after that, which means that whoever killed him wouldn't have been able to leave. Not without being turned back by one of your men.'

Causon nodded, looking impressed. It wasn't many people who could keep their head and think straight at times like this. Let alone civilians.

'You're quite right, Miss Starling,' he acknowledged, with reluctant respect.

'And there's something else, while I think about it,' Jenny added. 'That cricket stump. It had to have been sharpened, hadn't it? I mean, it's one thing to be able to pound a fairly blunt stump into turf with a mallet or something, but not so easy to stab someone in the chest like that.' She didn't look at the body on the ground, but waved towards it.

'Probably,' Causon said. 'Why? Did you see someone interfering with the sporting equipment earlier on?' he asked sharply. 'The killer would have needed a penknife, or . . . Have any of your kitchen knives gone missing?' he suddenly demanded.

Jenny shook her head. 'No, that's not what I'm getting at. And I'd know straight away if one of my knives had gone missing. But what if the killer didn't need to do any whittling of the stump? Or at least, not that much?'

Causon walked quickly towards her, and Lane followed just as fast. 'What do you mean? What do you know?' There was suspicion in his voice now, and a sharp, cold light in his eye.

Jenny wasted no time in telling him about needing to find a bigger chair for herself and going into the store room to find one, and exactly what she'd seen in the old equipment room.

'And amongst the old bats and balls and stuff, there *was* an old penknife,' she finished, 'but there was also an old cricket stump that had been split, almost halfway down to the middle, leaving a really jagged, thin, splintered end,' she concluded. 'Just the sort of thing that would easily pierce . . . well . . .' She wasn't quite able to complete the gruesome sentence. Not that she needed to.

'Yes, I see,' Causon said grimly. 'We'd better check out this storeroom then and see if it's still there. Lane, you stay here and oversee this latest crime scene. Get SOCO over here as soon as they've finished processing Tristan Jones.'

'Sir.'

Causon detoured slightly on the way back to the pavilion to talk to the old man who'd first found the body, but he wasn't able to add much. He was still clearly shaken by his ordeal, but he, like Jenny, was made of stern stuff, and managed to give his evidence clearly and without any hesitation.

As Jenny had already guessed, he'd been forced to seek the trees in order to discreetly answer a call of nature, since the only toilets were in the pavilion, and someone had been in the men's room for ages. Unable to wait any longer, he'd been forced to go 'al fresco.' He'd just relieved himself against the tree, when he'd seen something white and red in the weeds and had found James. He'd stumbled out and attracted the attention of the first police officer he'd seen — the PC who was now watching over him.

In answer to Causon's quiet but pertinent questions, he'd confirmed that he hadn't seen anyone leaving the stand of trees as he'd approached, and that no, he hadn't seen James Cluley go in there, either. Although if he had, he'd have assumed the groundsman had been going in there for the same reason as himself. Men of their age tended to be at the mercy of their bladders, he'd confessed, blushing slightly in the presence of the two women. And no, he hadn't noticed anyone else under the trees at any point during the afternoon.

Causon thanked him, placed a gentle hand on his shoulder for a moment or two, and then strode off toward the pavilion, with Jenny in tow. Like the old man they'd just talked to, she too was feeling a bit wobbly about the knees, and could have done with a good sit down and a hot cup of strong, sweet tea, but Causon was a man on a mission.

Obligingly, Jenny took him straight through the changing room, ignoring the curious looks of the people milling around outside, and led him straight to the storage room.

As they'd both tacitly expected, the broken cricket stump was nowhere in evidence. Neither was the old penknife.

'So, at some point the killer must have been in here,' Causon said more to himself than to Jenny, and stood looking around the dirty, dim room thoughtfully. 'I'll tell SOCO I want this place processed next as a top priority.'

Jenny nodded uneasily. 'They'll want my fingerprints then. For elimination purposes,' she added unhappily.

She was very much aware that if the killer had been careful, then the only traces they might find in here would lead only to herself. And she didn't fancy being hauled off to the nearest station house for the old third degree.

Causon grinned at her knowingly. 'Don't worry, Miss Starling. I don't suspect you of killing James Cluley,' he said comfortingly.

'You don't?' she said, relieved. Then frowned suspiciously. 'Why not? I've just admitted to knowing all about the murder weapon.'

'Yes, but your alibi is twenty-four carat gold,' the policeman laughed.

It took her a moment to see why, but when she did, she almost laughed too. Of course. After James Cluley had left the pavilion, Jenny had stayed inside with Causon until the old man's body was found.

Her alibi was none other than the inspector himself!

Seeing her shoulders slump in relief, Causon just couldn't help himself. 'Of course, I've no solid reason to rule you out of killing Tristan Jones just yet,' he informed her amiably. 'For all

I know, you might have known him before and been another in his long line of women friends. You might have only taken on this catering job so that you could keep an eye on him, and then became insanely jealous when you realized you weren't the only woman in his life. After all, I only have your word for it so far that you didn't know him from Adam.'

Jenny shot him a sour look. 'Gee, thanks,' she muttered. 'Nice to know you have such faith in my taste in men,' she teased right back.

And then she frowned. Although she appreciated a little levity now after the shocks she'd just been through, her mind was still whirling like a dervish. 'Seriously, though. You don't think we might have two separate killers on our hands, do you?'

Causon cocked his head thoughtfully to one side as he gave this some consideration. 'What? That someone killed Tris, for whatever reason, and then someone else decided to kill Cluley. It doesn't seem very likely, does it?'

'No, it doesn't,' she admitted. 'Unless the motives were very different,' she added thoughtfully. 'Or unless someone else was protecting Tristan's killer?' She paced up and down quickly. 'What if someone else besides Tris's killer knew that James had seen whoever it was who had gone behind the pavilion? If that person wanted to stop him from talking . . .'

But Causon was already shaking his head impatiently. 'Now, don't you go complicating matters,' he advised her. 'It's only in television dramas or in the pages of those complicated thriller books that you get multiple-murderers or twist-in-the-tale conundrums. Usually, killings are very straightforward. I think you'll find that someone killed lover boy because he bedded the wrong woman, and then that same someone later killed James Cluley because he was stupid enough to try and sell his silence to whoever he saw leaving the back of the pavilion after doing the deed. Or, if you still refuse to see the old man as a blackmailer, the killer went after him because he believed that Cluley represented some other kind of danger to him. Or her.'

Jenny slowly nodded. 'Yes,' she said. 'You're probably right.'

But then again . . .

Jenny wasn't able to follow that thought to its logical conclusion because just then, a man she hadn't seen before, and not one in uniform, pushed into the room behind them. 'Sir, you have to come to the gents' toilet,' this individual demanded.

It took both Causon and Jenny a moment to grasp that the man, dressed in casual jeans and a white T-shirt, had to be one of the volunteers from Traffic, who'd given up their day off to help out.

'Oh?' Causon, in spite of everything, play-acted looking very amused. 'And why, pray tell, do I need to do something as unsavoury as that, er . . . Constable . . . ?'

'Tripp, sir.'

He was a tall, brown-haired man in his early twenties, and his rather plain face was flushed with excitement. No doubt they didn't get many double murders in Traffic. In any case, the older man's caustic amusement slid right over his head. And given what he said next, Jenny could understand why.

'Sir, we've found a man in the gents trying to clean himself up. And he's got blood all over him!'

Causon leapt forward. 'Well, why the bloody hell didn't you just say so in the first place, son?'

The youngster simply goggled at him, and Causon sighed wearily. 'Well, all right. Let the dog see the rabbit, Tripp.' And as the now thoroughly bemused constable simply goggled at him some more, added, 'Bring him in here, Constable.'

'Yes, sir.'

And so it was that Lorcan Greeves was frogmarched, protesting vehemently, into the storeroom. And it quite quickly became evident that he was indeed very blood-spattered, and was also cradling his right hand gingerly in his left.

'What's going on?' he said at once, trying to look both aggrieved but determined to be reasonable, and failing to achieve either effect. His eyes shot nervously from the inspector, then with evident and perhaps understandable bewilderment to Jenny, whom he vaguely recognized as being the caterer. 'Why was I manhandled out of the lavatory in that way?' His chin was thrust out in an effort to bolster his bluster, but he lacked the necessary backbone to bring the look off, and instead he looked merely ridiculous.

Causon looked him over carefully, then said to Jenny, 'Do you know this man, Miss Starling?'

Jenny nodded briefly. 'I think his name is Lorcan Greeves,' she said quietly.

'Yes, that's me,' Lorcan piped up, trying to wrest control of the situation back into his own hands, and failing yet again. 'All you had to do was ask me,' he added, a shade petulantly.

Causon nodded. 'Indeed, sir. You seem to be in some difficulties,' he said, nodding down at the newcomer's injured hand.

Greeves had obviously attempted to clean it up and then bandage it, no doubt with the help of the first aid kit stashed somewhere on the premises. But he hadn't done a particularly good job of it, and blood still oozed from his wound, situated, by the looks of the seepage, somewhere on the meaty part of his palm.

'Oh, this,' Lorcan tried for breezy unconcern next. 'This is nothing,' he added nonchalantly, right on cue.

'It hardly looks like nothing to me, sir,' Causon said affably, feigning concern. 'And from the way it's leaking, it looks as if it needs stitching. I didn't realize cricket was such a dangerous game.'

The inspector watched him carefully to see if he might go for the bait, and even Jenny could see the sudden look of speculation leap into Lorcan's eyes. Should he take the line that he'd hurt himself at the match? But then she saw him reluctantly abandon the idea — as appealing as it obviously was. And it didn't exactly take a genius to understand his reasoning. There would be far too many witnesses to the fact that Lorcan hadn't sustained his injury on the pitch to try and pass it off that way.

Indeed, when you thought about it logically, Jenny mused, it was hard to see how he *could* have come by such an injury while playing cricket, when surely the only real hazard was a flying ball? Concussion or painful bruising might result from that, but surely not such a bloody hand wound.

'Er, no. I didn't get it out on the field, as it happens,' Lorcan finally admitted miserably.

'No? I didn't think so,' Causon said, still in that friendly, vaguely curious way that was so transparently fake that it made you want to grit your teeth. 'It looks like a nasty cut to me. Got it whittling some wood, did you, sir?' Causon slipped in.

Lorcan Greeves frowned uncertainly, looking at the older man in what appeared, to Jenny at any rate, to be genuine puzzlement.

'Whittling wood?' he repeated blankly. 'No.'

Jenny could almost hear his brain buzzing as he tried to figure out the significance of the words.

'Why on earth should I have been whittling some wood?' he finally asked, very cautiously indeed, clearly sensing some sort of trap in the policeman's words.

'Oh, just speculating, sir,' Causon said, more cautiously himself now, making Jenny wonder if he, too, hadn't picked up on what seemed to be Greeves's genuine bafflement. 'So, how did you come by such a cut? Hardly a paper cut, is it, sir?' he asked, deciding that the time for playing games was over.

'Er . . . no. I er . . . broke a glass. Yes, very clumsy of me, I know,' Lorcan said, trying to look embarrassed. 'It was so hot, I had a nice cold beer, but what with the condensation on the glass and what have you, it just slipped out of my hand and shattered. And when I went to pick up the pieces, I stumbled and almost fell, and put my hand out to save myself, you know, like you do.' He was all but gabbling now. 'And . . . well, ouch! There you have it. Brought my hand down rather hard on a jagged piece of glass and there you have it. Gashed my palm pretty badly, I don't mind saying.' He shrugged again. 'My ex-wife always said I was hopelessly cack-handed.'

Causon nodded. 'Quite a tale of woe, sir,' he said sympathetically.

Lorcan blinked. 'Well, yes,' he said. 'But it'll be fine.'

'Oh, I think we should get you some proper first aid for that, sir. We can't have allegations of police brutality or inhumane treatment being bandied about, can we?' Causon said earnestly. 'I'm sure there's someone outside qualified to help you out. A nurse, or someone with medical training.'

'No!' Lorcan said precipitously, his voice rising to a near squeak. And when the inspector raised his eyebrows and all but pantomimed a man being taken considerably aback, he managed yet another painful attempt at laughter. 'Really, there's no need to bother anyone, Inspector, I can assure you. I can always take myself off to A&E later, if it doesn't stop bleeding soon.'

Causon nodded. 'Very well, sir. If you say so. And where did you drop this glass, exactly?' he asked, still in that reasonable, amiable voice that was beginning to get on Jenny's nerves, even though it wasn't aimed at her. 'Not outside on the grass, I imagine. It would hardly break on grass, would it?'

'What?' Lorcan said blankly. He'd begun, quite visibly, to sweat. Then, 'No. I mean, why do you want to know where I was?'

Causon shrugged his hefty shoulders. 'Oh, I just want to be sure that all that nasty glass is properly cleared away, sir. After all, we wouldn't want a little kiddie falling down and hurting themselves on it as well, would we?'

'Oh, there's absolutely no chance of that,' Lorcan said airily, going to wave his hand loftily in the air, and realizing just in time that that wouldn't be a good idea. 'I made sure to clear it all up, Inspector. I was very careful, I promise.'

The chubby stockbroker's eyes were darting around the storeroom, like a mouse desperately searching for a way out of a maze.

'That was very public-minded of you, sir, considering that you must have been bleeding profusely all that time. You seem to have got a good deal of blood all down your shirt and on your trousers too.'

'Yes, it did drip rather. It does look bad, I know, especially since I'm wearing white and all,' Lorcan admitted cheerfully. 'But I haven't bled as much as it looks. I was just going to change out of my cricket whites into my day clothes anyway.'

'Yes, I'm sure you were.' Causon's crocodile smile made the most of his rather crooked set of teeth. 'If you'll just tell me which bin you put the broken glass into, I'll have my constable here bag it for evidence.'

He nodded at the young man from Traffic, who had been listening to the interview with evident fascination.

'What? What do you mean? Evidence of what?' Lorcan blustered anxiously. 'I thought Tris had been hit over the head? There wasn't any blood at the scene . . .' He trailed off as Causon shot him a very keen glance indeed, and then gave a shamefaced smile and a brief shrug. 'All right, I have to admit it. Along with a lot of other people, I did just have a quick peek at Tris, before your people first arrived. I was curious and concerned. He was my friend and business associate, after all. Oh, James made sure that nobody went behind the pavilion and disturbed the scene, of course, but he couldn't stop any of us just looking, could he?'

'No, I don't suppose he could, sir,' Causon concurred flatly.

'Well then . . . I don't see what my cut hand has to do with anything,' Lorcan said, trying to work his way up to some righteous anger now. 'I understand that you have your duty to do, of course, but there's no need to be so officious.' He looked rather proud of this sentence, and tried to follow up on it. 'So, if you don't mind . . .' He made vague, about-to-leave gestures.

'Oh but I *do* mind, sir,' Causon said incisively. 'Collecting evidence of your broken beer glass will be crucial to my case.

But I'm not referring to the murder of Tristan Jones. I'm referring to the murder of James Cluley.'

Lorcan Greeves literally gaped at him. It wasn't often that Jenny had seen anybody actually do that before, but there was no other way to describe it. Lorcan's jaw literally dropped, his eyes bugged out a little, and he looked like nothing so much as a seriously surprised frog.

'*James!* James is dead?' Lorcan gasped.

Causon sighed heavily. 'Yes, sir. His body was found a little while ago. He'd been stabbed.' He very carefully didn't add any further details about the murder weapon. 'And his killer must have got covered with blood,' he continued, his voice heavy with accusation now. 'And the funny thing about stabbing someone is that, very often, the one doing the stabbing also gets cut as well. Not many members of the public are aware of this fact, but it's very easy to nick yourself when you're wielding a blade of some kind. Especially if you're not familiar with a weapon, or how to use it properly.' Lorcan slowly but comprehensively went a very pale shade of sickly green, which only reinforced Jenny's mental image of him as a thunderstruck amphibian.

'But . . . but . . . but . . .' he spluttered. He seemed to find it both hard to breathe and to string together a coherent sentence.

'Yes, sir?' Causon prompted genially.

'But . . . but . . . I didn't kill James,' Lorcan finally managed to gasp out.

'But you *did* kill Tristan Jones?' Causon asked casually, slipping in the question smoothly.

'What? No! No, I haven't killed anybody!' Lorcan denied, so panic-stricken he sounded ready to burst into tears.

'No? Well, unless you feel like telling me the truth about how you came to slice open your hand, I shall have no choice but to arrest you for the murder of James Cluley,' Causon informed him, almost blandly. 'In point of fact, my superintendent would be most miffed with me if I didn't.

And you can't expect me to get in my superior officer's bad books, can you?'

Jenny glanced at Causon curiously. She was finding his unorthodox policing methods interesting. Presumably his brand of caustic humour worked on a suspect's nerves to the point that they confessed, simply to get him to stop speaking.

'But why would I want to kill James?' Lorcan asked, sounding genuinely wounded now. 'I didn't know him all that well, but he seemed a perfectly pleasant sort of fellow to me.'

Causon sighed. 'Your hand, sir. How did you cut it? And no more of this guff about a dropped beer glass if you please,' he rapped out.

Lorcan's eyes slowly began to widen in horror. 'But . . . but . . . but . . .'

Causon rolled his eyes. 'This again, sir?' he asked wearily. 'Really?'

'But I can't tell you that!' Lorcan wailed, almost comically.

'No?' Causon said, finally losing patience. 'In that case, Lorcan Greeves, I'm arresting you on—'

'No! Wait,' Lorcan rushed in, his face going from green back to white again. 'All right! I'll tell you. It was Marie Rawley. She cut me. It was an accident. I mean, she didn't mean to do it or anything . . . It was just an accident,' Lorcan trailed off miserably.

Whatever either Jenny or the inspector had expected him to say, it certainly wasn't that, and Causon stared at him for some moments, his mind doing a whole series of mental twists.

'Let me get this straight,' he finally said. 'Marie Rawley attacked you with a knife?' He carefully enunciated each word.

'Yes. No.'

'Please make up your mind, sir. Either she did or she didn't.'

'Yes, she cut me, but no, she didn't attack me. It was an accident, like I said,' Lorcan pleaded desperately.

'And how did this accident happen, exactly?' Causon asked, clearly not believing a word of it.

'We were just . . . er . . . talking . . . and we got into something of an argument . . .'

Lorcan hesitated, as if suddenly aware of just how dangerous the ground was becoming underneath him.

'And this argument entailed the use of a knife, did it? A bit drastic for your regular, run-of-the-mill argument, isn't it? Do you often bring a knife to a conversation with a lady, sir?'

'No, I do not!' Greeves denied indignantly. 'It was her knife. That is, she brought it with her.'

'Oh? Did she have reason to suspect that you might attack her?'

'What? No, of course not!'

'Were you and she an item, sir? Had she ended the relationship and you wouldn't take no for an answer? Defending her honour, was she?'

'Don't be so ridiculous! Me and Mrs Rawley? I barely know the woman!' Lorcan yelped, looking genuinely appalled. 'And I can assure you, she's not my type.'

'No?' Causon's patent disbelief was relentless. 'So she was a woman scorned, was she? She made advances and you disdained her, so she set about you with a knife. Is that what you'd have me believe?'

Lorcan stared at the inspector like a rabbit staring at a pair of approaching car headlights. 'No! No, no, no, no. It was nothing of the sort. If you'd just let me explain how it really was.'

'Perhaps that might be best,' Causon agreed.

'She was . . . just . . . er . . . waving it around and . . .' But again Greeves stumbled to a halt.

'And just what exactly was it that you were discussing that resulted in Mrs Rawley "just waving a knife around", sir?'

And it was then that Lorcan Greeves finally had the sense to call a halt. Clearly he felt too battered and bamboozled by the inspector's interrogation to come up with even the most pitiful of lies. His shoulders slumped in defeat. 'I want a solicitor,' he said flatly. 'I'm not saying another word until I have a solicitor present.'

Causon's lips twisted bitterly, and Jenny could easily guess why. Once a suspect called for a solicitor, the police couldn't continue the questioning.

'Very good, sir. I'll just get my sergeant to take you back to the station. There we'll get the police surgeon to take a look at that hand of yours, and you will be formally charged.'

Causon asked the Traffic officer to go and fetch Graham Lane, and then the three of them waited in awkward silence for the sergeant to arrive.

CHAPTER NINE

The sergeant duly arrived and was given a quick rundown on the situation by his superior officer. The younger man seemed quite excited by the new development, and Jenny could see that, as far as the sergeant was concerned, the case was all over, bar the mopping up.

She herself, however, wasn't feeling quite so sanguine.

After Lane left with his prisoner, Causon paced restlessly back into the corridor and then on through to the kitchen.

He'd told his sergeant to process Greeves as quickly as possible, hand him over for a formal interview to whichever senior was available, and then get back as quickly as possible. He'd need Lane back at the cricket ground to help organize the search for bloodied clothing, and once the much-needed reinforcements started rolling in, there was going to be a lot to do. Whether or not he was as convinced as his sergeant that with the arrest of Lorcan Greeves all their troubles were now over, it was hard to say. He remained grim-faced and thoughtful as he stood staring out of the window at the activity beyond.

Jenny, naturally, had followed Causon back to her preferred domain, and immediately went to the sink to fill the kettle for a cup of tea. She had never had any trouble arranging her priorities, and couldn't help but sneak a quick look at the barbecue meats she had marinating in the fridge. They looked good. Now if only she could convince the inspector that there was no harm in letting her cook them later on. After all, even if the spectators were allowed home, there would still be plenty of police and forensics personnel on site who were bound to be hungry.

And thinking of food . . . She automatically began to arrange some of the delicious tea leftovers on a large plate, and pushed it towards the inspector with an encouraging nod. At which, he visibly brightened a little.

'Well, what do you make of all that?' the inspector asked gruffly, sitting down at the kitchen table and eyeing the plate happily before selecting a fruity nut-topped slice. He bit into the slice gingerly, and then, after chewing a few times, continued with much more gusto. He gave a definite smile and helped himself to a second slice.

After that, he selected a jam tart. Then some sort of pastry parcel. Then another jam tart.

He licked one finger free of sugar as he watched and listened to the cook give her verdict, his shoulders gradually relaxing slightly.

Jenny beamed at him. She liked to see a man eat. Well, she liked to see anybody eat. It made everything seem better. 'Well, I think that if Lorcan Greeves *has* got James Cluley's blood on him, as well as his own, your forensics people will very quickly be able to prove it,' she said, absently nudging a wedge of neglected meringue to the front of the plate. 'And as an intelligent man, Lorcan Greeves would be aware of that, too.'

She felt safe in offering up this obvious objection first. Although she had no reason not to believe that Lorcan Greeves was the killer, she was by no means convinced yet, and they might just as well start picking holes in the theory now as later. It might save them having to wipe egg off their faces.

Causon grunted. And selected a strawberry scone. 'So you think he's too smart to lie about something so easily verified?' He thought she was probably right, but was too busy eating to confirm it. 'Well, whether or not his solicitor advises him to confess all,' he said sardonically, 'we still need to speak to Marie Rawley as a matter of some urgency, and see if she's willing to be any more forthcoming about what they were arguing about. If they were, that is. And even if she does confirm his story, it doesn't automatically leave him out of it. He could conceivably have argued with her and then killed James later.'

Jenny sighed, and reached for her handbag. 'Well, it would be rather a stupid story for him to tell if it wasn't true, don't you think?' she parried. 'Presumably, Marie Rawley is not likely to lie and say that she *was* brandishing a knife about if she wasn't. And it's not as if she has much incentive to confirm it, even if she had been.'

'Yes, but then he could just say she's denying it — as you've pointed out, even if it *were* true she's unlikely to confirm it.' He sighed thoughtfully. 'Unless the two were in cahoots to kill Tristan Jones . . . and all this is some sort of half-baked story they've concocted between them to give them a weird alibi,' Causon theorized. He champed down on a deliciously cooked, slightly gooey meringue and walnut concoction with a sigh of bliss, and then eyed the denuded plate thoughtfully.

He decided not to take the last pastry parcel. He didn't want to look like a greedy pig.

'But you don't really think that he argued with Marie, got a cut on his hand, and then killed James, do you?' Jenny demurred, harking back to his earlier comment. 'Surely he wouldn't have been able to. He'd have needed both his hands working properly if he was going to stab James with a cricket stump,' she objected.

Causon sighed. 'You're right. Besides, if he was already bleeding badly, the last thing he'd want to do is leave traces of his blood and DNA all over his second murder victim.'

'And he couldn't have killed James before he and Marie had the fight,' Jenny pointed out, with irrefutable logic.

'James was found only ten minutes or so after he left here, so it would mean Lorcan having his confrontation with Marie immediately afterwards and then going into the gents to clean up, which wouldn't give him enough time. And hadn't somebody said he'd been in there a long while? I guess we won't really know anything for sure until we get Marie's side of the story.'

'And she could still lie about it. If they were in cahoots, that is,' Causon said glumly.

Jenny shook her head helplessly. This was all getting rather complicated and messy to her mind. And in spite of Causon's speculations, Jenny wasn't a conspiracy theorist. She thought it highly unlikely that there were two killers, or two people acting in tandem.

But it was still possible that she was wrong about that. As surprising as it sounded, even she wasn't infallible! Still grinning self-mockingly over this unfortunately true fact, she picked up her handbag and slung it casually over one shoulder.

This time when they attempted to leave in order to interview a prime suspect, they were able to make their way to the village without further incident. Nobody rushed up to them with yet another body for them to inspect, nor were they presented with a suspect trying to flee the playing field. Causon had received directions to the Rawley residence from Lane before he left with Lorcan Greeves, and within a few minutes they were walking up the garden path of the Rawleys' neat little semi.

He rang the bell in a brisk no-nonsense way, and muttered quietly, 'I don't think we'll break the news of the death of her father just yet. Not until after she's given her version of her argument with Greeves. All right?' He looked at her sternly.

Jenny had no other option but to nod unhappily, although she felt distinctly uneasy about keeping such a tragic fact a secret, even for so short a time. She couldn't help but feel that a daughter had a right to know immediately when she'd lost a parent. But then, this wasn't her call, and if

Inspector Causon's methods might appear somewhat brutal, she could understand his reasoning. If his witness broke down on hearing such devastating news, any statement she might have to make concerning the murder of the first victim would have to wait. And, as the policeman whose job it was to find out the facts as quickly as possible, she supposed he could claim some justification for his hard-headedness.

Jenny's unhappy musings halted when the door in front of them was abruptly opened, and a pale-faced, dark-haired woman regarded them bitterly. Already she had a mutinous, stubborn look on her face, indicating that she'd recognized Causon as being a police officer. She looked slightly more puzzled when her gaze flitted to Jenny, however, since the cook didn't look much like anybody's idea of a female police officer, even in plain clothes.

The woman stood firmly in the doorway and made no effort to move to one side or invite them in. 'Yes?' she shot at them belligerently instead.

But for all her apparent bravado, Causon could see what Graham Lane had meant about sensing something fragile about her. There was a tense, white and tight look about the woman's face that spoke of someone who'd received a severe shock, and not too long ago.

Jenny flinched as she wondered what the death of her father would do to someone already so brittle with tension. She hoped the woman's husband was home, and that he had the telephone number of their GP to hand.

'Mrs Rawley?' Causon was already showing her his ID card, which, it had to be said, didn't seem to impress her much. 'Inspector Laurence Causon. This is Miss Jenny Starling. We'd like a word—'

'You're not talking to my Mark,' Marie Rawley interrupted him flatly. 'I told that other policeman that came and I'm tell—'

'It's you we want to talk to, Mrs Rawley,' Causon interrupted her in his own turn, and saw the woman blink in surprise. 'We can either do it here or at the station, that's up to you.'

For a moment, Jenny thought Marie Rawley was going to opt for the police station just to be awkward, but then she clearly thought twice about it. No doubt she realized that if she were to be taken from her home, her son would be left unguarded. And she was obviously determined that that wouldn't happen.

It made Jenny wonder why she was so terrified of letting the police talk to Mark. Did she really think he might have killed Tris? In which case, what did she know that they didn't? The fact that she'd been keeping a close eye on her son during the course of the day was becoming clear. Perhaps she'd seen something that had convinced her of his guilt?

'You'd better come in then, I suppose,' Marie said reluctantly, curling her arms around her middle, as if warding off a sudden chill — which, in the fierce heat of the early evening, was patently ridiculous.

'This way,' she said quickly as they stepped into the hall, opening the door to their immediate right. She seemed afraid that, once having gained admittance to the house, either the inspector or she herself might make a sudden dash for the stairs, or towards one of the other rooms, where her son might be found.

The lounge she showed them to was small, rectangular in shape, and decorated in muted tones of peach and mint green.

'Have a seat.' Marie half-heartedly indicated a plush green sofa, and perched herself on one of two matching armchairs, grouped around a gas fire with a faux-marble fireplace. She sat so near to the edge of the seat that it must have been putting tremendous strain on her calves, but she didn't seem to notice. Jenny sat more comfortably back in the other armchair, whilst Causon settled his bulk onto the sofa.

It sagged somewhat, but he didn't seem to mind.

'As you know, we're investigating the murder of Tristan Jones,' Causon began. 'You knew him, of course?'

'I knew *of* him more than knew him,' Marie corrected cautiously. 'He visits his father regularly, and I've seen him about the village. We exchanged a few words in passing, you know, the way you do. To be polite.'

'You've never been romantically involved with him then?' Causon asked blandly.

Marie stared at him as if he'd suddenly grown two heads, and Jenny could almost see him give a mental shrug. Well, she supposed, he'd had to ask, if only to get that possibility off the table.

'I'm a married woman,' Marie finally said, flushing angrily.

'It's no secret that Mr Jones had something of a reputation with women, Mrs Rawley,' Causon said, mildly enough. 'And I don't suppose he drew the line at married women, necessarily.'

'Huh! But my name's not Michelle Wilson,' Marie Rawley said, a shade vindictively. 'And I don't believe in adultery,' she added. 'I daresay that makes me old-fashioned nowadays, but . . .' She shrugged her shoulders, and fixed her gaze steadily ahead. 'Was that all you wanted to ask me? If so . . .' She made a hopeful move to half-rise, but was quickly waved back by one of Causon's large, expressive mitts.

'We've only just started, Mrs Rawley,' Causon warned her, and watched her shoulders slump. 'I understand you visited the playing field this afternoon. On at least one occasion, maybe even two?' He was, to some extent, chancing a shot in the dark here, for the primary interviews for the majority of the people attending the cricket match were yet to be collated. And so far he had no definitive information of anybody's movements.

But this time he struck lucky.

'I may have done,' Marie admitted warily, obviously realizing the futility of denying it. No doubt some of her neighbours had seen her on the playing field and would, in due course, admit as much.

'Can you tell me what you did there, Mrs Rawley?'

'Can't I have gone to watch the cricket?' she asked mockingly, and for the first time displaying a flash of bitter humour.

'Did you?' Causon asked her levelly.

Marie sighed. 'No. If you must know, I went to talk to Sir Robert.'

This time it was Causon's turn to blink in surprise. He clearly hadn't been expecting that. And neither had Jenny.

'Oh?' Causon, seriously wrong-footed, became more cautious. 'And what did you want to see the Lord of the Manor about?' he asked. He'd clearly picked up the locals' somewhat irreverent title for the man, and it made Marie's lips twist in a parody of a smile.

'You might well ask. If you must know, I wanted to know what he meant to do about that son of his,' she flared.

'Tristan Jones?' Causon clarified.

'He's only got the one son as far as we know,' she flashed back. 'Although if it's a case of like father like son, who knows how many bastards he might have scattered across the county.'

'And what did you want Sir Robert to do, exactly?' Causon asked, careful to keep his own tendency to sarcasm firmly under control for once.

'I wanted to know if he had a conscience that I could prick,' Marie said finally. 'I know that Tris didn't possess any such thing, but I thought if I could talk to Sir Robert directly, as a mother, he might feel guilty enough to make sure Dad got his money back.'

She looked down at her hands now, as if ashamed of having to admit to pleading with the big man.

'You may not know, but Dad promised Mark he'd pay to put him through university. Mark's really bright — all his teachers say so, and that he could have a really bright future in the IT industry. Dad thought the same, so he invested his savings with their firm — well, with Tris specifically. Mark insisted that Tris was a real genius with money, and that he could make Dad's savings double in a year. Hah!' Marie laughed bitterly. 'Instead he lost the lot.' Her fingers were twisting restlessly in her lap now. 'And Tris, of course, made like it wasn't his fault — all innocence and Mr Be-Reasonable. He blamed the economic downturn . .

. Oh, what does it matter what financial gobbledygook he came out with to justify his incompetence? Let's just say that he wiggled out, like he's done all his life. We consulted a solicitor, of course, but there was nothing we could do. Dad signed all the forms giving Tris permission to invest, you see. No doubt all that fine print covered the Joneses from any personal liability. Those people are all the same, anyway,' she concluded bitterly. 'They always stick together.'

Causon nodded. 'I see. So your son had real reason to hate Tris Jones, didn't he? Because of him, his future's been severely blighted.'

'You leave Mark out of this,' Marie instantly snapped. 'We'll see he gets to university. He can always get a student loan to fund his degree. We'll see him get there, all right. No matter what.'

Causon smiled thinly. 'I'm sure you will, Mrs Rawley,' he said soothingly. 'So, what did Sir Robert have to say?' he asked curiously. 'Was he willing to do anything to help?'

Marie snorted. 'He said he'd talk to Tris. As if that would make any difference — that boy didn't care what anyone thought or said about him, not even his own father. He had the hide of a rhinoceros. He didn't give two hoots about the damage he caused. And I reckon his father was beginning to realize it too,' she added, a malicious gleam coming to her eyes now.

'Did you kill Tris?' Causon asked her calmly.

'No, I didn't, though I'd have liked to. I certainly felt like it,' Marie said with defiant candour.

'What can you tell me about Lorcan Greeves?' the inspector suddenly asked, deliberately changing the subject so abruptly in a clear attempt to keep her off-balance.

And apparently it worked, because instantly she went pale. Then she swallowed hard. She opened her mouth to say something, then closed it again and once more swallowed hard. The hands in her lap began to twist frantically.

'What about him?' she muttered. 'He works at the same firm — the one that the Lord of the Manor runs. He and Tris

155

were supposed to be friends. Well, until he broke up Lorcan's engagement. Slept with his fiancée, didn't he?' she said, with a grim smile. 'It caused a right stink, I can tell you.'

But Causon refused to take this particular bit of bait. 'Mr Greeves is currently receiving medical treatment,' he swept on instead, watching with interest as her hands convulsed into fists, and her breathing became a little laboured. 'He was attacked with a knife,' he added starkly.

'What? No, that's not . . .' Marie half-rose from her chair, and then sank back down again.

'That's not what? Mrs Rawley?'

'Why are you telling me this?' Marie whispered back.

'Because Mr Greeves was found trying to clean himself up in the gents' toilets in the cricket pavilion. And naturally, we were very intrigued by this,' Causon said in massive understatement. 'At first he tried to tell us some fairy story about cutting himself on a broken beer glass.'

Her face lit up. 'Well then . . .'

'But when he couldn't produce the evidence of this by pointing us to the broken pieces of glass,' Causon ploughed on, 'he finally had to admit that he'd been in an argument with someone.'

Marie went so still that for a moment Jenny thought she might actually have stopped breathing.

'A woman,' Causon went on inexorably. 'A woman, apparently, who'd sought him out, and had brought a knife along with her.'

Marie let out a long, shuddering breath.

'Care to comment on that, Mrs Rawley?'

Marie shook her head helplessly. 'What does Mr Greeves say happened?' she asked at last, licking her lips nervously.

But Causon was far too wily to fall for the likes of that. He batted away the question like a pesky fly. 'Oh, I'm not at liberty to discuss an ongoing case, Mrs Rawley. In a case of causing grievous bodily harm, or assault with a deadly weapon . . .' he began, turning his voice deliberately portentous and ominous.

'No! You're making it sound like it's so much worse than it is . . . was . . . That's not how it happened,' Marie rushed in. 'If he told you that I attacked him with a knife then he's lying. That's simply not true. He made a grab for it — I have no idea why. It was so stupid. So *stupid*!' Marie slumped back in the chair, looking defeated. 'Why on earth would you do something like that? I mean, grab the blade of a knife with your bare hand?' she asked, looking from Jenny to Causon, then back to Jenny again. 'That's just plain daft, isn't it?'

Jenny nodded. She didn't quite know what else to do.

Besides, it *was* daft.

'Of course he cut his hand,' Marie said, shaking her head. 'Good grief, it bled so much.' Her voice was slightly awed now with remembered horror. 'I just didn't know what to do. I don't think he did, either. We just stood there, both of us like idiots, me gawping at the blood on the knife blade and him staring down at his hand, bleeding all over the place. I don't know what he was thinking, really I don't,' she said, again shaking her head in remembered disbelief. 'It wasn't as if I was going to actually hurt the silly sod. I only wanted to make him worried, see? He's such a rabbit, I thought that I could scare him off.'

'Scare him off?' Causon echoed sharply. 'Scare him off from doing what, Mrs Rawley?' he demanded.

And Marie went pale again. 'What? What do you mean?' she stammered, clearly playing for time.

But Causon was in no mood to indulge her.

'Mrs Rawley, you just admitted to stabbing Mr Greeves—'

'I did no such thing!' she cried. 'I didn't stab him at all. I didn't even take a step towards him. I was just waving my old kitchen knife about, warning him to leave us alone, and he just reached out and grabbed it. It cut his palm. That's all. It was his fault that happened! All of it is his fault!' She was beginning to pant now, and tears were pooling in her eyes.

'He shouldn't have . . . shouldn't have—'

She came to a gasping halt and the tears finally ran freely down her cheeks. They plopped off her small chin and fell, unnoticed, onto her cold-looking hands, which were still restlessly twisting about in her lap.

'What shouldn't he have done, Mrs Rawley?' Causon asked intensely.

'Leave her alone!'

The voice that suddenly, shockingly, cut across the room came from the doorway. It was young, male, impassioned, and it galvanized Marie Rawley to her feet. Inspector Laurence Causon was only a second or two behind her. He turned, instantly tense and alert and ready to defend himself, and narrowed his eyes on the youngster standing in the doorway.

Jenny, who'd seen him before, remained seated and quiet.

'Mark! Go back to your bedroom,' Marie all but screamed at him.

'What? And let this copper bully you?' her son said scornfully. 'No can do, Mum. Feel big, do you?' he demanded of Causon, walking further into the room and glaring at him. 'Can't you see Mum's close to collapse? I never really believed all those liberal bleeding-heart types when they cried "police brutality" but they had it right, didn't they?'

Of average height, skinny, dressed in jeans and a much-washed T-shirt, he looked a bit like a little cock bantam, strutting grandiosely in front of Causon's big bad Brer Fox.

Causon, seeing that the lad wasn't armed, and was more bark than bite, relaxed visibly.

'Your mum and I were just discussing why she attacked Lorcan Greeves with a knife. And I don't believe any brutality came into it. Not on my part, anyway,' he added mildly, but with a distinct twinkle in his eye now.

Mark Rawley looked distinctly shell-shocked. 'What?' His eyes flew to those of his distressed mother. 'What?'

'No, it's not . . . Mark, I didn't . . .' She held out her hands towards him in a helpless gesture. 'That's not really what happened. It was an accident,' his mother pleaded, her eyes fixed desperately on his face, willing him to be careful.

'Come on in and sit down, young man, and let's see if we can't sort this out,' Causon invited craftily, moving back to the sofa and patting the seat next to him in an encouraging gesture.

Marie instantly saw the danger of that, and again cried out, 'No! Mark, go back upstairs. I can handle this.'

'Oh, but the boy wants to protect his mother,' Causon said with a jovial smile. 'And more power to him, I say. It does my cynical heart good to see the younger generation showing some backbone. Please, feel free to come and listen in,' Causon repeated. 'That way you can make sure for yourself that your mum's all right and that I'm not being mean to her.'

'No! Don't listen to him, Mark. Can't you see he's trying to trick you?' Marie wailed.

'Mum, did you really hurt Lorcan?' the boy asked her, ignoring her words of wisdom as if she'd never spoken them. 'But why? What on earth's been going on?' He looked from the big policeman to his distraught mother, and was clearly bewildered.

'That's just what I was trying to find out, son,' Causon said comfortably, again patting the sofa next to him, once more inviting the youngster to get comfortable. And to Marie, he added more firmly, 'Please sit down as well, Mrs Rawley, otherwise I may have to arrest you and take you into custody.'

Marie's legs seemed to give out at this point, and she fell, rather than sat, back down in her chair, her shoulders slumping in defeat.

'Now, as far as things stand at the moment,' Causon began, almost amiably, 'Mr Greeves hasn't said that he wants to press any charges against you for assault. But then, he *is* getting his wounds tended to, so one can see that he has other things on his mind. But priorities can quickly change, and he might want to do so once he's had a chance to talk to his solicitor.'

'No! Lorcan won't—' Mark began hotly, but didn't get the chance to finish.

'Shut up! Don't say a word, you silly boy!' Marie said at the same time.

The last thing she wanted was for her son to provide evidence that he and Lorcan Greeves were in any way friendly.

Mark Rawley gaped at his mother. Causon beamed at them both.

Jenny Starling simply sat and wondered.

'Now, why don't we just get this all sorted out, hmm?' Causon took charge brightly. 'Mrs Rawley, perhaps you'd like to start by telling us why you sought out Mr Greeves, and what was so urgent that you felt you needed to bring a knife with you.'

Mark, who'd just sat down next to Causon on the sofa, suddenly stiffened. 'I think I might know why . . .'

Marie groaned and shook her head. 'No. No, we want a solicitor. Mark, be quiet. I mean it.'

It was, Jenny thought pensively, probably excellent advice, and she saw Causon wince sourly as yet another of his witnesses 'lawyered up' on him.

But Mark — who was, after all, just a teenage boy when all was said and done, and was thus convinced that he knew it all, or at the very least, that he had to know better than his own mother — stubbornly shook his head.

'No, this is . . . this is all getting out of hand. We need to sort it out. Mum, what on earth were you thinking?'

'Mark, don't,' his mother implored. 'Tris has been murdered. Don't you understand, this man doesn't want to help us. He only wants to make an arrest. Don't help him . . .'

Mark Rawley gave a small, stunned yelp. There really was no other way to describe it. '*Murdered?* Tris has been *murdered?*' he repeated, as if he couldn't quite get his head around the concept. His eyes became enormous as he turned to the man beside him, seeking confirmation.

Causon merely looked back at him impassively.

'Yes,' Marie said urgently. 'He has. Do you see now? Why we have to be careful?'

'But I didn't kill Tris,' Mark said, sounding surprised. 'And I know that Lorcan didn't, either. And I know you didn't, Mum, so wha—'

'Of course I didn't,' Marie wailed. 'But that's not—'

'Listen, son,' Causon said loudly, clearly not wanting to give the mother any time to talk any sense into her son. 'I think that you should just tell me all that you know about whatever it is that's been going on here. Otherwise you or your mum could both be facing all sorts of charges like attempting to pervert the course of justice, accessory before or after the fact, aiding and abetting an offender, and who knows what else. Once the CPS gets started, sometimes they don't know when to stop. They have to hit government targets, you see. I've seen it all before — those on the fringes of things can sometimes come off worse than those doing the real crimes,' he warned craftily. 'Now, you don't need any of that on your record, dragging you down, do you? Not if you want to get on in life.'

And to Marie, he said flatly, 'You say you want your son to go to university? And that you don't want the likes of Tristan Jones to succeed in robbing him of his future? Then don't you do it, either,' he warned her starkly. 'Come clean, and I promise I'll do my best for the both of you. But you need to start talking now.'

In the face of such grim reality, Marie began to weep helplessly. 'I've tried to look out for him,' she sniffed. 'I spent nearly an hour this afternoon, standing under the trees at the top of the field, watching over him.'

Jenny and Causon exchanged a quick look. So that was why there was a distinct patch of cow parsley trampled down, but only a narrow path leading further in. The bigger patch must have been made by Marie, and later . . . Jenny swallowed hard. Later, a killer had taken Marie's father further in and killed him. And she wondered just what sort of nightmares that would give the poor woman when she learned about it.

'I didn't know you were there,' the boy said to his mother. And after a moment or two of thought, a much more subdued Mark Rawley looked at Causon and said quietly, but more cautiously now, 'Just what is it that you want to know?'

'Anything and everything you know about Tris Jones and Lorcan Greeves. And what your mother's so desperate for you to keep quiet about,' Causon said simply.

The boy thought about it for a long moment, and Jenny could see that the big policeman was almost quivering with tension now that it looked as if they might finally be getting somewhere. She could almost feel the inspector mentally urging him on, and with some surprise she noticed that her own hands were clenched tightly with nerves.

Then Mark Rawley finally let out a long slow breath as he came to a decision.

'OK then,' he agreed. And it seemed as if the whole room relaxed. Even his mother gave a little sigh that might have been relief. Or despair.

'It all started about a week ago,' Mark began, and Jenny saw the inspector's eyes gleam in satisfaction. 'Lorcan approached me with a plan.'

'A plan to kill Tristan Jones?' Causon asked quickly.

Too quickly, Jenny thought, and mentally urged him not to let his impatience get the better of him.

'What? No!' Mark Rawley shot him a scathing look. 'Don't be so bloody stupid,' he added in patent disgust.

Jenny had to hide a quick smile behind her hand, and she saw that even Causon's lips quivered with suppressed humour. Because there really was something distinctly funny about the teenager's self-absorbed disdain.

'We didn't want Tris *dead*,' Mark Rawley carried on witheringly. 'We just wanted him to suffer. For once, me and Lorcan were determined that he wouldn't get away with it, and that he would be made to pay. You see, Tris had really done us both down. You know about Lorcan's girlfriend, right?' Mark began.

'Yes, yes, we know all about that,' Causon urged him on impatiently.

'Right. And has Mum told you about how he lost all of Granddad's money?'

'Yes,' Causon snapped, and Jenny shot him a warning look. But the big, grumpy detective was paying her no heed.

'Right. Well then, you can see why we both had good reason to want to teach him a lesson, right?' the boy went on. 'I really used to think Tris was so cool,' he confessed bitterly. 'He was so good-looking that all the girls fell for him, and he drove this amazing Aston Martin — not the James Bond car, I mean not the one Sean Connery had, but still . . . a really cool car. And he lived in London, in a really cool pad by Canary Wharf, and he . . . oh, I don't know how to explain it really. He just knew a lot of stuff about life, and going abroad, and . . . well, just stuff. You know?'

Causon smiled. Oh yes. He knew. And you wanted to be just like him, didn't you, the cynical old policeman thought. 'Go on, son,' he said heavily.

'Well. Anyway, that's why I advised Granddad to give Tris all his money to invest, because I really believed him when he said that he could make it accrue enough in returns to put me through uni. I mean, it never occurred to me that he couldn't.'

Jenny sighed, ever so gently.

The boy heard it however, and flushed in mortification as he glanced over at her.

'Yeah, yeah, I know, you don't have to say it,' he mumbled bitterly. 'I was a gullible twit, all right? I know that now — I acted like a silly little kid. But believe me, when it all went wrong, I really got to see another side of Tris then.'

'You hated him for what he'd done,' Causon said flatly.

'Oh yeah.'

'Mark!' Marie wailed in warning, but her voice lacked hope now.

'But I didn't hate him enough to kill him,' Mark clarified quickly. 'So when Lorcan came to me with his plan, I jumped at it.'

'Let's have it then, son,' Causon said impatiently. 'What exactly was this marvellous plan of yours?'

'We were going to ruin him,' Mark said simply.

'Ruin him? How?' Causon demanded.

'Like, financially. See, Lorcan had access to all sorts of company stuff. He's one of Sir Robert's stockbrokers, like Tris is. Was. So he could get into the computer files. He was going to be the inside man, see?'

Causon bit back a sigh at this. No doubt the kid had visions of himself as some sort of spy-cum-action-hero so beloved of big-money Hollywood blockbusters.

Marie Rawley merely moaned softly.

'But of course, Tris's accounts were all password protected, and had firewalls,' Mark continued, 'and Lorcan's no computer guru, so he needed help with all of that. And that's where I came in.'

Then he looked at Causon with a gentle sort of pity in his expression. 'I don't suppose you know much about computers, right?' he added.

Causon's lips again twitched with suppressed humour. 'That's right. Just think of me as your average Luddite, son,' he advised.

But there was something about his smile that made Jenny wonder just how truthful the canny old fox was being. And she rather suspected that should the youngster talk to him about software, hacking and viruses, the wily old policeman would probably have been able to follow him easily enough. But it clearly suited him to have Mark Rawley underestimate him, and she wasn't about to second-guess his tactics.

'OK. Well, before I go on then, I suppose I should tell you that I'm something of an expert,' Mark said, not immodestly. And looked at his softly weeping mother with an abashed expression. 'And a little while ago I sort of got into a little bit of trouble because of it. Oh, nothing major,' he added hastily. 'It was just meant as a joke. I hacked into my old school's computer system and changed some stuff around. Well, in the Education Department's system, actually.'

Jenny blinked. She wasn't particularly IT savvy herself, but she knew enough to know that you had to have considerable skills to be able to hack into government software.

Causon did too, because he gave a long, slow whistle.

Mark Rawley flushed — half with guilt, but also, Jenny suspected, with secret pride.

'Anyway, we got it all sorted out, and I agreed that I wouldn't use a computer . . .' Mark stuttered a bit as he realized that he was about to admit to breaking that agreement, then he shrugged and stiffened his shoulders. 'Anyway, Lorcan knew all about it and asked me if I would be willing to do a little . . . er . . .'

'Hacking of Sir Robert's firm?' Causon put in delicately.

'Yes. Well, no. I mean, nothing criminal,' the lad at least had the sense to qualify quickly. 'Nothing that would affect anybody else, I mean!' Mark said, sounding scandalized that the inspector could ever suspect that he wasn't on the side of the angels. 'After what happened to Granddad, I wasn't going to interfere with anyone else's money. I mean, we weren't going to touch anybody else's investments, or steal their identities or leak their personal details or stuff like that. In fact, we weren't really going to go into the clients' files at all much. Only to leave traces behind, proving that Tris had swindled them. But mostly we were going to go into Tris's personal stuff, and maybe one or two other accountancy files. Stuff like that. Just to change details of his transactions. Dates, mostly. I didn't really understand some of it — I haven't studied to be a stockbroker or anything. But Lorcan knew all about what was needed.'

'Needed to do what?' the inspector asked, but like Jenny, he already had a good idea.

'To drop Tris in it with the tax people,' Mark Rawley said, a flash of definite pride in his voice now. 'Lorcan knew just how to make it look like Tris was doing that insider trading stuff, you know, like in that film, *Wall Street*?' he added enthusiastically. 'He knew all this stuff about what was legal and what wasn't, and how we could make it look like Tris was really bent. That's why we met up today. He gave me a dossier on what I needed to look out for. Then we were going to meet up again, and work together to get it done. Me doing the tech stuff, making sure we didn't leave any digital traces of what we'd done, and Lorcan doing all the stockbroker things that would make it look like Tris was dirty.'

When he'd finished, his face was flushed with excited enthusiasm for the project, even now. He seemed almost totally unaware of the breadth and scope of the offences he would have been committing, let alone the consequences of being found out. But his poor mother began to rock silently on her chair, hugging her middle, and shaking her head helplessly from side to side.

'So let me get this straight,' Causon said calmly, not wanting to frighten the boy into silence by reading him the Riot Act. 'Mr Greeves approached you, and asked you to hack into the company's records and plant evidence that would implicate Tristan Jones in financial improprieties?'

'Yes. That's why I went to the cricket match earlier on. Like I said, we'd arranged to meet so that Lorcan could give me the latest passwords and the access codes I'd need.'

Marie shook her head. 'I knew it. I knew he was involving you in something bad. That's why I tried to warn him off,' she moaned.

Mark reached out and put his hand over hers, squeezing it gently. 'I'm sorry, Mum. Really. But it *would* have worked. We had it all figured out. Tris would have been prosecuted for tax evasion and insider dealing. And he wouldn't have been able to wiggle out of it this time — his daddy wouldn't have been able to step in and save his skin, like he always does. He'd have lost his licence for sure, and maybe even gone to jail for a bit. I know that's what Lorcan was hoping for. Me too, I guess,' he added, not quite so confidently now. Then he looked across at the inspector. 'So you see, Lorcan and me, we already had our plans ready. We didn't have any reason to want him dead,' he pointed out with growing confidence. 'You see that, don't you?'

Causon nodded. He saw all right. And Jenny could see that, like herself, he was reasonably convinced that the boy

166

had been nothing but a dupe for Lorcan Greeves. But he didn't seem so convinced that Greeves was out of the frame yet.

There had been something very brutal and *emotional* about the killing of Tristan Jones. She'd felt it instinctively. And although she wasn't sure if the inspector thought of it in those terms — or would admit it, if he did — she was sure that he felt, as she did, that whoever had killed the handsome young man had done so with real feeling. And Lorcan Greeves was an emotional sort of individual.

Then the inspector's face became heavy, and he glanced thoughtfully at the boy, then across at Marie Rawley. He stiffened his shoulders, getting ready to do something deeply unpleasant, and Jenny, suddenly aware of just what that was, began to feel sick.

'Mrs Rawley, Mark, I'm afraid I have some more bad news for you . . .' he began gently.

But Marie held up a hand. 'You don't need to say it. You're arresting us. Both of us,' she said miserably. 'I just don't know what Chris is going to say,' she wailed.

But Causon shook his head. 'No, it's not that, Mrs Rawley, although criminal charges may be made against you, further down the line.' He felt impelled to be honest. 'No, I'm very sorry, but this is about something else entirely. And I'm afraid it's bad. Very bad,' he warned her gravely. 'It's about your father.'

'Granddad?' Mark Rawley said, his young voice breaking on the last syllable, as if he sensed, way before his mother, just how bad the news was going to be. 'Why? What's happened to Granddad?' he demanded.

Causon sighed heavily, and reluctantly began to speak.

CHAPTER TEN

It was every bit as bad as they'd thought it would be, of course. How could it be otherwise when you had to tell someone that a member of their family had been irrevocably taken away from them? And in such a cruel and devastatingly unpredictable way?

And although Inspector Causon had been as gentle as anyone could be, nevertheless, when they left the house barely a quarter of an hour later, both mother and son were still in tears. But a next-door neighbour, a kindly, middle-aged woman who had a competent air about her, had been called in, and seemed to be coping admirably. She'd also dispatched her own son to go to the allotments to bring back Christopher Rawley, who was working on his plot there, and the local family doctor was on the way, too.

'That was awful,' Jenny said glumly to Causon, as they tramped to the top of the playing field, and once more had to give their names to the constable on duty there before they could re-enter the sports ground.

'It always is,' Causon grunted moodily. 'I'll have a family liaison officer go over there as soon as possible. We'll need to question them further at some point, about who they think might have wanted James dead. It's just possible that they might know of someone with some sort of independent grudge against Cluley.' He sighed deeply. 'Not that I expect I'll get much joy there. I can't help but think that the old man was murdered as a direct result of the Tris Jones killing.'

Jenny nodded her head in silent agreement.

They paused at the top of the field and looked around them. And although they'd been gone less than an hour, obviously things had been moving fast in their absence. There were more emergency vehicles in the car park, and the spectators and cricketers alike seemed to have been shepherded into more defined groups by uniformed men and women.

Causon regarded this with a happy yet resigned air. 'Well, better late than never, I suppose,' he grumbled under his breath as they set off back towards the bottom of the field. But Jenny knew that his superiors would be hearing just what the inspector thought about being left so short-handed for many months to come yet. And probably for a lot longer than that, if there was an official inquiry launched.

That Sergeant Lane was also back from escorting Lorcan Greeves to the nearest police station was immediately apparent, for as they approached the cricket pavilion he briskly descended the wooden steps and walked forward to make his interim report to his senior officer.

'Sir! The medicos have given the go-ahead to remove Tristan Jones's body, but they're still processing Mr Cluley. More men have arrived as you can see, and we're just starting to get back some preliminary interview reports. I also sent two teams to do a quick visual survey of everybody on the premises, but no one is wearing any obviously bloodstained clothing. The search of the changing rooms has also revealed no hidden bloodstained clothing, either, and just before you arrived, the teams I sent out to do an initial search of the grounds have come back, and they say they can't find any bloodstained clothing hidden anywhere.'

Lane paused for breath, which gave Causon time to scowl ferociously.

'What?' he barked, looking clearly thunderstruck. 'But that's not possible. James Cluley was killed after the exits were all covered, so no one could have left. Someone, somewhere, must be either covered in blood, or have hidden some bloody clothing.'

He was so agitated that he didn't notice the way that, by his side, Jenny Starling suddenly stiffened, or the look of intense enlightenment that came into her bright blue eyes.

'I know that, sir,' Lane said, sounding slightly aggrieved himself now. It was not, after all, his fault. 'Which means it has to be Greeves, doesn't it?' he slipped in urgently, before his boss could really get the bit between his teeth. Nobody knew better than he did that Causon, in a bellicose mood, could be extremely wearing on the nerves. 'I mean, he's the only one we've found with blood on him,' he finished with a shrug.

'Yes,' Causon said slowly. But he didn't sound particularly convinced. It was almost as if the solution was so obvious that he couldn't bring himself to trust it. 'And what *about* Greeves?' he prompted heavily. 'Everything went smoothly, I trust?'

'Yes, sir. I had someone at the station make it a top priority to remove his clothes and get them off to the lab, but the forensics boys probably won't get back to us with the results of the blood tests until tomorrow at the earliest. Not that that's a problem — we've got plenty of time to hold on to him,' Lane said with satisfaction. 'And once forensics confirm that some of the blood on him is James Cluley's, we'll be able to charge him.'

'I don't suppose he's confessed?' Causon asked dryly, and without much hope.

'No, sir,' his sergeant confirmed ruefully and just as dryly. 'When I called the station ten minutes ago, he was still waiting for his solicitor to show up and wasn't saying a word.' Then he brightened, and said inquisitively, 'And just what did Mrs Rawley have to say?'

But before the inspector could start to fill Lane in about his recent interview and all the latest revelations that it had thrown up, Jenny sidled up to him quietly and put a soft hand on his forearm.

'Excuse me,' Jenny said meekly. 'Inspector, I just want to go and have a word with somebody. I won't be a moment.'

'What? Oh, yes, go ahead,' Causon said abruptly, waving a vague gesture of dismissal her way.

Jenny smiled briefly at them both, relieved that the inspector was too preoccupied to care about what she was up to, and moved off towards a group of villagers who were chatting to one another by the deckchairs. So far, it didn't seem as if news of James Cluley's death had filtered down to everyone, and Jenny was glad. It was bound to cause both panic and real dismay.

And she didn't want anyone to realize what she might be on to just yet. Not until she was even more sure of her ground.

It didn't take Jenny long to find someone who'd lived in the village all their life. And once she'd found him — an elderly gent, who'd been enjoying the cricket and a quiet nap before all the excitement — it only took her a few moments to ask him one simple question.

He looked a little surprised by it, and then quietly speculative, but he was able to give her a full and comprehensive answer, with a few added descriptive hand gestures, and a pointing finger thrown in for good measure.

She thanked him profusely, and warned him that he would almost certainly have to make another statement to the police a little later on. She further asked him not to mention it to anyone until then — not even his closest friend — and then left him looking a little pleased at the thought that he'd suddenly become someone of even mild importance.

* * *

As Jenny approached the cricket pavilion, where Causon and Lane were just mounting the steps prior to going inside, she saw Erica Jones walking up from the right-hand side, and then hesitate as she spied the policemen. She then idled by the edge of the building, waiting for them to pass fully inside before climbing the wooden steps herself.

Clearly, she was not about to risk another run-in with the abrasive inspector.

So it was that Jenny had caught up with her, and was right behind her as they stepped into the main changing room.

Caroline and her friend Ettie were already in situ. Obviously a number of the regulars had given their statements and been allowed back inside, and they had, of all things, opened some of the bottles of wine, and were busy pouring several glasses. Not that Jenny could really blame them. It was getting on for evening now, and she could have done with a stiff drink herself.

She guessed that the two policemen had retired to the kitchen for some privacy, and began to make her way there herself. As she passed Erica, she saw the Lady of the Manor reach into her bag and extract a small vial of expensive perfume. Jenny vaguely recognized the packaging as belonging to one of the more exclusive French fashion designers, and the redhead elegantly sprayed a fine mist of exquisite perfume (which had probably cost a three-figure sum) behind each ear, and then at each wrist. She hesitated for a moment, gave a shrug, and then squirted some more down the column of her throat and along her sternum, which was, Jenny thought, coughing just a little as she walked into a misty patch caused by the atomizer, rather overegging it somewhat.

Apparently she wasn't the only one to think so, because she distinctly heard Caroline whisper cattily to her friend, 'Why doesn't she just bathe in it?' To which Ettie gave a slightly nervous giggle in reply.

Jenny too hid a smile, and watched as Erica Jones shot the two women a dirty look before slipping the perfume bottle back into her bag, then sitting down in her favourite deckchair in the doorway. The elegant redhead was now, Jenny noticed, sitting in the full evening sunlight, but was once again wearing her long-sleeved blouse. She crossed her elegant, trouser-clad legs, and once more reached into her bag, this time to withdraw a nail file. And with short, sharp, angry strokes, she proceeded to vigorously attack one of her scarlet-tipped nails.

Jenny watched her for a moment or two, then turned away.

In the kitchen, she did indeed find the two policemen, and was happy to see that Sergeant Lane had had the good sense to tuck into some of the leftovers.

'Try the Bakewell tarts,' she advised him happily, as he polished off a mini cheese and onion flan. And that reminded her — with the evening well and truly upon them, she should really get to barbecuing that meat.

'Thank you, I will, they look delicious,' Lane mumbled around his savoury mouthful. He turned back to Causon, saying, 'About those preliminary interview reports we've got back — there's a couple of things that are interesting. The lad who interviewed the Wilsons is sure they're hiding something. Or at the very least, not being particularly truthful. He says he got the distinct feeling that they'd been colluding beforehand, and they insisted on giving their statements together instead of one at a time.'

Causon grunted. 'There's really nothing particularly surprising in that,' he said. 'Hubby wanted to make sure that his wife didn't say anything about having an affair with the victim. He looked like the sort who would always be careful to take care of his own skin,' he added darkly. In his view, if a man was capable of captaining a cricket team, he was probably capable of anything. 'And not only that, he looked like he thought a lot of himself anyway, and no doubt it would bruise his ego to have all and sundry knowing that his wife had strayed on him.'

Lane nodded. 'Yes, sir, I think you're spot on there. The lad who took their statement said they were both acting decidedly antsy anyway. Mrs Wilson kept shooting daggers at her husband but she was careful not to contradict anything he said. I daresay he can be a bit of a bully, and she's probably used to towing the line. But that's not the really interesting bit, sir. There was one other thing that I thought you'd want to know about straight away.'

'Oh?' Causon looked distinctly interested now.

'Yes. Several people noticed, earlier on, that our murder victim—'

'Which one?' Causon interrupted grumpily.

'Tristan Jones, sir.'

'Right.'

'Well, they say they saw Tristan and his father arguing.'

Causon blinked. 'His *father*? Arguing?' Whatever he'd expected his sergeant to come up with, this was obviously taking him by surprise. 'What, fighting-arguing as in coming-to-blows arguing, or just talking in an animated fashion?' Causon asked, a shade cautiously.

Whilst it certainly sounded interesting, he was too old a hand at this sort of thing to get too excited just yet.

And apparently his lack of real excitement seemed to communicate itself to Sergeant Lane, who had to rein in a strong desire to roll his eyes. 'They were definitely having hot words, sir,' he clarified patiently. 'One witness says Sir Robert looked really steamed up about something, and that rather than soothing his ruffled feathers, his son seemed hell-bent on goading him. Anyway, most agree that they didn't seem to part on the best of terms.'

'Hmm. But no one actually saw Sir Robert go behind the pavilion with his son? Or any time after that on his own?'

'I'm afraid not, sir,' he confirmed regretfully. 'But it's something new, isn't it?' he persisted hopefully. 'And Sir Robert *was* very careful not to mention anything about it when we questioned him, wasn't he?'

Causon heaved a sigh. 'Yes, that's true enough. Not that it seems all that likely that we're dealing with a case of filicide here. I can think of quite a number of reasons why the man wouldn't have mentioned it. He was still in shock and it might genuinely have slipped his mind. Or he might simply have found it too painful to think about, let alone confess to strangers. Or, like Max Wilson, it might have been his sense of pride that kept him silent. No man likes to admit he can't handle his own offspring.' He smiled grimly, thinking of his own children, who could run rings around him. 'Still, I suppose we'd better get to the bottom of it. All right, go and fetch his nibs, will you?' he ordered, pulling out a wooden chair and slumping into it.

And before Lane could reach for it, he nabbed the last of the Bakewell tarts and began stuffing it into his maw.

'Sir,' Lane said wearily.

Without a word, Jenny reached into a Tupperware box and handed him a strawberry scone.

The sergeant smiled his thanks at her.

* * *

When Sir Robert stepped into the kitchen a few minutes later, Causon didn't look particularly happy to see that Lady Jones was following on right behind him. But then, Jenny thought, from her prime vantage point sitting right by the open pavilion doorway, there had been no way that Erica could have missed the spectacle of seeing her husband being rounded up by the sergeant and brought in for questioning.

And the redhead was obviously solicitous of her husband's wellbeing — or at least, wanted to appear to be so. For she made sure that he was sitting down comfortably, before taking up a position standing possessively behind him, with one hand laid protectively on his shoulder.

Absently, Sir Robert reached up and laid his hand briefly across hers in a gesture of acknowledgement before letting it drop listlessly once more into his lap. The stockbroker still looked ill, Jenny noticed with a pang, and had a flushed look to him that almost certainly had little to do with the oppressive heat. His colour wasn't particularly good, either, she noticed.

She only hoped that the inspector had also noted the signs of a man coming to the end of his tether, and went easy on him. Well, as easy as Inspector Laurence Causon ever got, that is. But the gaze that the Lady of the Manor focused on Causon looked distinctly unfriendly, making Jenny relax a little. If the inspector thought that he could bully Sir Robert, she had no doubts that his wife would very soon come to his rescue.

Causon, for his part, smiled his favourite crocodile smile at her, then looked firmly down at her husband. 'Sir Robert,' he began formally.

'Have you found out who killed my son yet?' The older man instantly put him on the defensive.

'The investigation has barely begun yet, sir,' Causon pointed out reasonably.

'What's going on at the top of the field, under the trees?' Robert Jones demanded next, once again wrong-footing the policeman. But whether he was doing it deliberately, in an attempt to deflect the questioning and emphasis away from himself, or whether he was just showing his usual take-charge attitude to life, it was hard to say.

'Perhaps, sir, if you wouldn't mind, *I* could ask a few questions,' Causon put in, not quite as politely now.

Jenny noticed that Erica's hand squeezed her husband's shoulder, no doubt in a gentle warning not to be so aggressive, and heard the older man sigh a little.

'Yes. Yes, of course. Sorry,' he muttered.

Causon smiled. 'That's all right, sir. If I haven't said so before, I'm very sorry for your loss and I know that this is a very distressing time for you. I'll try to be brief. Now, if you could just cast your mind back to the last time that you saw Tristan. We understand that your talk with him wasn't very . . . well, we've been informed that it didn't look like a friendly exchange, sir. Would you say that's fair?'

Causon, trying to be tactful, was quite a sight, and Jenny had to hide a smile as she busied herself fine-chopping some dill.

Erica Jones made that sort of 'tcha' noise between her lips that indicated general disgust, and shook her head.

'Bloody vultures. Nothing better to do than gossip,' she muttered. 'This village — it's like living in a goldfish bowl.'

Sir Robert, for his part, had gone quite pale at this untimely reminder of his last moments with his only son, and he swallowed hard. 'No. No, you're quite right, Inspector,' he confirmed gruffly. 'Tris and I . . . yes, we had words, I'm afraid. And I'm going to have to live with the fact that the last things I said to Tris, I said in anger.'

There was a sad, awkward moment of silence.

Causon shifted restlessly.

'They wouldn't have been about young Mark Rawley, would they, sir?' he finally asked.

Sir Robert jerked a little on the chair, looking for a moment in wide-eyed surprise at the inspector, as if suspecting him of a hitherto unexpected talent for clairvoyance. Then, abruptly, common sense took over, because he slowly nodded. 'Oh yes. I see. You've been talking to Mrs Rawley,' he said.

As an example of quick and intelligent thinking under extreme circumstances, it was quite some feat, and Jenny realized that it was a timely reminder, as if she needed one, that Sir Robert Jones was a very clever man indeed. And one who was used to acting decisively in fraught times. After all, steering your firm and other people's fortunes through the economic roller coaster of the last few years had to take nerves of steel, right?

'Yes, sir. She told me that she'd tackled you earlier on about your son's handling of James Cluley's investments, and demanded that you do something about it,' the inspector confirmed blandly.

'Yes. Yes, so she did.' He nodded wearily. 'And I *did* talk to Tris about it, for all the notice he took of me,' Sir Robert said a shade bitterly. But his eyes were now moving restlessly from face to face and finally resting on the large, rather attractive cook, who was now pounding spices with a pestle and mortar. He looked surprised for a moment, as if the rather domestic and comforting scene struck him as being incongruously out of place. Which, of course, it undoubtedly was.

'Er, yes, that's what we were arguing about,' Sir Robert said, a bit too thankfully.

The answer obviously struck both his wife and Causon as evasive, for Causon's eyes instantly narrowed on his suspect in suspicion, and Erica Jones tensed, her hand unconsciously digging into Robert's shoulder bone.

'I take it that your son wasn't very happy about your criticisms of his handling of James Cluley's money.' Causon was sure that the man was holding something back, and began testing the waters cautiously.

'No. He said that it had been just one of those things. Even the best and most experienced financial advisers can't always predict the markets, you know. He felt bad about it, of course, especially since the grandson, Mark, was a friend of Tris's but . . .' Sir Robert shrugged. 'Stockbrokers always get the blame when things go wrong.'

'So there was no question of incompetence on Tris's part, then?' Causon said, watching the older man closely. Because he had the feeling that if Tristan Jones had been guilty of anything that might have brought real trouble to his father's company, Sir Robert wouldn't have hesitated to cast his son adrift — flesh and blood or not. You didn't get to be as big a shark as Sir Robert and not learn to keep on swimming, no matter what.

But would that include killing your only son? Somehow it didn't seem likely. Unless there was more to this argument than he was hearing about so far.

'There was no question of Tris being careless,' Sir Robert denied with some heat. 'My son had a very good success rate for the majority of his clients,' he added. But again there was something evasive about the words that struck Causon as distinctly interesting.

'So if our fraud squad were to examine your son's dealings, they'd find nothing noteworthy?' he pressed.

Sir Robert leaned abruptly forward on his chair. He looked instantly ready to do battle. 'What? Now just a minute—'

But it was Erica Jones's voice that cut clearly across that of her outraged husband.

'I rather think you're over-reaching yourself now, Inspector,' Erica said icily. 'My husband's firm has one of the best reputations in the financial sector. And you'd better be very careful about starting, or being responsible for, any rumours to the contrary. Otherwise I think you'll find that our legal team will have something to say about it. And that won't please your chief constable.'

Inspector Causon grinned another crocodile smile. 'I'll bear that in mind. Your ladyship.'

Erica smiled glacially. 'Do that, Inspector,' she warned him.

'So, Sir Robert,' Causon turned back to the stockbroker with a brief smile. 'You're saying that that was the only thing that caused harsh words between you and your son. There was nothing else worrying you about your son's behaviour perhaps?'

Sir Robert's eyes darted about the kitchen for a moment, but the inspector's quiet bulk seemed to attract him like a magnet, and he found himself, much against his will, having to meet the other man's gaze.

'Well, there were one or two other matters that had been brought to my attention by the senior partners just lately,' he finally admitted.

Erica made another 'tcha' sound, but everyone ignored her.

'Tris had great luck in the past with some of his more speculative investments, and that had led to us acquiring some really top-notch portfolios. But just lately . . .' he trailed off as Erica's hand once more squeezed his shoulder tightly in warning.

'You really don't have to go into details with this man, darling,' she advised him quietly. 'After all, he's only interested in . . . what happened here. He's not an accountant or a financial expert. And since there were none of your clients here, and no one from the firm — well, apart from Lorcan — then whatever little mishaps Tris might have had at work couldn't possibly have had any bearing on who killed him, or why.'

'Yes, that's true,' Sir Robert said, with evident relief. 'Thank you, darling. I know I can always trust you to keep a clear head.'

Causon bit back a weary sigh.

'The inspector is just being over-thorough,' Erica finished, shooting daggers at the inspector, and daring him to disagree.

But in point of fact, her words had given him just the opening he needed, and for once he found himself feeling almost grateful for the catty redhead's interruption. It wasn't something he'd ever have thought could happen, and certainly wild horses wouldn't have dragged the admission from him, if anyone had been foolish enough to challenge him on it.

'Talking of Lorcan Greeves,' Causon said smoothly instead, 'were you aware of any particular friction between himself and your son?'

'If you're talking about that so-called fiancée of his,' Erica put in, once more speaking before her husband could be made to do so, 'yes, we know all about it. Tris and she had a little fling, resulting in Lorcan discovering the truth about her. That was just typical of Tris — it didn't mean a thing to him, naturally. But no doubt it was painful for Lorcan to learn the truth about her in that way.'

Sir Robert's eyes closed momentarily, and when he opened them again, they looked both sad and embarrassed. 'I'm afraid that my son could be rather . . .' Sir Robert broke off, obviously struggling to find the right words. 'I'm afraid he rather lacked discernment and compassion sometimes, when it came to affairs of the heart. Let's just say that Tris . . . well, that my son liked women, Inspector, and they liked him back,' he said simply.

'Yes, Sir Robert,' Causon said mildly. 'Did James Cluley approach you at any time this afternoon?' he asked next, abruptly changing the subject, as was his wont. Jenny, who'd observed this phenomenon before, was able to take it very much in her stride, but she could see that it had disconcerted both of the Joneses. 'And did you have any reason to, shall we say, take issue with him about anything?'

Sir Robert looked bewildered. 'James? No. He wouldn't let me go behind the pavilion to see Tris, and I thought that was going too far. The man had no authority to do that!' he admitted angrily. But then his shoulders slumped. 'But I think on the whole he was just trying to save me from . . . well . . . from seeing my boy like that . . . But apart from that, I don't think I've ever had much to do with the man.'

'When *was* the last time you saw Mr Cluley?' Causon asked.

'When? I don't know . . . He was guarding the way to the back of the pavilion until your policemen arrived. And I think I saw him go into the pavilion some time later, I presume to give you a statement.' Sir Robert shrugged helplessly.

'Did you see him leave again?' Causon asked abruptly, watching him closely.

But Sir Robert merely frowned, then slowly shook his head. 'No. I don't think so. I was talking to Max Wilson, I think. No, come to think of it, I haven't seen James around for some time. Why? Have you let him leave? Or have you arrested him?' Sir Robert leaned forward eagerly on his seat. 'Did he kill my son? Is that how he knew where to find him? Is that what all these questions are about?'

'No, sir, we haven't arrested Mr Cluley,' Causon said gravely, and watched the older man slump miserably back in his chair. He gave a small sigh. 'All right, sir, I think that's all for the moment,' he added quietly.

'When can we go home, Inspector?' Erica asked, as her husband with some difficulty, got to his feet. 'As you can see, my husband is exhausted and really should be in bed. He's had a profound shock. I can understand why you haven't let any of the others leave yet, but surely you can let *us* go now?' she wheedled.

Causon gave yet another crocodile smile. 'I'll see what I can do, Lady Jones,' he said. 'But just for the moment, if you can bear it a little longer, sir . . . ?'

'Yes, of course, whatever you need.' It was Erica's husband who spoke, waving his hands in a weary and defeated gesture, and together the two of them left the kitchen.

'Well, that seems to be that, sir,' Graham Lane said once they were safely out of earshot. 'I can't see why Sir Robert would kill his own son. And Marie and Mark Rawley wouldn't kill their own father and granddad. The Wilsons might have had a motive for killing Tristan, but not James Cluley, unless he saw them do it and was trying his hand at blackmail, but Max Wilson couldn't have killed Tris because he was batting at the time with more than two dozen witnesses. So it has to be Lorcan, doesn't it? He wanted Tristan dead, and he wouldn't have any reason not to kill James Cluley if the old man tried to blackmail him.'

Causon sighed. 'Yes. Yes, I suppose so. It has to be him, doesn't it? All right, Lane, apply for a warrant for his arrest, charging him with both murders.'

But from her position by the sink, where she was just rinsing out some dishes, Jenny Starling said quietly, 'You know, Inspector, I wouldn't do that if I were you.'

There was something quiet but certain in her voice that instantly made Graham Lane feel a shiver run up his spine.

'Oh? Why not?' Causon turned in his chair to eye her warily.

'Because I don't think he did it,' Jenny said simply.

Causon's lips twitched. 'I rather think that my superiors will want me to come up with a better answer than that, Miss Starling. Even coming from such an august body as yourself, I doubt they'd simply take your word for it.'

Sarky sod, Jenny thought fondly. She was really getting to like this bluff, unusual policeman.

'OK, so you don't think Greeves is our man,' Causon continued, prepared to play along. 'I don't suppose you have someone in mind that you like better?'

'Oh yes,' Jenny Starling said simply. 'I think I know just who killed Tristan, and why. And why it was that James Cluley also had to die.'

Both policemen stared at her for a moment, and then Causon got slowly to his feet. He'd heard about this phenomenon before from other police officers who'd had the luck (either good or bad, depending on your point of view) of working with this renowned cook. And they'd all reported how there came a moment in the case when Jenny Starling seemed to just pull the answer out of thin air.

Now he had the distinct impression that it was his turn to have a front-row view of this particular magic trick, and he was both looking forward to it and resenting it in equal measure.

'And just who do you think the killer is?' he asked ominously.

Jenny looked at him, sighed, and said flatly, 'I think Erica Jones did it.'

CHAPTER ELEVEN

For a moment, the big policeman looked at her blankly, and then slowly began to smile.

Then he frowned. Perhaps it was because what she'd just said had pleased him so enormously (since nothing would give him more pleasure than to snap the handcuffs on the snooty Lady of the Manor) that he felt suddenly obliged to pull himself up and be a little less receptive to the idea.

'Oh?' he said, glancing across at his sergeant, who was staring at Jenny Starling like a cobra that had just spotted a particularly sleek and multi-striped mongoose in the shrubbery. 'OK. I'll bite.' He grinned savagely. 'And for a start, there's something I'm just dying to know. Namely — just how in the hell do you think Erica Jones managed to kill her stepson without ever leaving this building? Because unless my memory is playing tricks with me, didn't you yourself tell me that she never left this pavilion once Tristan had finished having his tea and was seen alive and well and blithely walking back out onto the field, munching on one of your world-famous scones? A fact that was backed up by Caroline what's-her-face and that Ettie woman?'

Jenny sighed. 'Oh that. Yes, right. That was what originally stumped me, too,' she admitted readily enough.

'On the face of it, it does seem to be a bit of a poser, doesn't it?'

Out of the corner of her eye, she could have sworn that she saw Graham Lane put a hand over his mouth in order to hide a big grin. But when she looked at him suspiciously, the sergeant was nonchalantly leaning against the wooden wall and making a show of examining his fingernails.

His boss, however, was merely watching her expectantly. Then he said heavily, 'It does rather have its drawbacks, yes.' Jenny lifted an eyebrow at him, but had to conclude that she couldn't really blame him for looking and sounding so sceptical. And, in fact, the more she thought about how she'd come to her conclusions, the more she thought that simply explaining it in words might not be the best way to go.

'Actually, it might be better if I just showed you something first,' she said slowly. 'Then I can tell you what I think must have happened, and show you how it could have worked, all at the same time.' She paused in the action of drying her hands on a small towel, and cocked her head slightly to one side. 'Mind you, I could have it all wrong,' she added, in order to be strictly fair. But she didn't really think that she had. 'I mean, just because a thing *could* have been done a certain way, it doesn't automatically follow that it *was* done that way. If you see what I mean.'

'Oh yes,' Inspector Causon lied calmly through gritted teeth.

'And it doesn't necessarily mean that Erica Jones was the only one who could have done it,' Jenny added, neatly folding the towel away.

'If you say so, Miss Starling.'

Jenny glanced across at the affably smiling inspector, and then at Graham Lane, who was now looking studiously down at his shoes. And if his shoulders seemed to be trembling just a little in unexpressed laughter, she supposed she couldn't blame him, either.

But sometimes she really just couldn't resist playing Stan Laurel to Inspector Causon's Oliver Hardy.

'OK then, so long as we've got that all clear.' And so saying, she rose and led the way into the tiny hall and then to the entrance of the storeroom next door. There she stopped abruptly in the doorway.

'I think it might be best if we don't go any further inside before your scene-of-crime people have had a chance to go over it thoroughly,' she said. 'I know they're already going to have to look in here for traces of whoever took the penknife and cricket stump. But if I *am* right, then they're going to be even busier in here than that. Because it's in here that they're going to find a good portion of the evidence needed to convict Erica Jones.'

Causon glanced around at the dim and dusty interior, looking less than impressed. 'They'll do a thorough job in here as soon as possible, naturally,' he conceded. 'But right now they have two murder sites to process first.'

And whilst he was hoping that he might have a viable suspect at last, if only to placate his angry superiors, even the infamous Jenny Starling, Causon supposed sourly, could fall flat on her face sometimes.

'All right. But I really do think that this is a murder scene, too, and one that's every bit as vital as the area around the trees where we found James,' Jenny insisted. 'Outside and around the back of here might be where Tris's *body* was actually found, but this is where the person who killed him was standing when she did it,' Jenny said firmly.

'*What?*' Causon said, clearly taken aback. Beside him, he felt his sergeant take an instinctive quick glance around.

'You see those shutters?' Jenny said, pointing at the darkened windows. 'I was in here earlier looking for a chair, like I told you before. And those shutters were both very dusty and hard to open — I know, I gave one a try. I don't think they'd been painted shut, as such. It was just that they'd never been opened much and had got very rusty and hard to move. Probably a good oiling would sort them out. But that's not the point.' She looked down at her hands and sighed. 'Unless I miss my guess, I think your SOCO people

186

will find that at least one of those shutters, if not both of them, are now more free of dust than the rest of the stuff in here. And what's more, that they've been forced open very recently — perhaps they'll even be able to find traces of rust from the hinges on the floor to prove it. Maybe even paint flakes from the window itself. I really don't think the shutters or the windows have been opened for quite some time — until today.'

Causon's eyes slowly widened as he finally saw what this marvellous cook was getting at. 'And you'd bet money that the victim's body was found lying right underneath the window that's been opened, I take it?' he said quietly. And whistled judiciously through his teeth. His eyes narrowed again as he pictured the scene.

'Wouldn't you?' Jenny said. 'The killer might have arranged to meet Tris behind the pavilion, but instead of going outside and around the back, out in open view of anyone who might happen to be looking . . .' She trailed off, deliberately urging him to follow her line of reasoning.

'The killer came in here, where he or she wouldn't be so easily spotted, opened the window and . . . bam!' Causon said, miming the action of someone swinging a cricket bat down against an unprotected head.

Graham Lane shifted excitedly.

'Look around,' Jenny continued. 'Even from where we're standing, I can see a couple of old bats lying around, not to mention some cricket gloves, which would be great for concealing fingerprints. And the killer would have seen the same things as we do. All she had to do was select one of the old bats, put on some gloves, open the window and beckon Tris over. He'd have been expecting to talk to her out there anyway, and whilst he might have been a little surprised to be beckoned to the window, instead of her coming around to join him out back, he wouldn't necessarily question it. Why would he?' Jenny sighed sadly. 'They probably talked for a little while about whatever it was Erica wanted to talk about. And I think we can easily guess what that was,' she added grimly.

Causon nodded. 'You still think that he and she had been doing the horizontal tango. And was desperate that her husband didn't get to know about it.'

'Yes. I definitely got that vibe off them. But whether or not you'd be able to prove that . . .' She trailed off and shrugged.

Causon glanced at Lane, who also shrugged.

'It all depends on how discreet they were. Some affairs are easy to prove, if they went to hotels or rented out a pad, or used a friend's place for their trysting,' the sergeant explained. 'But if they were really careful — and we know Tristan had his own place in the city — who can say? And I doubt that the lady was the sentimental kind who kept his loving text messages.'

Jenny gave a grim smile. Luckily, it was not her job to go grubbing about in other people's dirty laundry. She gave a quick shudder.

'Anyway,' she picked up the thread from where she'd left off. 'Let's say that Erica and Tris talked for a little while, with Erica failing to get what she wanted from Tris. He turns to walk away and . . .' She shrugged uneasily. 'Well, as you so graphically put it, Inspector — bam.'

For a moment, all three of them were silent as they contemplated the shocking suddenness with which death could sometimes come.

'And that would explain how it was possible for James Cluley to see Tris go behind the pavilion, but no one else come out again,' she added.

And both men could see that it clearly pleased her to be able to exonerate the old man from lying. Indeed, it had always been obvious to Causon, at least, that the cook had never really believed in the concept of James Cluley as a heartless blackmailer, or someone who would try to profit from something as sordid as murder.

The inspector again whistled silently through his teeth. It did all sound pretty believable.

'Yes. That's all very clever, Miss Starling, I grant you,' the inspector acknowledged willingly, though still inclined to be cautious. 'But Erica won't have been kind enough to leave us a clear set of her prints. And now we know how it might have been done, the field is more or less wide open again. *Anyone* could have sneaked in here after tea and done the deed.'

'Oh, not just anyone,' Jenny denied. 'And certainly not anyone with a reasonable motive. Max Wilson was batting in plain sight for all to see, so he couldn't have done it. That lets him out. And I imagine Sergeant Lane checked Michelle Wilson's alibi, that she was still chatting away in her chair?'

She looked at him, and he quickly nodded.

'And Lorcan Greeves and young Mark were still away from the field and plotting their revenge,' she pointed out. 'Yes, they could have been in it together, I know. But you *have* got that independent witness who saw Lorcan come back to the cricket field after handing over the computer passwords to young Mark, haven't you?'

She glanced across at Sergeant Lane again. 'And presumably it won't take long to collate the witness statements and see if anyone saw Lorcan go into the pavilion just after Tris was last seen alive.'

Causon nodded. 'That shouldn't be a problem,' he agreed. 'And you clearly don't expect to find anyone who *did* see him go inside, do you?'

Jenny merely shrugged. She'd never been overly partial to sticking her neck out.

Causon contented himself with a cynical smile. 'Well, let's just hope that the blood results confirm that none of the blood we found on Greeves belonged to James Cluley,' he said hopefully.

'So who does that leave us with?' Sergeant Lane decided to take up the baton. He gave it a moment's thought, frowned, then pursed his lips and glanced warily across at his superior. 'I know it doesn't seem very likely on the face of it, sir, but I suppose we *do* have to include James Cluley on our list of suspects at this point? After all, he could still have killed Tris and then been killed by someone else.'

Causon snorted, clearly indicating what he thought of *that* theory.

'Yes, sir, I know, it does seem rather far-fetched,' Graham agreed quickly. 'Two different victims and two different killers, with two different motives, resulting in two dead bodies in the space of less than an hour or so. But a defence lawyer will try and put any theory out there if it can confuse a jury,' he added defensively. 'So we'd better have an answer for it.'

Causon sighed, and Jenny felt obliged to come to his rescue before the irascible policeman could pepper them with yet more of his sardonic outbursts.

'Except that James never came back in here that I know of,' she pointed out helpfully. 'I was working in the kitchen, ferrying food to and fro, but you don't only have to take my word for it. You can ask Caroline and Ettie or any of the others who were in here after tea, but I think you'll find that they'll agree with me about James not coming in.'

She regarded Causon firmly.

'No, as I see it, there's only one person who could possibly have done it.' She held up a hand and began to tick things off on her fingers. 'One, Erica had a motive. Two, she was always present in the pavilion, because she didn't want to go out and get burned, so her being seen in here wouldn't even cause comment. Three,' she tapped another finger, 'during the course of the afternoon she excused herself to use the loo — or so she said — thus giving her the perfect excuse to be absent for five minutes or so. Which is certainly long enough to have a quick chat with Tris, and then hit him over the head. And four, I even saw her dusting down her expensive clothes before going back to her seat in the doorway. As she'd have needed to, if she'd just come from being in here, and had been battling with dusty shutters and stubborn windows. This place is filthy.'

Graham Lane began to feel really excited now. When he heard it all laid out like that . . .

'Erica Jones,' Causon said, nodding slowly. 'And you're saying the reason she killed him was simple jealousy? Because he'd tossed her aside for Michelle Wilson?' He sounded a little sceptical now. 'She doesn't particularly strike me as being all that emotionally unstable. In my experience, men or women who kill out of "hopeless love" suffer from low self-esteem and all that malarkey. And it strikes me that the Lady of the Manor has a perfectly healthy ego, thank you very much.'

Jenny couldn't help but smile. 'Well, I have a feeling that it's not so much love or emotional revenge that's behind all this. Unless, of course, you count a love of money.' Jenny now had the rapt attention of both policemen, who were listening to her intently. 'I didn't overhear *much* of what they said when she and Tris were having their argument earlier, but I *did* hear Tristan mention a pre-nup that she'd been forced to sign.'

Causon nodded. 'Gotcha,' he said. 'And no husband is going to be generous in a divorce settlement if he finds out his younger bride has been bedding his own son.'

'Er . . . no,' Jenny agreed succinctly. 'And it would be no skin off Tris's nose if his father divorced her,' she pointed out. 'In fact, he might have found it amusing to taunt her with the possibility.'

'And our Lady of the Manor does strike you as a woman who likes to spend big,' Graham Lane felt obliged to put in. 'Like I said before, that outfit she's wearing today—'

'Yes, all right, Mr Fashion Expert,' Causon interrupted him before Lane could give him another lecture about haute couture.

'Mind you, there's nothing to say that it couldn't have been a combination of the two things that motivated her to lash out at him,' Jenny speculated, with world-weary cynicism. 'Knowing that Tris was probably sleeping with half the female population of the county would be bound to seriously wound her vanity. But I still think that, mostly, she was fighting to hold on to her cushy and easy way of life.'

'Quite,' Causon agreed. 'And if sonny boy was teasing her with the threat of telling his father about their affair, well, Sir Robert would kick her out, and the pre-nup would hold up in any divorce under those circumstances. Which would mean that Erica Jones would not only be facing one hell of a scandal, leaving her reputation in the mud, she would also have to make do with far less than she was used to.' He nodded. 'And if killing him meant that she got some emotional payback for being dumped for Michelle Wilson — well, why not? Yes, I think a jury would buy into that scenario all right.'

Jenny sighed wearily. 'You know, Tris *did* strike me as just the kind of silly, unthinking fool who *would* torment his stepmother, just for the fun of it. But whether or not he'd ever have actually spoken to his father . . .' Jenny shrugged philosophically. 'Who can say? It would have put him in as bad a light as his stepmother, after all, if you think about it. And Tris, who knew how to look after number one, would hardly want to get on his father's bad side, would he? Sir Robert might have disinherited him as well, and that wouldn't have suited him at all.'

'So she might well have killed him for nothing,' Sergeant Lane said, aghast.

Jenny winced at such a horrible thought. 'I suppose, in the end, she decided that she just couldn't take that risk. And since he was leaving her bed for Michelle's, she realized that she might be about to lose any hold over him that she might once have had and . . . well, decided to kill him.'

'And planned it really well,' Causon said grimly. 'She minimized the risk of getting any blood or trace evidence on her, because the wooden wall and glass window shielded her. And afterwards, all she'd had to do was toss the bat outside to land beside the body in order to maintain the fiction that the killer had been outside with Tris all along. Then close the windows and shutters, put the gloves she was wearing back on the shelf, then come back in here and take her place, as if nothing had happened. Thus reinforcing her alibi. Neat. Very neat. You have to hand it to her.'

'And later she could swear — perfectly truthfully — that she'd never left the pavilion,' Jenny agreed, 'and we'd all have to confirm that. We were her witnesses.'

The cheek of it, Jenny suddenly thought angrily. Using me as an alibi!

'You're right. I need to get SOCO in here right away,' Causon said. 'The gloves she was wearing must still be in here somewhere, and they'll have her DNA all over the inside of them. Then there'll be the dust on her clothes, which will be a perfect match for the dust in here. Oh yes, we'll get her for it all right, now we know where to look for the evidence,' the policeman said, with satisfaction.

'Hang on a minute, though,' the sergeant interrupted softly. 'What about James Cluley?'

Jenny looked at him, surprised. 'What about James?' she echoed, as she heard Causon swear softly under his breath. 'She killed him, too, of course.'

'Now hold on a minute, there have to be problems with *that*,' Causon began to object, but Jenny was already shaking her head.

'No — it had to be her, don't you see? All these theories that were flying around about who would want to kill both Tris and James, and the possibility that there might be two killers was never going to wash. Because once Erica had killed Tris, she then found herself with no other choice but to kill James too. She simply had to.'

'I don't see how that follows,' Causon objected. 'If your theory about how she killed Tris is true, then James Cluley couldn't have tried to blackmail her, because he'd have had no more idea than anyone else of who the killer was.'

But again Jenny was vigorously shaking her head. 'No, no, that's not why she had to kill him,' she explained patiently. 'Of course James didn't approach her, or try anything on. In fact, *she* must have approached *him*. At some point very soon after he left here. She'd have needed to act as fast as she could before more police reinforcements arrived.'

Jenny looked at both policemen a little sadly now. 'I don't really want to have to say it, but I'm afraid it's true. She realized just how lucky a break it was for her to have you so dangerously understaffed. It was because you *were* so short of people on the ground that she could plan and execute his killing with at least a realistic chance of success. If you'd been able to police this place properly right from the get-go,' she waved a hand around to include the pavilion and the grounds outside, 'then she never would have been able to get away with it.'

Causon was visibly grinding his teeth, and she winced in real sympathy.

'I'm not accusing you of anything, you understand,' she said hastily, desperate not to be misunderstood. 'I know it wasn't your fault. And I don't see how we could have known about it in time to prevent it anyway,' she added bitterly.

'But I still don't understand why she had to kill the old man,' Graham Lane said, both to change the subject and because he was genuinely baffled. 'If he didn't know she was the killer, and he wasn't blackmailing her, what danger did he pose?'

Jenny looked at him wide-eyed. 'Because of his evidence, of course,' she said simply. 'When James told us that he didn't see anybody come out from either side of the pavilion once Tris had gone behind it — well, she realized the danger at once. She must have eavesdropped on your questioning of him. Although I don't suppose that James himself would have made any secret of what he'd told you.'

'But I still don't see why it's relevant,' Causon continued.

'But can't you see what a fix Erica suddenly found herself in?' Jenny said. 'Her whole plan relied on the fact that nobody would look at her seriously as a suspect, because she hadn't left the building, and thus had an unimpeachable alibi. She knew that if you dug deep enough you might find out about her fling with Tris, which would put her on the radar, but whilst she was in the position of not possibly being able to have done it, she felt safe enough. But when James told us what he'd seen — or rather, what he'd *not* seen — well, then it became a whole different ball game. You immediately thought that James was either lying about it, or was intent on sheltering someone, like his daughter or grandson. Or that he intended to try and use the knowledge to blackmail someone,' Jenny reminded him. 'But only Erica would have known that James was literally *telling the truth*. And that it was imperative that he must be made to stop telling the truth as soon as possible. Because if she didn't shut him up, and he kept sticking to his story, you might just start to believe him. And who knows where that would have led you?'

'Yes. We might just have started thinking like this,' Graham Lane said.

'We'd have got there eventually too,' Causon said sharply, glowering at his sergeant, who dragged his admiring gaze away from the attractive cook, and flushed slightly.

'Of course we would, sir,' Lane said stoutly.

Jenny shivered. 'Erica probably approached James with some excuse or other — maybe that she wanted to hear for herself how he had found her stepson. Maybe she told him that she needed to ask his advice about something. Either way, James would have felt no reason to fear her. Even when she led him to that quiet spot under the trees, he wouldn't be prepared for such an attack . . .' She shuddered to a halt.

No, she just didn't want to think about such things.

Instead, she forced her mind onto something else, and as it always did when asked to come up with an alternative, pleasant solution, found herself conjuring up images of food.

And that led her on to remember why she was here in the first place, and she began to think about the barbecue instead. If she could just persuade Causon that it should go ahead, she could make some proper coleslaw. She could easily whisk up some of her quick-fire mayonnaise, and she had onions and carrots and some cabbage left over from—

'Miss Starling!' She heard her name being bellowed, and jumped a little guiltily. She knew she had a tendency to zone out when she was contemplating menus.

'Yes? Sorry, what?' She looked at Causon, who was staring at her.

'I said,' he relayed between gritted teeth, obviously repeating himself, 'that we understand now why she had to kill James. But we still don't see how she could possibly have managed to do it. She couldn't have anticipated having to kill someone else, so she wouldn't have brought a change of clothes with her. Besides, I myself noticed that she's still wearing the same outfit now that she had on when I first saw her. And no doubt my sergeant,' and here he shot a fulminating look at the innocent-faced Graham Lane, 'who should be an editor for *Vogue* in his spare time, can confirm that. Yet we've already established that the killer of James Cluley *must* have got blood spattered all over their body and clothing. And the medical examiner confirmed it.'

'Oh yes,' Jenny Starling agreed amiably. 'Erica must have got considerably bloodstained.'

Causon gaped at her easygoing admission, his eyes bulging a little as he did so. It made Jenny wish that he really wouldn't do that. He did so remind her of a startled bullfrog.

'Well then . . . we've just seen her and her husband not ten minutes ago, and she didn't have a speck of blood on her,' Causon huffed and puffed the sentence out, going a little red-faced as he did so.

Clearly he was holding on to his temper by the skin of his teeth.

'Oh no, she wouldn't have,' Jenny agreed placidly. 'Not now, anyway. And before you say it, Erica wouldn't have dared to risk trying to get into the ladies' loo,' Jenny said at once. 'For that, she'd have had to come in through the changing room, and neither Caroline nor Ettie could have failed to notice if she'd been covered in blood. Even if she'd somehow managed to clean her hands and face with a wet-wipe or something from her handbag, they'd still have noticed the state of her clothes. I know Erica is wearing dark trousers and a multi-coloured blouse, but they're mostly in shades of blue and green with splashes of white. Red or a rust colour would have been unmistakable, seen up close. Oh no,' Jenny shook her head emphatically. 'Erica couldn't have chanced anyone getting up close to her after killing James.'

Causon looked at Lane, who looked blankly back at him and gave a shrug.

'Then just where and how in hell *did* she clean herself up?' Causon almost shouted in frustration.

Jenny blinked at him. 'Well, in the river of course. Where else?' she said.

To her it was perfectly obvious. The only other source of water anywhere close was the river that ran behind the field.

'But . . . how . . .' Causon began to splutter, and Jenny suddenly smacked her forehead with her palm.

'Oh, sorry. Of course, I haven't mentioned it yet, have I?'

Causon began to growl ominously, and Jenny held up a hand.

'Sorry, it really just slipped my mind. And I only talked to the old man just before we came back in here, after seeing the Rawleys, so this is literally the first opportunity I've had to pass it along.'

'What old man?' Causon asked suspiciously.

'Well, when I realized that the only place the killer could have cleaned themselves up was in the river, I found a local, and asked him if there was any other access from the field to the river that we didn't know about. And of course there was. Well, there had to be really, knowing how lazy human nature is,' Jenny said pleasantly. 'Apparently, the fishermen of the village made the shortcut, so that they didn't have to go the long way around. Don't worry,' she said, mistaking Causon's blank-eyed gaze as one of scepticism. 'He gave me clear directions to it. Apparently it's not far down from the stand of horse chestnut trees, just where some elder bushes take over from the hawthorn for a few yards. And it makes sense that they'd choose to go through the gap in the fence there, doesn't it?'

'It does?' Causon echoed.

'Yes. Well, they wouldn't make a gap in the fence where there are hawthorns, would they?' Jenny Starling pointed out sweetly. 'It's too prickly. They'd get scratched and their clothes would get snagged.'

Graham Lane stepped in before his chief could blow his top quite spectacularly, which experience told him was likely to happen any moment now. 'You're saying that there's a way for someone to get through from here to the river, without going through any of the normal gates or exits?' he clarified gently.

'Yes,' Jenny said, looking from one of them to the other with a slightly puzzled frown. Wasn't she being clear? 'According to the old-timer I asked, you simply pull one section of the chain-link fence along, a bit like a sliding door, and slip through. But everyone remembers to put it back again, in case the farmer has sheep in the field — it wouldn't do to have them stray onto the sports ground. Then all you have to do is just squeeze through the elder bushes, which is quite easy apparently, and you're in the next field, right by the river.'

'That must be why our men searching for hidden clothing didn't find it, sir,' Lane said hastily. 'If the chain-link fence panel was still in place, they'd have no reason to suspect that it *could* be moved.'

'And if there was room for a person to squeeze past the elders, there must be a fairly wide space there, and one quick look through the fence would confirm that nothing had been tossed over and hidden in there,' Jenny put in quickly. 'So you see, your men weren't being incompetent. You told them to look for bundled-up, bloodied clothing — not a bit of a pathway through some bushes on the other side of the fence.'

'Yes, yes, fine,' Causon snapped. 'So you're maintaining that Erica Jones lured James Cluley to the stand of trees, killed him, used this secret shortcut and cleaned up in the river? That's a bit far-fetched, isn't it?'

'Why?' Jenny asked bluntly. 'As a villager of some years standing, she would have known all about the shortcut.'

'I'm not questioning that,' Causon said wearily.

'But if she'd washed up in the river, surely we'd have been able to tell.' It was Sergeant Lane, the fashion aficionado, who made the objection. 'I mean, she'd still have been damp for one thing.'

'Would she? Really? In this heat?' Jenny asked sceptically. 'I don't think so. It's been hot enough to fry an egg on the pavement all day. And don't forget, the trousers Erica's wearing are made of a very thin material — they'd dry as quick as winking. As is the top she's got on. And as for the long, floating blouse over that, I don't think she was even wearing that when she killed James. But even if she had been, in this heat, every stitch she had on would have dried in twenty minutes easily. Half an hour max.'

Lane slowly nodded, realizing she was right.

'Why don't you think she was wearing her blouse?' Causon asked, a bit distracted.

Jenny sighed. 'Now, I was a bit slow there,' she admitted, looking abashed. 'Before we went to talk to the Rawleys, I noticed Erica walking past the kitchen window, and that she had taken her long-sleeved blouse off, and draped it over one arm. I remembered thinking at the time that she obviously couldn't be that worried about getting sunburned anymore. But I didn't follow the thought through to its logical conclusion until later. She's red-haired and fair-skinned. Of course she'd have got sunburned. Now, of course, I realize what she must have been doing.'

'Which was?' Causon asked.

'Going to meet James Cluley — with the sharpened cricket stump hidden by her hanging blouse,' Jenny said flatly. 'If you think about it, it's decidedly odd that nobody noticed somebody walking around with a bizarre object like a broken cricket stump in their hand, isn't it? It's not as if it's the sort of thing that you can shove into a pocket or fit into your handbag.'

'I suppose you could stick it down your trousers,' Lane said. Then promptly wished he hadn't, when both of them looked at him in amusement.

'Er, yes, maybe,' Jenny said, trying to spare his blushes. 'But I think holding it along your forearm, and hiding it with a piece of clothing would be easier.'

'She truly thought of everything, didn't she?' Causon mused bitterly. 'Considering that she had to make it up as she went along. I presume you think that she *had* planned to kill Tris long beforehand?' He shot the question suddenly at Jenny.

The cook shrugged. 'I'm not sure. She might have had the idea in the back of her mind for some time.' This was as far as she was willing to go, when it came to guessing whether or not Tris's murder had been premeditated. After all, Erica could just as easily have thought it up on the spur of the moment. She was clearly good at improvising. But surely there would've been much easier, less public ways for her to kill him if she'd planned it ahead of time?

'Anyway — to get back to James's murder. I think that when she got to the stand of trees, she'd have been careful to leave the blouse to one side,' Jenny said. 'That way, after she'd . . . done what she had to do, she'd have been able to slip the blouse back on over her bloodied top and at least hide some of the bloodstains from view, if she'd been unlucky enough to meet anyone else roaming around up there. But nearly everyone was congregated down here, where all the action was, and wouldn't have had any reason to be up the top end of the field. Whatever, she was just lucky that, in the event, no one seems to have noticed her. And don't forget, she knew that the shortcut through the fence wasn't that far away from the trees, which is another good reason for luring James in there.'

Graham Lane frowned. 'But why, if she'd made her way out of the grounds undetected, didn't she just go home and wash up there?'

'Because she couldn't risk walking through the village in her bloodstained clothes in case she was seen,' Jenny said. 'There was no guarantee that the village would be deserted. Not everyone loves cricket, and people walk their dogs or go out in their cars. And if she'd been seen going past by anyone who happened to be out in their garden or something, you'd have found out about it when you did your house-to-house interviews later.'

'Yes, and she didn't have a lot of time, either,' Causon ruminated. 'She'd want to get herself and her clothes clean right away, and get back in sight of witnesses here in the playing field as soon as possible.'

'OK, that makes sense,' Lane agreed. 'So the river it had to be. She kills James Cluley, runs down to the river, washes her clothes, hangs them out to dry on the bushes, bathes herself and then returns back here as bold as brass.'

'Yes. And of course, she tried to minimize the risk of anybody figuring out what she'd done by dousing herself in perfume,' Jenny added.

'Perfume?' Causon repeated.

Jenny nodded. 'Yes. When we came back from interviewing the Rawleys, she was just getting back from the river herself. And I noticed that when she came back into the pavilion, she used far too much perfume. A lady only needs to use a few dabs. Anything more is a bit . . . well . . . naff.' Jenny struggled to explain this bit of feminine etiquette to the big and burly policeman. 'It struck me as odd, and not something that someone with Erica's finesse would ever do. Even Caroline and Ettie noticed it. But of course, what she was trying to do was disguise any lingering odour of river water that she might have had coming from her skin or clothes.'

'Ah.' Causon nodded. 'Yes. The rivers around here are relatively clean, but even so . . .'

'Yes. Washing yourself and your clothes in a river isn't something you'd do by choice. Especially in a field where the farmer keeps sheep.' Jenny grimaced fastidiously. 'But, looking on the bright side, at least that'll help prove that she did it,' she pointed out. 'I mean, don't rivers have bits of weed, and diatoms and whatnot, as well as their own unique individual chemical make-up or whatever? It shouldn't be a hard task for your forensics lab to confirm that her clothes had been washed in it, right?'

She looked at Graham Lane and smiled.

'And she's going to have a very hard time explaining why she dunked her thousand-pound outfit in river water, isn't she?'

Causon began to grin.

'And Erica's shoes aren't leather, but those fabric-type ballet pumps, so they'll probably have traces of river water and mud on them as well, no matter how clean they might look to the naked eye,' Jenny pointed out brightly. 'Then there's her nails to consider.'

Causon heaved another portentous sigh. 'Nails? As in fingernails?'

'Yes,' Jenny said. 'You might have noticed that she's had a manicure very recently, and her nails painted bright red. But when I came in here just now, she was sitting in her deckchair, rather vigorously filing one of her nails. Now, no woman would do that unless they absolutely had to, because it would ruin the look and symmetry of them,' Jenny explained, and Graham Lane was already nodding in perfect understanding.

No doubt his wife had taught him all about the importance of maintaining lovely nails.

'So she must have broken a nail during her attack on James,' Lane confirmed her reasoning. 'Or when she was preparing the broken cricket stump to be used as a weapon.'

'Yes,' Jenny said grimly. 'Murder can be . . . well, murder on your manicure, it seems.'

'All right, all right,' Causon butted in. 'I'm not so sure that a broken nail is going to add much to the evidence against her — but as for the rest, yes, you've convinced me we've got enough to take it to the CPS. Sergeant, get on the phone and arrange for an arrest warrant for our Lady Jones. If her ladyship thinks she's got away with murder, she's going to have to think again.'

* * *

Ten minutes later, Jenny was standing outside the pavilion, watching a violently cursing Erica Jones being helped into a police car. Her husband, white-faced and ominously silent, watched the proceedings stoically.

As expected, the Lady of the Manor had vigorously denied all the charges put to her, and had instantly demanded the services of a first-class solicitor. No one was in any doubt that she'd get one. She was just the sort of woman who *would* know high-flying QCs and had probably been the hostess at her husband's business parties where top-notch legal people abounded.

But Sergeant Lane, sitting beside her in the back of the police car, doubted that even the best legal brains in the country would do her much good. Now that they knew where to look, he was confident that the forensic evidence alone would nail her superior and snooty hide to the wall.

Causon was standing at the entrance to the car park, watching the police car depart, a beneficent smile for once wreathing his face. And Jenny, now that all that other business had been attended to, realized that she had something very important to ask him. And since he was obviously in such a good mood, now was the perfect time to do it.

She approached him with a wide smile.

The crates of beer that Caroline's husband had brought were still nestling in the shade under the pavilion, and the barbecues wouldn't take long to set up. It would be light for another hour or so yet, but the sports fields had floodlighting anyway, so that hardly mattered.

She could almost hear the sizzle of meat, and the scent of her best-recipe barbecue sauce floated like a tantalizing culinary phantasm somewhere out in the ether.

'You know, Inspector,' she began wheedling gently, 'you've all been working so hard, you must be starving. And I've got all this food for the barbecue supper just waiting to be used—'

Causon shot her a quick, scandalized look. 'No,' he interrupted her flatly. 'This is still an active crime scene. I can't have you cooking up a barbecue, for Pete's sake. I'm already in hot water with the powers that be.'

'Oh I know, but I've had a word with someone on the committee, and they have no objection to using the food to feed you and your men. And since you're still doing a lot of interviewing, some of the spectators will be getting hungry too, and don't you have some sort of obligation to see that witnesses are fed?'

Causon eyed her grimly. 'No, we don't,' he said flatly. 'You're thinking of people we're holding down at the station. These people,' he waved at those who were still giving statements to the officers, 'can go home as soon as we have their details.'

Jenny sighed, but wasn't inclined to give up yet. She had bread rolls that had been expertly proved and would be perfect, when baked, for burger buns. 'It's just that I do so hate to waste food,' she persisted hopefully. Surely the man could be persuaded to see reason? 'And I bet your mother did, too, and brought you up the same. And since it's all here and ready to . . .'

But the inspector was now glowering at her.

'No! Get the idea out of your head. You're *not* going to cook for us and that's that,' Causon all but yelled at her. It made several of his officers and a few of the SOCOs glance over and grin at them. No doubt they were glad that it was someone else, and not them, who was getting the sharp end of Causon's tongue for once.

He ran a harassed hand through his hair and sighed. 'Look, Miss Starling, it's not that I don't appreciate all the help you've given us these past few hours. But you need to leave now, and let us get on with what needs to be done. And we can't have you underfoot whilst we're doing that,' he said, forcing his voice to sound reasonable. 'You can see that, can't you?'

'Look, I understand that it's a bit unconventional and all that,' Jenny concurred magnanimously. 'And I have no intention of messing with a crime scene,' she reassured him fulsomely, holding up both hands in an appeasing gesture. 'But there's nothing stopping me from setting up the barbecue outside in the lane, is there? I mean, that's a public place, right, and well away from the pavilion, and all this.

And I really don't mind trekking all the food and things out there . . .'

'No!' Causon howled now, going a quite spectacular shade of puce. There was just no getting through to this woman!

Jenny sighed. 'Oh, come on.' She gave his forearm a gentle nudge with her own, willing to give it one last shot. 'Every man loves a barbecue,' she insisted. 'There are steaks, and my home-made Oxfordshire herb sausages . . .'

Causon took a step away from her, stared at her balefully for about thirty seconds, then pointed imperiously at her van. 'Out,' he thundered through gritted teeth.

Jenny Starling stared back at him, then sighed sadly. Her shoulders slumped as she turned and walked dejectedly away.

There was just no helping some people, she acknowledged to herself sadly.

In fact, she thought, with a spurt of resentment, some people could be just downright unreasonable.

Which, by an odd coincidence, happened to be exactly what Inspector Laurence Causon was also thinking.

THE END

THE JOFFE BOOKS STORY

We began in 2014 when Jasper agreed to publish his mum's much-rejected romance novel and it became a bestseller.

Since then we've grown into the largest independent publisher in the UK. We're extremely proud to publish some of the very best writers in the world, including Joy Ellis, Faith Martin, Caro Ramsay, Helen Forrester, Simon Brett and Robert Goddard. Everyone at Joffe Books loves reading and we never forget that it all begins with the magic of an author telling a story.

We are proud to publish talented first-time authors, as well as established writers whose books we love introducing to a new generation of readers.

We won Trade Publisher of the Year at the Independent Publishing Awards in 2023. We have been shortlisted for Independent Publisher of the Year at the British Book Awards for the last four years, and were shortlisted for the Diversity and Inclusivity Award at the 2022 Independent Publishing Awards. In 2023 we were shortlisted for Publisher of the Year at the RNA Industry Awards.

We built this company with your help, and we love to hear from you, so please email us about absolutely anything bookish at feedback@joffebooks.com

If you want to receive free books every Friday and hear about all our new releases, join our mailing list: www.joffebooks.com/contact

And when you tell your friends about us, just remember: it's pronounced Joffe as in coffee or toffee!

ALSO BY FAITH MARTIN

DI HILLARY GREENE SERIES
Book 1: MURDER ON THE OXFORD CANAL
Book 2: MURDER AT THE UNIVERSITY
Book 3: MURDER OF THE BRIDE
Book 4: MURDER IN THE VILLAGE
Book 5: MURDER IN THE FAMILY
Book 6: MURDER AT HOME
Book 7: MURDER IN THE MEADOW
Book 8: MURDER IN THE MANSION
Book 9: MURDER IN THE GARDEN
Book 10: MURDER BY FIRE
Book 11: MURDER AT WORK
Book 12: MURDER NEVER RETIRES
Book 13: MURDER OF A LOVER
Book 14: MURDER NEVER MISSES
Book 15: MURDER AT MIDNIGHT
Book 16: MURDER IN MIND
Book 17: HILLARY'S FINAL CASE
Book 18: HILLARY'S BACK
Book 19: MURDER NOW AND THEN
Book 20: MURDER IN THE PARISH

MONICA NOBLE MYSTERIES
Book 1: THE VICARAGE MURDER
Book 2: THE FLOWER SHOW MURDER
Book 3: THE MANOR HOUSE MURDER

TRAVELLING COOK MYSTERIES
Book 1: THE BIRTHDAY MYSTERY
Book 2: THE WINTER MYSTERY
Book 3: THE RIVERBOAT MYSTERY
Book 4: THE CASTLE MYSTERY
Book 5: THE OXFORD MYSTERY
Book 6: THE TEATIME MYSTERY
Book 7: THE COUNTRY INN MYSTERY